Search for the Alien God

By David C. Flynn

Search for the Alien God

8th Edition

To Father Robert Bradley, S.J., my professor at the
Notre Dame Graduate School of Christendom
College; his help and patience were an inspiration.

Edited by Anna Macdonald

Drawings by Madalena Noyes

The books in this series:

1. **Search for the Alien God**
    Published January 2013

2. **Dangerous Alien Robot**
    Published October 2013

3. **Battle of the Queens**
    Due spring 2015

See the website at www.sftag.net

Contents

Foreword

The story that follows was created as a best guess based on current science and theology regarding the events that could arise if other civilizations were found in space. The sheer vastness of the known universe makes this idea more plausible with each new mission from NASA. Christians, Muslims and Jews all profess to hold to the faith of Abraham and adore God who is credited as the originator of all that is known. For those faiths, any other civilization found in the vast universe must also come from the same God we know here on Earth. Christians most notably identify God as "Jesus" who came here in person 2,000 years ago. Christians believe Christ's death on the Cross redeemed ALL of creation, meaning even the darkest corners of the universe as yet undiscovered. If that is true, then the firsthand account of salvation and redemption is here on Earth alone. As the Jews were a chosen people, Earth is a chosen world. But as surely as all people here and beyond share the same God, so do they share the same demons. These agents of Hell have a vested interest in seeing to it that no advanced civilization ever succeeds in leaving Earth to spread the word of God throughout the universe. So, they have effectively quarantined Earth. In our story, prophets in distant worlds tell their people that they were passed over, and must travel to Earth to get the meaning of everything. So, the demons had their ships destroyed in orbit. Until eventually, the most advanced alien society, that has conquered every mystery of physics, sets out to travel to Earth. They also have the technology to defend themselves, even from Hell itself.

What follows is the story of their search for the Alien God, who is our same Christian God, right here on Earth.

Author's Note

The story that follows contains excerpts from a recurring dream that has taken place across twenty years. After a high score on an IQ test as a child, I recall the test examiner telling me that ninety percent of my mind was subconscious. Therefore, its activities were unknown to me. This didn't sit well with a 13 year old boy, so I decided to spy on my subconscious. I created a plan to set my alarm clock for 2 and 4 AM in the morning and copiously notate what I was dreaming. This story was one that I captured, in part, and it has continued in pieces ever since. Friends I told inspired me to write it all down, which I finally did after assembling the jigsaw of disordered pieces gathered from dreams across the years. Every attempt was made to render accurate science and theology. The book of Enoch was also used as a source for the names and histories of the bad angels throughout the novel. The Bible and works from Catherine of Genoa serve to frame many ideas characterized here. I hope you enjoy "Search for the Alien God," because for all we know, somewhere in the vastness of space, this may actually be a reality.

Chapter 1
The Question that Started Everything

My life is now one escape after another from creatures of Hell. Luckily, I have Alta to protect me. Unfortunately, right now, I don't know what to do with her, either. This beautiful and powerful robot, made by aliens who were attempting to build angels, can bend physics and twist the nature of reality itself, but as we sit on the edge of the bed in her spaceship's quarters, she is CRYING! I mean, gosh! I don't even know what to do when human females cry. I know why she is sad; she is sad because she lacks the one thing her makers couldn't give her. But how can I comfort her for THAT? I'm just a lowly human. Like an angry mother bear, though, she will protect me to the death, a death which is looking more likely by the day. I have the worst luck.

Why me?

Looking back, I suppose I set myself up for this whole thing.

In October 1969, I recall attending my first Boy Scout Camporee in Howard County, Maryland. It was a special time in

1

history, because earlier that year Neil Armstrong had landed Apollo 11 on the moon. Our Boy Scout patches for the Camporee had "Moon Year" written right across the top. Everyone was fascinated with space, Tang and Velcro. My tent mate even had Space Food Sticks on the trip; they were a cigar-shaped early version of the modern Power Bar. On a Saturday night, after the big group campfire and ceremony that was held for all the troops in attendance, a friend from my same troop hung out with me on the parade ground looking up at all the stars. You could see everything in space that night. The entire hub of the Milky Way was as clear as I can ever recall seeing it.

Everyone had departed back up to the various troop camps in the woods, leaving no one but us on the field. Lying on our backs, we both looked up at space and pondered. I thought out loud.

"You know, I wonder if there are other people out there looking back at us."

My friend responded, "Yeah ... "

I continued, "I wonder if they have Boy Scouts out there and a Camporee like ours. Perhaps they are marrying, going to school, or driving cars." The driving thing was important to every kid under 16 here on Earth, so why not out there in space.

"Yeaahh, ... ", my friend said in response.

"You know ... Church is tomorrow ... I wonder if they have God, or even the same God as us?" I said.

My friend said nothing, but just lay there reflecting on the matter and staring straight up at the sky. So, I kept going.

"You know, and I wonder if their God will have to go and die on their cross as He did here … ".

My friend finally did respond with the usual "Yeaaahhhh," while still lying on his back, looking up. Shortly thereafter, my friend and I got up and left the spot and never spoke of it again.

Reflecting on this event years later, I'm amazed at my thought processes at the time, for being just 11 years old. I never dreamt that, in my lifetime, I would get an answer to all of those questions.

A month ago, I was driving my SUV south on 95 towards Washington, D.C., intently listening to my favorite AM radio talk show "Coast to Coast." It was a daily program that discussed strange occurrences, UFOs and other unusual phenomenon. Like everyone else, I was completely unaware that aliens were looking for my quiet little planet in a relative galactic backwater, or that I would be at the top of the list of Earthlings that alien visitors would choose to meet.

My name is Tom Ford, and by all outward appearances, I am an ordinary guy. I do have my hobbies, though. I have been a triathlete for over twenty years. At the same gym where I ran my triathlon training program, I taught salsa, swing and hustle dancing. It was in those classes and through social dancing, that I had met most of the girls I knew. As a rule, I felt comfortable in any sport that didn't have a ball. Diplomas in the living room testified to my long time in school. My first grad degree in computer science took up so much of my life that I had to stop doing triathlon to study. I recall once joking I needed to take a course on how to get out of school. Right now, though, I was still in school, finishing the MA in theology, a subject I was passionate about.

Visitors at my place would say I had a propensity for large expensive toys, among which, was the huge Meade SCT telescope sitting in the living room. I always had an avid interest in astronomy. The telescope was a usual fixture on the front lawn at any party held at my house. A trip into my den would also reveal numerous ham radios all together on a table charging. I had gotten my extra-class Ham radio license after years on a CB Radio where my alter ego "Space Rabbit" became a local phenomenon.

But the thing people usually noticed most about me was that I was religious. Not just spiritual in a vague sense, but deeply dedicated to my religion, and faithful to my moral code with the same discipline that was required to complete a triathlon. In total, I have never known a moment in my life where I didn't feel the close presence of God. That was undoubtedly God's choice as well as my own. My role in the events that unfolded later that same week was also due to closeness of another sort, but not of this world.

Chapter 2

Strange Presence at the Funeral

After a twenty minute drive, my Infiniti's navigation system had zeroed in on the field that I was driving to. I was bound for a funeral at an outdoor site that I'd never been to before, so I used the car's navigation system to get me close. It put me in back of a Dim Sum place on the edge of the green, or rather, the cemetery. Darn GPS system. I was on the opposite side of the field and in the wrong lot. I was still close enough to walk, however. So, I parked there and hoofed it all the way over to where I saw people, probably a quarter of a mile from my car.

As I arrived, Jane was there, a girl from my theology class. I had met her at a class break and asked her name. Normally I forget people's names, but not this girl. Jane was simply stunning: long straight blonde hair, a soft face, and a figure that some girls would kill for. I made a point of standing next to her, even though most of the people present were on the other side of the coffin. We stood together in silence at the gravesite. I wondered how she knew the girl whose funeral it was. It seemed quite a coincidence that one of my theology classmates would know a girl who had been the daughter of one of my father's friends.

As the service went on, Jane asked me the strangest thing. "How many people do you see across from us?"

What an odd question. "Twenty or so," I answered, "Why, how many people do you see?"

"I see about twenty more than you perhaps, behind and above those you see."

Normally I would write such a comment off as the sayings of a nut case, but my curiosity got the better of me, and I just had to ask.

"So, … umm … what do they look like?"

Jane paused before answering, and then said, "They have no faces and are neither boys nor girls. They are a translucent white. I can see right through them. They're floating behind the procession across from us. There may be others that I do not see."

"Who do you think they are?" I asked with a shiver. She was nuts, for sure, but her description gave me the creeps anyway.

"I believe they are those souls that might have arisen from this girl who is being buried, after this generation or the next, if she had married, that is. But now that she's dead, her future blood line is cut off."

"Why would they be here?" I asked doubtfully.

"I am not certain, but I believe they are less than a real creation. Perhaps they have gathered here for a last instant as their potential existence ends with this girl's demise. We know that God creates by mere thought and has foreknown all things, including those that might have arisen had this girl lived. So, I surmise that they are less than a creation and more than a thought by God. They have no immortal component yet and cease to exist when her timeline expires."

Well, at that point I had heard enough of her nonsensical rambling. Why was a girl this pretty in a graduate theology class? Apparently there was a catch, namely that Jane was a nut. So, I said nothing more to her, paid my respects to the family, and did a 180 to get back to my car after the ceremony. I knew I was the only one who had parked in the wrong lot behind the funeral gathering; no other cars had been parked near me. But as I walked back to the car, I saw Jane following me. Oddly, I got a streak of fear from head to toe at that thought. The fear quickly turned to anger. I stopped and turned around to her and barked, "Why are you following me?"

"I actually came here to find you." That stopped me dead in my tracks.

"You came here to find me? Why me? And, how could that be in the first place?" I said, raising my voice. "NO one from theology knew I would be here. Not to mention, we're in Maryland now. Our school in Annandale, Virginia, is twenty miles south. What do you want with me?" After all, I figured Jane lived in Virginia where our classes were held. The questions just spilled out from me, one on top the other, without giving her a chance to respond.

Jane realized I was concerned and she tried to pacify the situation. She made a calming gesture with both hands, lightly waving her palms towards the ground as she spoke.

"Listen, I have a proposition to make to you," she said in a quiet and gentle tone. "You may actually like it in fact. Believe me, I'm on the level with this request, because, to be honest, I need your help." A hint of pleading had entered her voice.

"I'm listening," I said. I was still stressed, but it's hard to resist a pretty girl who's asking for your help.

"I can't explain everything right now, but you may have guessed that I am not from around here. Nor am I exactly average," she replied.

Hot looks, sees the ghosts of the never-conceived, and stalks fellow classmates at funerals—definitely not average. "No kidding," I said. "So, what does that have to do with me?"

Jane cut to the chase, saying, "I came to your school to find someone who could make a case for their faith to me, and for various reasons, I believe the best person to do that is you."

Faith? This was about theology? What an odd request! I mean, I dream of people—especially beautiful girls—asking me to explain everything I know about God to them, but it's not like it's ever actually happened before. If she just wanted to talk, why didn't she ask me after class sometime? Why would she follow me miles away and ask me in a cemetery? But it was a different question that I spoke aloud.

"Jane," I said, "our teacher, Father Mark, is nearly world-renowned, and we're in a Pontifical Institution to start with, at Christendom. Anyone at school would be a better bet than me. Have you asked Father Mark? They have people on staff that make me look like I'm still in grade school. For a person who sees ghosts at funerals, I suspect you already know that. So, why pick me?"

She answered, "You have other qualifications that make you a good choice. But who cares, since I'll pay you."

"Pay me for what exactly?" I asked. I was intrigued now, and the offer of payment distracted me, as Jane probably meant it to, from wondering what my "other qualifications" were. If payment was involved, this amounted to a contract, and I wanted to be explicit on the terms.

9

"Either by words or in print, explain why a completely neutral person would pick the Catholic faith over the 33,000 other Christian choices," she said.

"33,000?" I said. "And, what do you mean by 'completely' neutral? No one is 'completely' neutral."

Jane responded, "Tom, imagine that the aliens landed tomorrow, and rather than saying 'Take me to your leader,' they came instead to find your world's God."

Jane motioned towards the heavens with one hand, and went on, "Or better yet, try to imagine a situation where the universe is teeming with intelligent life in every direction and your Earth is the only inhabited world God actually came to. Just as prophets here on Earth heralded God's coming to the Jews; assume prophets in other worlds told believers they had to travel to an alien world for the first-hand account of salvation. That location happens to be your Earth."

I responded, "So, basically, Jane, that would make Earth a chosen world the way the Jews are a chosen people." It was obvious that Jane wanted me to believe her scenario, despite the fact that she had phrased it as a hypothetical. I played along for now, although I thought that making a theological argument to someone who was nuts might present some extra difficulties.

"Right!" Jane said with excitement. "But here's the problem. When others come here, rather than finding one true faith, they find an entire array of beliefs that number in the thousands. There are about 33,000 flavors of Christianity alone at current count. Not to mention other barriers to getting at the truth that I needn't bore you with right now."

"Well, Jane, people smart enough to travel across space could sort that out with a visit to the Library of Congress and a complete review of the history of human civilization," I said.

"Great suggestion, Tom! I knew you'd know where to look! We'll consider your suggestion as a top priority. But I still want to hear your case, so let me make it worth your while," she replied.

Did I just hear Jane say "we?"

"Take the job and I'll pay you," Jane wheedled.

I asked, "What kind of payment do you have in mind?"

Jane picked up a small dark stone from the ground. Holding it in her hand and looking at it, she said, "Become gold." A shimmer passed over the stone, leaving it gold-colored.

She handed it to me and waited for my answer. I felt the stone in my hand and thought about it. The stone was heavy, heavier than lead, and did indeed look like gold. I could see that this was gonna be interesting. Now, I was born at night, but not last night, and I was not going to be taken in this easily. But Jane was, at the very least, the most interesting girl I'd met all week, alien or not. Even if she was a complete liar, she was a helluva magician, and an even more imaginative story teller. Worst-case scenario, maybe I could teach her to dance. I told Jane I accepted her offer, and I resolved to have the stone tested the first chance I got, to see if I would be getting anything more out of this deal than an interesting time.

I reflected upon the gravity of the challenge I had just accepted. How do you make a case for your faith to all-knowing aliens, who may already have the complete human history and a stunning science fact-base due to their star-traveling technology? Could the aliens find the one planet in a billion that God actually came to thousands of years ago, and leave in modern Earth-like confusion over what the truth was? Somehow, if they were smart enough to find us, they just had to be smart enough to sort out the specific truths that underlie all the sordid human history and confusion on matters of a correct religion. I suppose some assumptions need to be made to parse the problem, which I could just tell them up front. I pulled out my calculator and realized that if I made a case against every faith but my own, I would be mired in 33,000 other Christian faiths alone. Giving just a paragraph to each would leave me with a five million word document that could fill sixty-four regular-sized novels. Who would even want to read a book that just slammed everyone else's faith?

Perhaps I could use a logical attack on the problem. In the case of Mormon theology, the book of Nephi says that Jesus visited the Americas. So, if He DID do that, He certainly could have visited Jane's world, removing her need to even come here. So, I would argue that her presence here removes Mormon theology as a real possibility. Perhaps that is partially true for Protestants also, who make no historically traceable requirement for apostolic succession. In those cases also, the true church could be moved by the spirit alone to any planet … but the fact is, Jane IS here. I suppose it's fair to surmise that God must have communicated the need to find us to her people, because we certainly didn't tell her.

It may even be worthwhile to consider my audience in this. Are they agnostic, or deists? Perhaps they are atheists seeking answers. Atheists prize their reputation for being open minded to ANY possibility, even things the less enlightened might write off as fantasy. I have my doubts about their fairness to this, personally, but I DO want to give the possibility a chance. The very act of Jane's people coming here removes the atheists as a possible "final" truth just as the Mormon's beliefs run into trouble. If there was no God, then who sent them here? If Jesus traveled to the Americas, then why not to other planets? These theologies fail the acid test for purely mechanical reasons. All of this is fascinating to consider, and upon reflection, I may be the only person who has ever needed to wrestle with these thoughts.

Hours later, I got home and was resting on top of the sheets of my bed. It was about dusk. After a moment or two, I began to see something appear off to my left, in the middle of the room. It looked like a disembodied head, floating. I froze in terror. This wasn't a human head. It was entirely covered with a thin black leathery skin, and taller than a normal human head, with no visible hair. Where the left eye should be was just smooth skin, as though

13

it had been omitted from the original design. When the face opened its mouth, no sound came out. It had no visible teeth. It appeared to let out a silent moan, a lengthy one. The interior space of its mouth, once opened, appeared utterly black and endless—almost like a doorway to someplace far worse.

I was completely stricken with fear. Just about ten seconds after it appeared I got an overwhelming feeling that I was looking at something that was more than one entity. Moreover, I got the distinct impression that it wanted to tear me limb from limb. Not kill me, mind you; death would only be an incidental side effect of tearing me to pieces. I felt that it wanted to rip me into shreds to satisfy the rage and pain that emanated from it like wind from a hurricane. This was no passing feeling either; I could SEE myself being ripped in half and thrown away, almost as though the entity was projecting the thought. A moment later, it disappeared. I was still frozen in a lightning-strike of terror. As I lay there, still glancing to my left out of the corner of my eye, I felt something invisible walk right over me and straight through the wall to my right. With that, I couldn't take anymore. I jumped up and ran over to my cell phone and dialed the number Jane had given me hours before.

I began, "Jane, since I met you, things have all gone to Hell around here." I told her the story, and she tried to calm my fears. I was still shaking.

"You have answered a couple of key questions I have had," Jane added, after not entirely succeeding at calming me. Then, she

14

summoned me to meet her the following morning at a ball field near the place where we had first met.

At the ball field the next morning, Jane said, "It appears that we have ruffled some feathers."

"What do you mean by that?" I nervously asked. I was calmer than the night before, since the disembodied head had not come back, but the encounter was still fresh in my mind. The bright sunshine on the perfectly ordinary ball field, and the dry green grass underfoot helped.

"We came here to find news of the creator of all things," Jane explained. "We suspect that demons have hunted us from the time we left our home."

"Demons?! Is that what that thing was? Why would they do that? Your home? What are you talking about?" I asked.

"It's simple, Tom. Yes, what you saw was a demon. The demons want to prevent any star-traveling civilization from spreading the truth of God to the rest of the galaxy. You see, I am the captain of an exploratory mission from Gihon, a planet like yours, about twenty light-years away from here in the constellation Libra. Your astronomers call our planet Gliese 581d," Jane said.

She went on, "Also, I can tell you we are not the only civilization that is seeking this very truth. Another planet that is gearing up to try sending a team here is Pishon, which you call exoplanet HD85512b. We will share our data with them if we are successful here, or they will send their own ship if we aren't. They

15

are thirty-six light-years away from you in the constellation Vela. Since they are technologically behind us, they preferred to see what we discovered first. Further from you still is Kepler 22b, a veritable paradise and inhabited with a civilization that is five hundred years ahead of Earth's technology but also of lesser technology than my world. Kepler 22b is only slightly larger than your Earth, but six hundred light years out in the constellation Cygnus."

She continued, "Of all these and many others, it appears that your world alone has had testimony of a visit from the creator. And, as you said yesterday, 'Just as the Jews were a chosen people, so Earth is a chosen world.' Your prayers and writings even say He died once for all. The 'all' part is the crux of this. Did He die for us too? Or would God die on each alien planet to redeem those people? So, Tom, here's my problem. Can we sort out which truth is the original accurate theology from God Himself? Can we do it before the demons destroy me and the remainder of my crew?"

"Destroy your crew? What do you mean?" I asked.

Jane answered in a grave tone, "We have had several people on our team mysteriously torn apart, limb from limb, while en-route here. Not just killed, but ripped into pieces." She shuddered at the gruesome memory.

I had told Jane about the apparition I saw in my room, but I had never mentioned my sense that it wanted to tear me in half. A shiver of terror shot through me. Not even the bright sunshine was enough to comfort me; not when Jane's words confirmed that that thing had been real and might come back.

Jane patiently continued to explain, "We are now in a race to get to the answer before the last of us is hunted down. And, we don't know which theological truth is THE truth. Despite our great technology, we still have the same problem figuring out if a traveling salesman is telling the truth about a cleaning product that your civilization has. Some things just don't get easier with time or technology. But we do know that the demons know the correct answer. They are a perfect reverse barometer."

"Wait a minute," I said, as things clicked into place, "I wondered why you didn't care about my religious credentials! You just selected some random theology student. You are using me as bait!" The demon encounter made Jane's story much more plausible than it had seemed yesterday, and I was starting to buy into it. But even if she belonged in an asylum, it infuriated me to think that she might have known that thing was coming for me and not even warned me about it.

Jane explained, "Tom, we had no way of knowing what might happen, but since we were running out of time, we wanted to try what we could quickly. And, what little I know of you, you are single, mentally tough and enduring, and there's no end you won't go to, to do the right thing in the bigger picture of God's will. Well, here's your chance. There are so many, beyond millions, of people who want you to help them find their salvation. Except in this case the people you are helping are not of this world."

"But we're not just abandoning you to the demons. Since I have involved you, and since your description has given me a better understanding of what has been killing my people, I will see to your protection," Jane said.

"You're gonna protect me from demons?" I said incredulously. "You mean the same ones that have already been killing your own people, by tearing them in half? How in the world could you protect me from something like that?!"

"Now that I realize what we're up against, the solution is easier than you might think," she said, with perhaps a hint of a smile. "Our physics isn't just beyond yours, it is way beyond yours."

"It's like this," she said abruptly, tracing out a square in front of her with her hands. As she did this, I couldn't help but notice how nicely shaped those hands were.

"Picture one of your Monopoly boards," she went on. "That board is the universe. You and I and other sentient species are the dog, the top hat, the thimble, and the other player pieces. At first, we think we move around the board by ourselves. But, like in the game, we are being moved by entities greater than us. My people are the first created beings who have risen to the point of being able to reach out beyond the monopoly board and have a conversation with those entities playing us as tokens. That's how much more advanced than yours my species is." Jane said this matter-of-factly, without any hint of superiority or arrogance in her tone.

"And now," she tacked on the end, with a sudden look of great intensity, "we have stumbled upon a greater question that supersedes physics. The question is, just how tightly did God seal the box of creation to prevent us from getting out?"

I tried to comprehend the reality of being in a society that could even think of asking such a question.

"We have resolved dark energy, dark flow, and the other seven unseen dimensions your string theory predicts," she said.

Pulling myself away from the image of escaping creation and back to the more normal topic of esoteric astronomy, I asked, "What about dark matter?"

Jane frowned, and said, "There is no such thing. Your astronomers think there is dark matter because it would explain how the outer stars in a galaxy spin as fast as they do. But they are observing an effect of black holes twisting space itself from the very start of galaxy formation. So, all the stars in a galaxy are on a space-time carousel of sorts where gravity and the twisting of space combine to make those stars turn at a uniform speed. Your people nearly hit the mark with Modified Newtonian Dynamics in 1983, but they didn't know why it worked. It works because of the black hole's effect on space itself. Black holes don't just curve space; because they spin, they also twist it."

"Think of a galaxy as an umbrella. Umm ... a polka-dotted one, I guess" she said with a self-conscious grin, "so that the polka-dots are the stars." As she spoke, she used her hands to mime an umbrella pointed at the ground with its handle coming up.

She continued, "The handle of the umbrella is the black hole at the center of the galaxy. As the umbrella opens," and here she mimed the umbrella spinning on the ground while it opened, "that is, as the galaxy forms, the twisting of the handle in the center keeps the rest of the umbrella turning in sync with it. That first quasar that pushes out the arms also stretches space. This is more than the localized effect of frame dragging."

"Or perhaps," she interrupted herself as another thought occurred to her, "another good analogy for this would be to put one of those mixing wands in the nose of a hand drill and stir up a large can of paint with it. The vortex created in the paint represents the added effect of gravity due to mass. The swirling paint represents the effect of the black holes on the twist of space. Each supermassive black hole has a characteristic 'drag' on space around it, in addition to the time-gravity bending. The first hint is that black holes all spin in the direction of their galactic rotation. The gravitational twist they give to space-time explains every observation your scientists have made, with the exception of colliding galaxies. In that case, more than two supermassive black holes exist that are revolving around each other, but the extra ones are not yet apparent to your observers here on Earth. A good example is the Bullet Cluster. If you happen to have the opportunity at some point, you can tell your scientists that I recommend that they first find all the black holes in the area and then collect the data. That should put them on the right path."

"And, since I know you're wondering, dark flow is a current in space-time that carries superclusters along like a river. Your people will figure that out in time, by analysis of the probes that come along after WMAP. That was the probe you used to measure the background microwave universe more than ten years ago," she said.

Jane was right; I had been wondering what dark flow was. That would have been my next question. I was a little surprised that she knew me that well.

"But I digress," Jane said, suddenly glancing at the Sun in the sky. "You already knew we understood space travel pretty well. What you didn't know is that our technological industry can use those other dimensions. We used them to design a team of super robots, made from the same fabric as the angels and demons. These robots possess properties of the dimension from which they are made and have power over our physical laws here in this dimension. They assist us in all things. They possess characteristics of men and the power of the angels."

"So, if they are the same as angels, how can I be sure that one of your robots is going to beat a demon in an attack?" I asked. Despite the interesting sidetrack into astronomy, I had not forgotten the demon from last night, or the fear it inspired. I asked, "If they are evenly matched, isn't there still a 50-50 chance that the demon is going to rip me to shreds after beating your robot?"

"Great question," Jane explained, "Angels were made to serve God, not made to do battle. They CAN do battle, but they

21

weren't designed especially for it. We, on the other hand, designed our robots to win in a fight because that is what we needed them for. Remember, in our world, we have had no visit from a savior. Because of this, we weren't the focus of a spiritual battleground, and so we have no angels as guardians. Once our technology developed enough that we could, more or less, make our own angels, the demons began to pay attention to us. We were in the middle of the fray, so we developed our technology to defend ourselves. You see, when you consider something like the angels or demons to be 'spiritual,' that's really no different than the early Puritans' view of science being witchcraft. They mistook something natural for something supernatural, and so do you. The so-called spiritual realm is the actual structural framework behind all of creation, including parts unknown to you like the dark flow and dark energy your people have just begun to see. Our robots posses the ability to control those forces the same as all the angels and demons—when permitted by God."

After this explanation, Jane walked with purpose over to the pitcher's mound. She bent over and picked up a handful of the rough brown sand that is ubiquitous in pitcher's mounds everywhere. Stretching up her arm to the sky and leaning forward, Jane let the sand fall from her fingers in a sprinkling stream.

Then, it felt as if my heart must have stopped.

For out of the falling sand materialized a second girl.

Chapter 3
Meeting Alta

Jane was certainly more attractive than average. She looked, moved, and talked like a normal human woman. Nothing about her screamed, "I'm an alien!" I learned later that her crew was similarly designed and coached to blend into Earth's fabric seamlessly. Jane's crew was carefully coached not to attract attention. Alta was a different matter.

At first glance, this new girl seemed normal enough. She was about 5′6″, with long brownish-blondish hair that had a bit of a wave to it. Her skin had a hint of a tan, and her body was athletic, like one of the triathletes I was used to training and racing with. Alta's face looked soft and lifelike even to the point of very minor human irregularities. If I had just met her on the street, I would have guessed her age to be mid-twenties at the most. She was quite attractive and had perfect proportions, and there was nothing obvious that would reveal her identity as an android.

Yet there was something subtly odd about her. Later, when I had time to think about it, I realized this must be because her design was an emergency contingency, less planned than that of

Jane and her crew. Alta had more of the raw properties that these other worldly visitors would have if they were completely unmodified.

After the girl materialized out of the stream of falling sand, Jane whispered something into her ear, and the girl came over to stand by me. Then Jane offered an explanation, "Tom, this is Alta. Alta will protect you from anything in this realm, or those realms beyond here. She can handle any eventuality, even those unknown to your people or your technology. In Earth terms, you might call Alta a robot, but that would be selling her short. She's far more than your usual idea of robots."

I had just seen a girl—a robot girl, apparently—materialize in front of my eyes. My mind was struggling to catch up. It would be a gross exaggeration to say that everything I knew turned out to be false, but that's about what it felt like. I was rebuilding my worldview from the ground up, building a picture of the universe which included aliens HERE, NOW, and girls who materialized out of falling sand. Still, I caught what Jane said, and I just had to ask the question that was pressing with understandable urgency on my consciousness.

"Jane, … these other realms? What are they? Are they sending more demons against me? Something worse than demons? What kind of realms are we talking about?" When Jane didn't immediately answer me, I continued, "I mean, you're not gonna just leave me with that hint, right Jane? Or, at least you'll tell Alta to explain?" I tried not to sound desperate, but I wasn't sure if I was succeeding.

Jane looked at me softly and clearly understood my concern, but all she said was, "You could not understand what those realms are until you have direct experience or are given the sight to see. Frankly, you wouldn't believe me until you do see for yourself anyway. I realize you don't really know me, but trust me on this, Tom; Alta is the best help you can get in the entire galaxy. She was created as a general researcher with a dark side forged for battle. So, day to day, she is not a soldier. But, that can change in an instant when needed."

"She won't turn on me … right?" I asked.

"Right!" Jane said with emphasis. "She will give her life to protect you, actually. Also, she can accurately detect threats that you cannot perceive. She will do as you ask, but you would be very wise to take her advice when offered."

"One more thing." I said, "There's no manual."

Jane looked puzzled. "What?" she asked.

I tried to explain, "I'm guessing Alta is a billion dollar machine. And, there's no manual."

Jane said, "Oh, I see what you mean. Tom, treat Alta as you would anyone else. Think of her as your house guest. She'll answer any question you have as you go. So, I guess, in a sense, she is her own manual. Just ask her anything you like."

"All righty then," I said in my best imitation of Jim Carey. I was starting to feel better about this whole proposition. The memory of the demon and the terror he inspired was not completely gone, but now I had my own robot girl to protect me, and the reality that aliens, real aliens, wanted ME to save them— save them in the real theological sense, even—was starting to sink in. I already loved discussing theology, so calling this the chance of a lifetime was an understatement. Souls were at stake. ALIENS were asking ME for help. With my own robot to protect me, the risk wasn't too serious, right? But I thought again of the demon, and a cold shiver went back down my back.

Turning to the girl standing next to me, I said, "Alta, I guess you'll be staying with me for a while, so let's go to my place and I'll show you around."

Alta and I hiked back across the ball field and headed for where I parked my car. I suddenly realized that Alta had maybe a grand total of ten minutes of "earthly" life experience. Since she was clearly not from around here, it might be good to do a guided tour. But to be a good tour guide, I'd need to ask her a few little questions.

As we walked across the field, I noticed Alta's feet sinking deeper into the ground than mine. I knew the ground I was walking on was dry, but I just assumed her feet were sinking deeper because there was mud under the grass she walked on. So, I said to her, "Alta, get outta that mud." After I said that, it briefly crossed my mind to wonder if it was wise or appropriate to order around an alien robot girl. I brushed that thought aside.

Alta looked down and saw the depressions her feet were making. "Compensate," she said.

She shot me an apologetic glance and said, "Sorry."

Alta then moved to walk the same course right beside me. I saw she was leaving almost no footprints at all. I almost laughed out loud when I thought of Alta as just a girl hiding her weight. Maybe she was a little more humanlike after all.

"Alta, I guess I can assume that you know all about our language and culture, because obviously, you speak perfect English. So, you probably have some knowledge of our science fiction genre?" I queried.

"Yes." The waves of her hair bounced down her chest and back up again as she nodded.

27

"Like Star Trek, Star Wars, Terminator, etc.?" I asked. I realized I sounded like a curious thirteen-year-old. Alta was unfazed by my inquiry.

"I have complete recall of every work of human culture and literature that has been broadcast into space since your invention of radio. Anything prior to that is unknown to us unless your transmissions were of a historical nature," Alta explained.

"So, Alta, do you speak French?" I asked.

She nodded yes again. Again, her hair bobbed with her head.

"So, you're like C3PO then?" I queried.

Alta answered, "Not at all. I am a creation like you, with will and intellect. But I have no immortal soul. The fabric of my being lets me operate here and in other dimensions with equal ease. The angels, by definition, have dominion over physics; so do I."

Here she paused for a moment, and then continued, "Rather than explaining things for which you have not yet achieved the understanding of physics, it would be better over time for me to just show you. But in short, I am more like a guardian angel that you can actually see than like the Terminator in your movies. I have the ability to alter, ignore, or change your physical laws."

She added, "At least within the sphere of my influence, which is considerable." If a human girl had said that, I would have expected her to add some body language that accentuated this bold claim. Alta's demeanor was so calm, it was unnerving.

I looked incredulously at Alta, but I figured it'd be better not to call the Terminator a liar. Jane had mentioned bending the laws of physics, too. Materializing out of sand was a neat trick, but that was a far cry from being a guardian angel or violating the laws of physics.

"Well, this I'll have to see," I answered. "And, just how considerable is 'considerable?'"

Alta, still leaving hardly any footprints, said, with a quirk of a smile, "What if I told you that, from another realm, your entire universe looks like a darkly glowing smoky orb, about seven feet across, floating above a marble console that was made to hold it? Now, do you think I could swing a tennis racket though seven feet of smoke?"

I figured it'd be wise to just let this one drop. If she thought she could swing a tennis racket through the entire universe, well, it probably wasn't going to do any good to prove to her how nonsensical that was.

As we got back to my car, I walked Alta over to the passenger side. I always held the door open for women when I drove them places, and this also seemed like the easiest way to show an alien robot where she should sit. As I came around the side of the car, I realized I had a flat tire. How had this happened? Maybe I had run over a nail. Alta saw me look at it, and without a word, I walked around to the back of my car and pulled out my road bike to get at the spare below.

"This needs fixing, right?" Alta asked matter-of-factly.

"It needs replacing … which is what I am about to do," I responded. I wondered if I would have to explain the whole process of changing the tire to her as I did it.

She interrupted, "Wait a second."

She walked around and looked at the tire on the other side of the front of the car and then walked back over to the flat one. She spoke as if casting a hex, her voice taking on a willowy tone.

"Make this tire like that one," she commanded.

The passenger side tire promptly re-inflated. It can't have taken even two seconds for the tire to be full and steady again. I think it even had more tread. The handlebars of my road bike were still in my hands as I stood staring at my car's tire.

"Okay, Alta," I said, "I think I am beginning to understand. Anything you speak as a command or a verbal prescription will happen as requested." I wondered what limits there were to her ability to control things just by saying so. I put the road bike back in the trunk of my car and closed the hatch.

"Yes, within limits," Alta said, echoing my thoughts. "Or I could just think the command. I revealed my thought with words for your sake." I held the passenger door open for her, and she climbed in without trouble.

"And the footprints back there?" I asked, once I had climbed in the driver's seat.

Alta responded, "I just compensated for the greater gravity here."

"How did you do that?" I asked, starting the car and pulling out.

"I changed my weight," Alta said. "I would be about 1500 pounds here unaltered."

"So, I gotta ask," I said, looking over at her, "with the kind of powers you people have, why have you traveled across the galaxy to find our God? I mean, if you wanted to create something, you could just say it, and there it would be."

When I glanced over at Alta, I saw her looking at me with disappointment. "It amazes you that we come looking for our mutual creator from clear across space? Well, it amazes US that, of the 100,000 known worlds with intelligent life, God chose to come to Earth and your people aren't looking for Him at all."

Gosh, that was deep. Her comment hit home; I realized it was shallow of me to focus just on the cool things these aliens could do with their powers. For all their advancement, they were still people, with at least some of the same longings and fears that we humans had. But, I wasn't quite ready to stop thinking about Alta's superpowers. That tennis racket comment suddenly didn't seem so far-fetched. I wasn't sure I wanted to know, but frankly I just had to tickle the dragon's tail on that one.

"So, when you made that comment about a tennis racket," I inquired nervously. Alta held up a perfectly-shaped hand, stopping me before I could finish.

31

"Trust me; I know that it's harder to build something than it is to destroy it. You may or may not be safe overall in this odyssey, but you are completely safe from me," she said.

I decided that it was probably a great time to stop questioning Alta entirely.

Chapter 4
The Doll

After driving for just a few minutes, I realized I was getting hungry. I thought it might be a good idea to get lunch, and stop at a park near my place. But considering my guest, well, honestly, I wondered, does Alta eat?

"Alta," I said, "let's pull into the park and do lunch, or hit the strip mall. What would you like? Can you eat?"

Alta said, "I can do anything you can do, but I do not require it." But she added, "Either is fine, and I do like parks."

As we drove, I decided that now was as good a time as any for one of the questions that was on my mind. I asked, "So, do you have a history before you showed up on the ball field today? Did you already exist somewhere else?"

"Yes," Alta said. "In my world, I walk about as freely as you and Jane do here. I can travel in the way you saw for excursions, like this trip to Earth."

"But, it is not the only way I can travel," she added thoughtfully, tilting her head to one side.

As we pulled up to the curb, we decided on a food court across from the park that had Chinese. We crossed the street, and I noticed curiously that Alta didn't look to her left or right to see if cars were coming. On the far sidewalk, three children were sitting together, playing some sort of game with stones. They had a whole pile of discarded stones next to them. Since they were blocking a large part of the sidewalk, I passed them carefully and watched to see how Alta would handle it. Without showing any trace of concern and without disturbing the children in any way, she followed my path around the kids.

Then, we passed a storefront en-route to the food, and Alta saw a little shop with expensive designer-looking collectable dolls. She stopped walking and pressed her face close to the glass. The dolls were made from beautiful porcelain, silk, and carved woods of every type. They had handcrafted clothes made to fit, including perfect little shoes. Alta looked excited.

"Please buy me that doll!" she politely requested.

I looked at the doll in the window. It was a musical doll about 18 inches tall, made of delicate white porcelain, with a pink silk ballerina's dress. The price tag was more than $500. The mechanical beauty of the doll made me think of Alta herself, and I saw odd irony in a doll like Alta wanting a doll.

"Alta, what would you do with a doll?" I asked dubiously. "I mean, aren't you kind of … "

She stopped me with a hand wave, picked up a medium-sized stone from the pile that the sidewalk children had discarded, looked at it, and said, "Become gold." This was just the same as Jane had done after the funeral. Alta handed the now-golden stone to me expectantly.

"Well, what do I care what you do with it anyway?" I said, feeling the heavy weight in my hand and wondering what the current price of gold was. "I wonder if they'll take Discover?"

Five minutes later Alta happily hugged her doll and explained that she had a whole collection of dolls in her world. This one was special, since it was a souvenir of her trip here. After a moment, she looked right at the doll, and it disappeared with an eerie wavering glow. I looked around nervously, wondering if anyone on the street had seen her little trick. Alta could see my concern.

"Not to worry, I just put the doll away," she said.

"Oh, like Jane puts you away?" I couldn't help but say with a snicker.

Alta ignored me and continued, "I get a doll at every place we visit, just like you might collect beer mugs."

I realized that Alta was revealing something deeper about herself here. If she wanted a doll, she could have easily just made one out of something else, like she fixed my tire or converted stones to gold. But she insisted on us buying it. Alta apparently wanted to follow a hidden set of ethical or practical "rules." There was more to her than just super robot powers. However, I was still concerned that I might have a problem on my hands, if anyone else saw Alta doing any of her "beyond physics" stunts. I decided to try to nip that in the bud.

"Alta, in order for me to do what Jane asked, we'll need to keep a low profile. So, you might want to try to blend in. There are some things you do that simply won't escape people's notice," I said.

Alta realized the importance of my concern. "I completely understand, sorry," she said with a look of contrition.

We finally arrived at the door of the Chinese place, and we shuttled over to the carryout line. I wanted Kung Pao Chicken, as always, and Alta ordered a broccoli and beef dish. When she got it, it was a bit cold for her taste. I was a bit surprised that she had such preferences, if she didn't need to eat, but we walked over to the microwave, where I figured I'd finally be useful as a tour guide and give her my first lesson on "use of Earth machines." Alta was balancing a left hand full of seasoning packets and napkins and a right hand full of a round aluminum serving tray with a bowl full of food on it. A little ways from the microwave, people were returning those serving trays to a stack for reuse. Alta realized that to use the microwave, she had the wrong type of dishes. I was just hoping she wouldn't say "become hot" to the food in a crowded room full of onlookers. As we came over to the front of the microwave, Alta lightly tossed the food bowl a foot above the aluminum tray that was carrying it, and threw the tray like a discus onto the appropriate stack 15 feet away, all with the same hand.

The plate somehow made a perfect silent landing on the stack of others just like it. She then caught the bowl of food in its downward flight like a professional juggler. Not a drop was spilled. This was a demonstration of accuracy and speed that was so subtle that if I hadn't been looking right at it, I would have missed the whole thing.

A little kid saw the whole thing and shouted to his mom, "Wow, did you see that?!"

Alta glanced their way and explained without missing a beat, "I used to work for the circus."

My amazement was sharp, and I felt I needed to do something about this. "Alta," I said in an emphatic whisper, "that's another one of those things that would be a good idea not to do in public." Then I added more gently, "But I admire your quick thinking with the kid and his mom."

"I didn't think, I knew. 'Already knew' is always faster than 'I figured it out,'" she said.

Alta put her food in the microwave while I tried to sort that statement out.

"I figured it would be enough that I didn't just say 'become hot', and used the microwave instead," she said.

Spooky ... I HAD thought precisely that, and now she said it. Could she read my mind? But something else also bothered me about what she had done.

"Alta. You worked for a circus? Lying to a kid! Shame."

Alta deflected, "Tom, our ship really is like a circus. Or maybe a game show, but it certainly isn't like your NASA."

We walked out and ate our lunch in the park without much conversation, as I tried to absorb everything that had happened.

After returning home, I put Alta in my guest room, and turned on the TV. I switched over to the Sci-fi channel, figuring it would amuse her. I left to run some errands, but upon my return I decided to check up on her. I found Alta watching some designer show on the wedding channel, and a show called "Say Yes to the Dress." She was sitting up straight on the couch, not lounging like a normal person would. I couldn't see what interest those shows could possibly have for her, so I asked her why she wasn't watching the Sci-fi channel anymore. She looked up at me with incomprehension and informed me that these were her two favorite shows. It was just then that I began to realize that I had absolutely no idea at all who or what I had as a guest in my house.

The next morning was a Saturday, and I had a long training bike ride scheduled with my friend James. He was gearing up for the physical test to make the county fire department, and I was training for my next triathlon. So, having similar goals, a 30-mile bike ride seemed about right. He was due to arrive at my place shortly, and I was still wondering how I'd explain Alta. She was checking out stuff in the weight room in my basement. I figured he'd just assume she was another outta-town dance partner training for the next competition; otherwise she'd be biking with us. I wasn't sure at this point if Alta would even want to let me go out alone after all that had happened. I was still looking over my shoulder for that floating head as it was. But the truth was, I needed somebody to share the craziest story I ever had to tell, and no one had told me not to tell James what was going on.

James pulled up with his pickup, and his bike was already set up in the back. I pulled mine out of the front of the garage; it was also set to go. As he came in, I introduced Alta and explained that we'd all do dinner after our return from the ride. Alta shook his hand, and I looked to see if she would crush it, or have robotic cold skin, but she acted completely normal. As we set out to go, I asked James about route choices, and we agreed on a trip north to Patapsco State Park and the Swinging Bridge. I figured I would wait till we were outta town to tell him the whole story about Jane and Alta.

We parked at the library, which was our usual starting point and unloaded our bikes to go. It was a decent day for riding; there were clouds overhead, but nothing that threatened rain. We set out on our bikes through the housing development to our trailhead. After getting northwest of Route 1, the road opened up to woods and rural countryside that surrounded us on all sides. We were riding front to back, so I pulled up next to James to talk as we rode.

"Remember that girl at my place this morning?" I asked. The exertion of bike riding may have hidden the eagerness and suspense in my tone, but perhaps not.

James asked routinely, his mind on the bike ride, "Sure. Another dance partner I assume?"

"Well, not exactly. Actually, she's not a dancer or a triathlete, nor is she a love interest. Oh, and she's not family either," I responded.

James gave me an incredulous look, and said, "I'm guessing that you're trying to tell me something here."

"Yeah, except I can't imagine what it would be like to be committed to an asylum after telling a friend something that convinced him I had lost my mind," I said.

James paused in the conversation to think about this for a moment and then asked, "Okay, Tom, does this involve anybody getting killed?"

"I don't believe so, but I'm not honestly sure what's involved," I said.

"Okay," James said, "Tell me and I promise I won't have you committed."

I took a breath and paused to think, still pedaling.

"You know I've been in grad school for theology, right?" I asked.

"Sure, in Northern Virginia right?" James said.

"Yes, and it's a very orthodox Catholic grad school. When I signed on a couple years ago, one of my girlfriends from the Catholic circles I hang out with told me something I never forgot. When I told her the school I was going to, she said, 'Well, Tom, don't count on meeting any beauty queens there. Beauty is a gift God rarely gets back,'" I said.

"Well, a girl came in midway through summer semester that looked like she just got off of a James Bond movie set. Her name was Jane and she was a doll. In the school environment, she stood out like a nine-year-old playing professional football. Even odder was the fact that she wasn't really there for classes. I now think she was there to find me. I had seen her in a class or two and assumed she was either auditing or a late addition. But yesterday it all came to a head. I was scheduled to attend the funeral of the daughter of my father's work friend. He was my friend also, but mostly through my Dad. She had been hit by a car I believe," I said.

James broke in, "Not on a bike ride, I hope." We both looked around us. There were no cars anywhere near us, but we both knew the risks.

I responded, "No, it was in the city, and she was hit crossing at an intersection. Whatever! That part doesn't matter in this story."

I then explained to James the weird conversation with Jane, the presences she had seen at the funeral, and even the thing that showed up in my bedroom. I was convinced that Jane and her team were from another world and I shared that with James just as a statement of fact.

"So, what do they want with you?" James asked. I couldn't tell, as we biked along, whether he believed me or was just playing along.

I tried to explain, "I don't think this is about me at all. Frankly, as far as I can tell, Jane and Alta came here on a religious fact-finding mission. But when they got here, they found thousands of choices instead of just one Earthly religion. Jane says that Earth is the only place that God has actually visited, at least according to their prophets or research or whatever. Alta even suggested that there are thousands of other worlds that might be interested in this. So, either they'd all come to Earth individually, or the news would spread to them from this mission Jane and Alta are on."

"So, Jane and company are like the Magi from the first Christmas. Maybe they brought cool space gifts!" James continued with excitement. I thought he must believe me now. Or else he was just thinking of it all as a good story. It was hard to tell. But that Magi thing struck me. I would keep that image in mind.

"Well," I said, "if they did bring gifts, they are 2,000 years late." The gold nuggets had temporarily slipped from my mind. "The trouble is that now the demons are onto them and have a vested interest in stopping any progress they might make."

"That very well might include anyone who helps them," James observed in a cautious tone, looking at me sidelong as we cycled.

"Right, that's why Alta is with me; she's a bodyguard … essentially." I said. Bodyguards and wedding shows did not usually go together in my mind.

"You know, Tom." James wasn't huffing at all as he spoke; we were both in good shape. "This concept isn't as surprising as you might think. I just saw a book about Giordano Bruno, a Catholic priest and philosopher who was burned at the stake in the Roman Inquisition … 1600 A.D. I believe. Anyway, Bruno suggested life on other worlds and other things very much like your story. Except in a way more familiar to his times. But they didn't like his expansive universe concept. He said that we were a portion of the whole rather than the center of everything. I just thought I'd toss that in."

"Well, here's the cool thing," I said. "I suspect that since Jane and Alta can speak our language, they have some encyclopedic knowledge, or who knows how much beyond what we know. It's awesome to ponder what could be learned from them."

"Listen," I added, glancing again at my friend, "I realize this is all a little bit thin, but I had to tell someone. And, Alta will be waiting for us when we get back."

James leaned my way to speak again while we pedaled up a slight grade, "I can't wait to meet her again."

Alta's powers flashed back into my mind. "Oh, by the way, James," I added, "She can turn anything into gold, and even fix flats with her words."

"Flats?" James said. "Well, looking at all the junk on this road, maybe we should have brought her." I looked around at the road we were on. Trees and lovely older houses lined the road, but we were going too fast to even see tire threats on the street below.

When we returned to my home 3 hours later, sweaty but fit, Alta was playing with the cat. My cat trusted no one, so I was almost surprised to see this. But I've seen enough science fiction on TV to know that it's pretty standard for alien robots to get along with otherwise skittish Earth pets. Alta had a strange rapport with all animals.

Chapter 5
Alta's Home

Back at my house, James couldn't resist the urge to interrogate Alta. But, rather than saying "Let's see some tricks," as I was expecting him to, and as I probably would have in his place, his questions were about her home and her basic composition. These were questions that I hadn't gotten around to asking about yet, so I listened with great interest. The three of us settled ourselves comfortably on the couch and chairs. I noticed that, once James and I had sat down, Alta observed our postures and adjusted hers to match, so that she was not sitting straight upright as she had been when watching the wedding shows. I was relieved to think that I wouldn't have to teach her how to sit.

"Alta," James started out, "The followers of St. Thomas Aquinas, the Thomists, say angels have no physical bodies. If the angels have no physical bodies, then it stands to reason that the demons have no bodies either. It seems that you DO have a body. So, how can you fight demons that are non-corporeal?"

Alta pondered for a second, and then answered, "The Thomists DO advocate for angels not having bodies, and depending on the choir, that is largely correct. There are nine choirs of angels, you know. Lower choirs are made like me. When Thomas Aquinas was writing of the angels, he was describing the higher choirs of angels, not advanced alien robots. There was another writer, a Franciscan named St. Bonaventure, who described angels differently. He said angelic bodies were made of Hylomorphic Matter. That's a better description for us robots. Remember, I was designed to best suit a mission on my own world. To make a good interface with physical species, I needed a supernatural body."

"What is your world like?" James asked next.

Alta said, "It is just like your world, but there are different species of trees and animals. You'd probably be surprised by how much the physical environment resembles yours. In fact, there are dozens of worlds that are very similar, all inhabited, all about the same size and gravity, all with oxygen-rich atmospheres. Most of these are like Earth and Gihon in their climate and wildlife forms."

She continued, "The biggest difference between these worlds isn't the place, but rather when they started on the technological timeline. Our timeline is more than 8,000 years ahead of yours. A lot can happen in just 100 years. Remember, only 150 years ago, you all had the Civil War. Your technology has made a big difference in your society since then. Now, picture your progress of the last 100 years, and multiply it by 800. In reality though, the difference is even greater. Technology snowballs. As time passes, the rate of discovery increases. On Earth, there was far more discovered between 1950 and 2000 than between 1800 and 1900, technologically speaking. So, the technological differences between your world and mine are astronomical."

Rather than waiting for James to ask what those differences were, Alta apparently decided to steer the question-and-answer session herself, because she next said, "James, rather than fielding questions, let me tell you the key differences that I see. The most impressive among them is the fingerprint of God upon your world. You people have guardian angels, ours do not."

James interrupted to ask, "How do you know that?"

Alta said, "Because I can see them. I can see any agent of the other dimension, the one which you call the spiritual realm. That dimension is the larger reality in which THIS universe you live in is embedded. The spiritual dimension is eternal and vast beyond imagination. There is no end to time there. Within its confines are Heaven, Hell, and other places whose theological classification is beyond my understanding."

I interrupted, "Do you know what those other places are like?"

She replied, "There are … compartments or zones; I guess you might call them, around those places. We hoped their significance and purpose would be explained by finding the true theology."

47

"Can you go to these places?" James asked.

"Technically yes, just like you could go to the President's house. Ability is one thing, permission is another. If it was that simple, I'd just fly to Heaven and ask God or the angels which religious path was best. But it's not set up that way. I now believe that sorting out the truth is our civilization's test of merit, as Eden was yours. Your people had the task of not eating the forbidden fruit; our people have the task of finding the right religion after Eden," Alta said.

"To understand the things I tell you," Alta went on, "you need to understand what lies beyond the shores of your reality. Tom, when you talk to your guardian angel, where do you think he is?" She looked directly at me as she asked this.

I said, "Gosh, I dunno … here I assume?" I shrugged and waved my hand around in a vague gesture to indicate the space around us.

Alta shook her head and replied, "No, neither angels nor demons are here, except with the explicit permission of God. Almost all of them live in Heaven or Hell. But they can exercise their influence from there, again if they have permission. If their will and intellect are located here, their influence is greater, but for most, their will and intellect reside in Heaven or Hell. There are two notable exceptions, one from Heaven, and one from Hell. Ostara and The Watchers roam the space between Heaven and Hell, seeking the destruction of intelligent species. Michael the Archangel and his team are commissioned from Heaven to fight against Ostara and The Watchers. I know very little about these groups, but I hope that we don't run into the ones from Hell. Unfortunately, I suspect that they are already on our trail."

"I am most similar to the higher angels in capability, but I am located right here on Earth. You can see and touch me. I can travel the spaces between, but I am not permitted to travel into Heaven or Hell directly. Those borders are guarded. So, I have the ability, but not the permission. Like, you can't just walk into Fort Knox," she said.

"So, if you did have permission … ," James speculated, eyebrows raised. Alta finished the sentence for him.

"Yes, if I had permission, I could go to any place in the next dimension, or in this one, for that matter, and I could even bring you with me."

James and I looked at each other with excitement, as James said, "This sounds like an invitation, even if it's just conditional."

"Well," Alta said hesitantly, "considering what we have subjected Tom to, it would be a fair trade, if only it were allowed. I should tell you, though, that while our prophets told us that there was a God who created everything, they also told us that we were to be passed over as regards a personal appearance. God is not going to show Himself to us here. We were instructed to find your world, and we were given the ability to see the greater spiritual reality, precisely BECAUSE we were passed over by God. So, I really don't think God's going to suddenly give us permission to come visit Him in Heaven."

49

"Alta," I said, leaning forward in my excitement, "I wasn't passed over, because I am from here, right? Would I incur the wrath of God for peeping under the curtain?"

"Tom," Alta answered, "You weren't a random pick. We were guided to you by your guardian angel who recommended you for this task." Hearing this, I sat back in shock. I knew I had a guardian angel; I even talked to him on a regular basis. But hearing that he had recommended me suddenly made him seem much more real. A wave of self-satisfaction flowed over me as I thought that I had earned the good opinion of such an exalted being.

Alta continued, "Since we know your guardian angel recommended you, we know that anything you do to spread the truth to other worlds therefore has the approval of God. But he's also given permission for the things that you may suffer in this quest. It is my job to protect you, but I have been given strict limits on what I can do. I am constrained to this place, to this time, and to do no more than match force with force, should anything attack us. For instance, when demons killed members of our crew on the way here, I was warned by my friend Raphael not to follow the demons back to Hell to destroy them in retaliation. Those crew members belong to God, not to me, even though they were my friends. I do not have the right or permission to avenge their deaths."

"But you could do that?" I asked. "You could go to Hell and destroy demons?"

"Absolutely! In fact, it might at some point be our best statistical chance of mission success, depending on how things play out," she replied.

That thought was too intimidating to absorb all at once. It was hard to imagine this attractive girl, with her doll collection and penchant for wedding shows, wreaking violence on the demons in Hell, so I changed the subject back to Alta's home. "Can you tell us more about Jane, your crew, and the journey that brought you here?"

"Sure," she said with a half-shrug, "where would you like me to start?"

"Alta, you said that you all are 8,000 years ahead of us on the time line. I assume that's Earth years. In OUR timeline, when did your people invent radio?" I asked.

Alta responded, "That's a very good question! It appears that in fact, you all have been around almost as long in total as us, but your technological evolution was slower. We believe this may have been due to time lost in your dark ages. We never had a Dark Age."

"Do the Gihonians look like you and Jane back at home?" Or is this appearance just for our benefit?" I asked.

"Interestingly," Alta continued, "we all look like your people. Our planet and virtually every inhabited one we have found has intelligent life on it that is nearly identical to ours. The genetic match is so close that any two of these inhabited worlds could interbreed. This was our first incontrovertible clue that there was a God to be found. It indicated the possibility of a single unique creator, whose fingerprint was on every sentient being we encountered. We have an expression in our world … 'They are all made in His image.'"

James got up and went to the kitchen, poured us a couple of Gatorades, and brought them over. I realized Alta's quote sounded very similar to one from Earth, a quote that Christians use from Genesis 1:27, "We were made in His image." Perhaps their people had some crude version of Genesis, I thought. But rather than asking Noah to build a huge boat to escape the flood, as happened in our version, their race was asked to accomplish space flight.

"Alta, tell us more of the big differences I would observe on your world?" I was surprised to hear that the Gihonians so closely resembled us, but I still wanted to get at the alien-ness of them.

"For starters, we use our minds more than you all do, and more diversely in everyday tasks," Alta said.

I said "Well sure, you ARE aliens. So, the Gihonians look mostly human, but with bigger brains, right? Like the Coneheads?"

"Very funny," Alta said, rolling her eyes at me. "Once again, we're biologically the same as you, and so is everyone else on all the other inhabited worlds we've found so far. There are no funny-looking Klingons. People all look basically the same, except variance by race, everywhere. You are unknowingly at the great biological stopping point of human evolution. And, yes, there is such a thing. The differences are between us are technological. But our technology has come to the point where our minds interface directly with our embedded systems, so we use our minds to do all of the functions that you use machines and external appliances to do here. In the guest stateroom on our ship, there's a physical remote control to adjust the room conditions. But no one in the crew needs it; it's just for guests like you. The crew merely thinks commands, like 'gravity off,' or 'TV on.'"

"Wait, you have TV?" James interrupted with a surprised look.

"Sure, but it's not like your TV," Alta shrugged.

"Then, are your minds better than ours?" I asked, trying to keep the discussion on point. If their brains weren't bigger, maybe their biology was more efficient.

Alta said, "No, not fundamentally. They are just better trained. After twenty generations of this 'better training,' babies on Gihon are now born with many of rudimentary abilities from the very start. But our machines are helping them along. I have the same ability to control our systems with my mind, but I also have a transcendental engine, because I am a machine. That transcendental engine lets me to do as the angels do."

"In a sense, you are a machine made of carbon. God has given each of you a soul, and you all share in the same human nature. The angels could also be viewed as machines, ones made beyond this world, by God. Angels don't all share in one angelic nature, though; each has a unique nature. We call them all angels, because it's convenient, but each of them is more like a whole separate species unto itself, than like one individual within an 'angel' species. We transcendental robots are also machines made of carbon in part, like you. But like the angels, each of us has a unique nature, not one common shared nature. But unlike both you and the angels, we have no soul, and thus no eternal destiny," she continued.

I was ready with my next question, "So, Alta, what would I see on your city streets?"

Instead of describing the streets of Gihon, as I expected, Alta said "I can show you," and reached over and touched my forehead.

Abruptly, I could see the two of us walking up a sidewalk that almost looked like Earth. I realized she must be showing me a vision of Gihon. In the town center to our right, there appeared buildings like on Earth, stone and metal and glass constructions that varied in height. But the sidewalk we were on led up a hill, curving around the outside of the hill in what I could see became a spiral leading to the top. To our right, and all along the length of the spiraling sidewalk, was a large retaining wall, made of rough light brown stone. Then there were a series of round minarets near the top of the walkway. They looked to be four or five stories tall, made of a very uniform white brick. Near the top, were two balconies that ringed each minaret, with a waist-high railing around the outside of the balcony. Reaching from the pointed roof to the floor of each of the top balconies were a set of narrow windows circling the minaret.

As we walked up the hill, I could sense something trying to reach my mind. There were no other conspicuous noises in this vision; we were too far from the other buildings for that. But this new sound in my head was not quite like an audible noise, either; I doubt anyone else could have heard it. It was like a siren song; it reached inside and called to me. I knew it was coming from one of the towers. I was deeply disturbed by all this and stepped backward. This motion within the vision apparently meant I leaned backward in real life as well. My head pulled out of reach of Alta's hand, and I snapped out of the vision.

"Alta," I said, breathing deep to dispel the tremors I felt inside, and trying to re-orient myself to the reality that I was sitting in my living room and not walking up a hill on a foreign world, "what was that, that was summoning me in your world?" I was too caught up in my experience to be thinking about James, but he was looking at me with an expression of curiosity. He hadn't seen what I had just seen. I took a drink of the Gatorade in my hand, and the familiar liquid helped restore a sense of normality.

Alta answered, "In our world, children normally gestate in nine months like they do on Earth. Many years ago, though, a few of our people chose to do something different with their children. They delivered their children early, typically at five months, and then gestated them for nine years in the tops of those white towers

55

that you saw. The children lived in special chambers inside the towers that restricted their physical growth. This was a lot like the earthly practice of cultivating Bonsai trees; the caretaker restricts the tree's growth in one direction so that the tree will grow in another. Not all aspects of growth are restricted; it is this way for Bonsai trees, and it was this way for these children, as well. The cerebral functions of these children expanded dramatically. Their mental powers and influence were markedly greater than the rest of society. They can reach the most sensitive of our people, and always each other. Moreover, they are clairvoyant."

"That's barbaric!" I exclaimed. No amount of mental powers could justify locking kids in a tower and not allowing them to develop to their natural physical potential. I shuddered at the thought of my parents not allowing me to develop my athletic body, my triathlete skills, in order to turn me into a telepathic monster.

Alta said, "That image was from 3,000 years ago on my world, more than 150 generations ago, but still 5,000 years ahead of your time, technologically. It was the very dawn of this mental control that we now have across all of society. But in today's world, we don't need these older methods anymore. Those methods pioneered the mental difference we now have, but we found we didn't need those methods to sustain it. As you know, I also have this mental ability; I can cause external events, with just my mind and no machines, because I am transcendental. What that means is that I am the machine that drives a change my own mind initiates. Jane, for example, can, with her mind, directly use one of our machines to do as she wishes. In my case, I am both the mind and the machine."

I sat thinking about this for a moment, but James could no longer contain his impatience. He insisted that I describe what I had seen in my vision, so I did the best I could to tell him what it was like. But there was still an elephant in the room.

"So, Alta, are you also clairvoyant?" I asked.

Alta said, "Yes, most definitely. I'd have been destroyed by demons the first week of my existence if I weren't. But we do not use the term quite as you do in your world."

"How so?" I asked.

She replied, "Clairvoyance applies to any extrasensory capability that allows us to see into the spiritual realm. The sight of the dead, the living, demons, and angels are as common to my people as seeing Canada Geese fly south is to yours. As far as we can tell, God has allowed people to develop this clairvoyance as a way of helping them get started in their search for the truth. The closer you are to the truth, the less clairvoyant. People on your world, Tom and James, have hardly any of this clairvoyance because God came here more directly. So, you just don't need it. But those of us less gifted by the appearance of a savior were given a different edge in our search for the truth—the ability to see the spiritual realm. As far as we know, the other intelligent species also share this clairvoyance with us, to varying degrees. Partly because of this and partly because of other evidence like the genetic resemblance I mentioned earlier, all these species are aware that there is a creator out there. They are all searching for the alien God. We were the first to come here, although it was not our first attempt to find you."

"How DID you find our planet?" I asked.

"Actually, we followed a star. Your people call it Cassiopeia A; it's the remnant of a supernova that first shed light on your world 350 years ago. Your astronomers discovered its radio signature just after World War II. We followed its radio emissions. It is one of the brightest radio features in the heavens," she said.

Alta quirked her head to one side and said quietly, "We know there is a God, but don't know very much about Him. We passionately desire to know Him better, and that is why we are on this search. But even though we don't know Him, we do have a glimmering of an idea of how to read the heavens. There are signs around us, if you keep your eyes open, that are guideposts to follow. Not all events are meaningful, but Cassiopeia A was one such sign. The light of its radio emissions shown on Earth with a special brilliance, and so we followed it here."

Alta continued in a more conversational tone, "When we first discovered Earth, many years ago, we sent an expedition at light speed, which was the fastest travel available at the time. The transit was twenty years, but before they could get here, we discovered how to travel faster than light, by leaving the interior of the universe. Essentially, we exit at the nearest point and travel on its outer surface to move faster than light. Then we re-enter the universe at the closest point to our goal. We would have sent a ship to catch up with them anyway, but ten years into the first ship's journey, they radioed back a distress signal, in what later was called a 'historic event.' They were never heard from again. When a new, faster ship was finally sent to investigate, they found a wrecked ship in a debris field, with bodies torn in half."

The memory of being frozen in bed, a disembodied head desiring to rip me to shreds, flashed vividly into my head, and I shivered. "I can guess what happened," I said, trying to sound nonchalant. "Demons, right?"

"It would now seem so." Alta nodded soberly.

Deciding to change the subject, James asked, "What about murder and suicide in your world, Alta?"

Alta turned to face him and said, "We have tools that you don't have yet, that nearly eliminate that sort of problem."

"How is that? What do you all do that we don't do here?" I inquired.

Alta faced me again and said, "Do you remember your dream from last night?"

"No one remembers their dreams, Alta," I said.

"You'll remember if I tell you," she said.

"Okay, what did I dream?" I asked skeptically.

Alta said, "You dreamt of entering a swimming race that had three laps of breast stroke."

"Yes!" I practically shouted, then with a less noisy surprise, "I DO remember dreaming that." It was eerie to realize that Alta could read what I was thinking. She had just demonstrated that she knew my own mind better than I did, down to subconscious thoughts I was not aware of. I had always assumed mind-reading to be impossible. A pit started to form in my stomach, and a wave of loss washed over me, as if my very selfhood was slipping away, because there was no part of me, no matter how tiny, which was private and inaccessible to others. I might have drowned in these thoughts if Alta had not continued to speak and thus distracted me.

"The rules were seventy-five yards," she said, "with one lap on top of the water, one under water, and the last lap on top again. You even told a friend of this format. For years, you have had dreams that established this as the rule for the race, so it was completely familiar to you, and you taught other racers."

"That may be true," I said, perplexity in my tone. "But it's not possible, because the race would finish on the far side of the pool. This makes no sense at all."

Then Alta asked, "Why did you tell the other swimmers that well-known format for the contest?"

"I don't know," I said. I was at a loss to explain any of this.

Alta gave me an intent look, and said "What you don't realize is that you are basically living a second life in your dreams. Your world's psychiatrists have yet to fully explore and manipulate this as we do. But there is a complete catalog of subconscious pseudo-realities and a history file of these events that shape your life, hopes, and experiences and even your self-image as you travel through, night after night. You have subconscious friends, associations, a job, and a pseudo-reality that has complete consistency both forward and back in time. You plan night to night, as we do day to day, and you remember your pseudo-history as it happens. All of this draws from and creates a complete catalog of subconscious realities that are used to shape optimism, depression, ambition and every facet of your real identity."

She continued, "This catalog is critical to your ability to process events of your day. People who are depressed have a couple bad cards in their file. You, for example, are a little bit more on edge today because your subconscious mind wants to reconcile what you know about how swimming races are actually held with your dream-memory of a whole history of races that were set up differently. On our world, we just remove or over-write the bad cards. Then they feel better about themselves without even knowing why. It's like getting an IV drip of water, so you no longer feel thirsty, even though you never took a drink. This card file is central to your identity and it's the undiscovered reason why only sleep will let you fully process the events that occur during the day."

"How do you your people overwrite these dream cards? Use an alien brain machine?" I liked the thought of pushing a button and suddenly feeling better about everything.

Alta shook her head and said, "No, our advanced technology has increasingly revealed that the very best machines

61

are the ones made by God. So, the solution is actually very simple. I could just take you to the pool, and have you swim, one lap on top, one under, one more on top, and the last lap under water. That would reformat the program so you'd finish on the right side of the pool. Your card would be re-written, and you would feel a bit better."

I pondered her answer for a moment. Although this was fascinating, I wasn't about to jump up and head to a pool right in the middle of this conversation. Sorting out my mental health into its ideal state didn't seem like a high priority in the face of, you know, aliens and demons and the mission I had accepted and all that. I was still curious about her crew, so I asked her about that next.

"Alta, tell us about your crew. Other than Jane, who manned the ship that brought you here?" I asked.

She replied, "We started with a crew of six, but, as we approached your world, two of our team were destroyed in orbit."

"Destroyed?" James said. "You mean killed in some sort of accident?" When I had told him about all that had happened, I had not mentioned Jane telling me of crewmates suffering the same fate that I felt from the demon. This wasn't a deliberate lapse on my part; it just hadn't been at the top of my list of things to mention, being somewhat overtaken by the existence of scary disembodied heads and aliens who wanted to argue theology.

"No," Alta said emphatically. "Being mysteriously ripped in half is not an accident. Something of tremendous power, something beyond this world, has been hunting us, and it has now turned its attention to you. That is why I am here. The crew has only one protector however, who is me. And now, Jane has given me to you. But the crew is working on another like me." I thought I detected in Alta's tone a note of … it was hard to put my finger on it. Wistfulness? Sadness? Anger? It suddenly flashed through my mind to wonder how Alta felt about being ordered to "babysit" me when her crew was in danger. Did she resent the job she had been given? Was she capable of loving her crewmates? She had wanted to go to Hell to avenge them, so maybe. I felt a stab of pity for her and guilt at taking her away from her crew that needed her protection as much as I did. But I needed her too so I wasn't about to offer to give her back.

"Another like you?" I asked.

"Yes," Alta said, "My sister Raven, who is mostly complete."

Chapter 6

The Alien Ship

Later that morning, Jane called and asked me to meet with her at the outdoor Mall in DC. She was interested in what I might have put together for her team so far on the theological front.

We planned to meet up at noon. So, when Alta said she didn't need me to drive her there, I figured I'd bike over and enjoy the sunshine on the way. Saturdays on the DC waterfront in summer are fantastic; there's just so much of everything going on. Volleyball games, Ultimate Frisbee, even people watching the planes take off at the airport from the adjoining soccer field. Once I arrived, Jane was there with another crew member, sitting nonchalantly at a picnic table, and they were discussing something. Alta also arrived, but I wasn't exactly sure how she got there.

"Where's all your stuff, Jane? I mean all the paperwork I had Alta send you?" I asked. I had worked on the project for awhile on Friday night, and then a little bit more after James had left this morning. Alta had zapped the paperwork to Jane the same way she had "put away" her doll. I had expected Jane to bring the paperwork with her so we could go over it at this meeting.

Jane answered, "Up on our ship, which is where I figured we'd conduct this meeting."

"Oh, really?" I said. "So, did I miss it when I biked up?" Inside I felt a rush of excitement. I was going to get to see a real spaceship up close?

"Very funny, Tom," Jane said, rolling her eyes. I thought she smiled a little as she said it, though. "It's parked in orbit, hidden from your air defense system's prying eyes."

"Well, can I bring my bike?" I asked.

Jane looked around at the outdoor mall. "I guess you'd better; it looks like something that'd get stolen pretty quickly if you left it here."

"Okay then, beam me up," I said with an excited grin.

Jane grimaced, hoping not to encourage my stupid joke, and said, "Alta, if you please."

Alta waved her hand at us and in an instant we were all on board. I wondered if anyone at the outdoor Mall had seen us disappear, but then I figured whatever, that was someone else's problem. I was on board a SPACESHIP. I looked around eagerly.

My first impression was of a Royal Caribbean luxury cruise liner, in space. At least, that was what the inside looked like. We had teleported into a sort of entrance hall that was absolutely huge. The ship seemed more like a resort destination than a space vehicle. There were tiled marble floors, glass balconies with red wood railings around the upper stories, warm lights atop golden stands, crystal chandeliers, and soft couches dotting the sides. The entire place was spotlessly clean. The air smelled fresh; I think I even felt a breeze! This was like nothing I'd seen on Star Trek, or any other futuristic show. This ship really reminded me of the giant cruise ship that I had been on when I took a vacation to the Bahamas. I stared around in awe.

As we walked down the hallway, I discovered a twist. As Alta walked with us, it almost seemed as if she was a walking remote control. By that I mean that something mysterious happened to the ship as we traveled through it. When I looked out of a port window, back at Earth, I saw stars, meaning we were on an edge of the ship. But on the same wall as that window was a door that presumably led to outer space. As Alta approached the door, it opened to another wing of the ship that simply couldn't have been there when I looked out the adjoining window. Before I could ask Alta what the trick was, Jane started talking about how the ship was designed.

"We are a spacefaring people, Tom. As your scientists have theorized, the universe is wrapped around itself, so that it is finite and contained but without ever having an edge that you can reach. For things that have mass, no amount of travel through the universe will ever bring you to a final boundary. Our ship is sort of like that, designed on the same paradigm. It's one set volume, but that volume always lies in your direct path of travel. So, I could pick a direction and run for ten miles without having to stop or swerve, even though the ship itself is in a volume less than one square mile," she said.

I tried to picture this and failed. "Okay, what if four runners went north, south, east, and west simultaneously. Then you'd run outta ship, right?"

Jane said, "If you sail ships in four directions of the universe, none of them ever stop or run out of space. Your four runners might end up meeting back up with each other in odd spaces, though. And, even if it were a problem, Alta could just instantly add to the ship's total volume, if that was needed. The current size that we have today seemed to be a good fit for our journey here. All the labs, observatory, sports equipment, and fields we have now represent a comfortable up-scaling from our average day-to-day use. Remember, we are coming great distances. This is our home, our lab, and everything else."

Then Jane pointed, and said, "Wanna see something cool?"

"Sure!" I said. Of COURSE I wanted to see something cool.

"See this hallway?" she said and led us to an eight-foot-wide corridor that connected two parts of the ship. At one point, there were doors on both sides of the hall, facing each other. She stopped in front of them. Then she wheeled to make a presentation of sorts.

"On my left is our lab." Jane presented it with both arms extended. She looked like Vanna White presenting a new prize on Wheel of Fortune.

Jane looked at the door and said, "Lab!"

It opened up and inside were two of her associates, working sophisticated equipment that appeared to be for some sort of electro-mechanical assembly plant. On the front left side of the room, it had all the makings of an exotic custom robot shop. One crew member even had a robotic arm in her hand that she was testing from an interface in the wrist. They were clearly in the finishing stages of building some sort of android. Jane called out "Hello" to them, and they waved.

She then closed the door with a verbal command, "Close!"

Next Jane redirected my attention as she pointed and said, "Now, on the right side of the hall is the same lab."

She looked at the door and said, "Lab."

The door opened and inside were the same two colleagues working the same equipment. She waved. They smiled, knowing Jane was teasing visitors who hadn't seen the trick.

I said, "Okay, Jane, open both doors at once." I think I had a silly grin on my face. Clearly, this was the same kind of ship re-arranging and moving that explained how Alta could open a door to a room that had previously been outer space.

Jane shook her head. "You get the trick. Obviously, it doesn't work that way. But, the way it DOES work is very convenient. Let's face it, at the end of a long day, it's awfully nice to have my quarters be only 100 feet from wherever I'm working. I just say 'quarters,'" which she did now with emphasis. At that command the left door opened, the one which had first gone to the lab, and it now was Jane's captain's quarters.

She invited us in, to a large working table where I could see all the documents I had given her were neatly laid out. Her suite was luxurious. The table looked as if it was made of mahogany, although I supposed it was the Gihon equivalent. A thick, soft carpet spread from wall to wall; it was beautifully colored in swirls of burgundy, cream, and dark brown. Tapestries hung on the walls.

Jane passed through to a door on the far side. She said, "Display Room," and we all entered.

The display room was huge, with 30-foot ceilings. It had massive flat screen displays containing some sort of charts. When I looked closer, they appeared to be some sort of hierarchical charts of the total religious and political history of our world. All the church fathers, religious founders, heretics, and principle religious branches or splits were listed there. Each part was scaled against a timeline that started from about 5000 BC and continued to the present. We stood around, looking at the screens as we talked. Jane waved her hand at sections to expand them, as she displayed what the crew had gathered. These pieces, properly connected, were meant to assess how philosophy and theology evolved from historical events. This even included kings and political factors that influenced outcomes.

"You guys have a vast collection of information here," I said. That may have been an understatement. I was impressed.

"Well, it's all that we aggregated from radio, TV, and other broadcasts while en route here. Plus a few disparate things we collected this week. But we need a more comprehensive data source, and then we'll need some private 'lessons' to sort out the right interpretation of it all," she said.

I responded, "What you have now is amazing, but the best total source for information would be a complete scan of the Library of Congress. I have often said that if the aliens dropped through the roof of the Library of Congress, they'd walk out the front door Catholic."

"To us, Tom, you are the aliens. But if I need to go there in search of your alien God, so be it. Tomorrow, we'll do just that," she said.

As I pictured a band of aliens—plus one alien robot—walking into the Library of Congress and demanding all the information stored there, I had some concerns about the plan. Jane and company didn't seem to get that their intrusion might not be welcome.

"Well, they do have rules there, and guards. Not to mention that all of the data might not be in the digital domain. So, you may only get a portion of what you seek," I said.

Jane waved her hand dismissively. "Yes, but that's a simple problem to resolve with our technology. Permit me to demonstrate with Alta. Just watch." She handed Alta a closed book and told her to read it. Alta grabbed it, but never opened it. Then Jane took it back and opened it to page 140.

"Alta, what is the second word on the third paragraph of page 140?" Jane asked.

"Fractal," Alta answered. Jane showed me that Alta was correct. She had read the whole book in an instant without even opening it. This was my day to be impressed, apparently. Aliens are so cool. They were living up to my every boyhood dream.

"Boy," I said. "Would Alta have been a big help in grad school! How many volumes can she ingest at once?"

Alta chimed in, "I could absorb the totality of the Library's contents in seconds, just by passing through the threshold of the building. But I need to know what I am looking for and what the boundaries of the search are. For instance, I would eliminate data from live wireless networks, or radio waves that penetrated the building. I also have no need for data regarding the food and material requisitions of their cafeteria or cleaning crew, or data on the cash register. All material already scanned or in print is equally accessible to me using this method. After collecting and parsing the total data load, I'd return it to the computers here to add detail to our current understanding."

"So, tomorrow, Alta is going to read the library with you guys?" I asked. I decided to ignore any intimidating thoughts about the lack of privacy around a being that could walk into a room and know how much money was in the cash register, or what I had eaten for lunch.

Jane said, "Not for this trip. However impressive this may have seemed to you, we can do the same thing with a portable device that any member of our team can carry in. We need Alta's other talents for your mission. You see, she IS your protector."

71

"Okay, Jane," I said. "So, let's get into it now." I waved my hand at the screens. "Based upon what you now know, without the Library of Congress stuff, what faiths appear to have the greatest likelihood of being the real deal?"

Jane thought for a second before commenting. "Now, you are asking me ahead of my chance to really look over the data, but here's what I can tell you so far. We did get a head start from our own prophets. They told us two things. First was that God had already come once to redeem all of creation. The second thing was to seek the God of Abraham."

Thinking of God redeeming all of creation, I quoted, "God wanted all fullness to be found in Him, and through Him to reconcile all things to Him, everything in Heaven and everything on Earth, by making peace through His death on the Cross."

Just like the smart kid in school, Alta spoke up with the source of the quote. "From Paul's letter to the Colossians, chapter 1, verses 19-20, found in your Christian Bible."

Jane appeared to consider this, but continued, "This leaves us with the earthly Muslim, Jewish, and Christian faiths to review. That's still a big footprint. But since we know from our prophets that God has already come, we can eliminate faiths that claim He is still being awaited. Obviously, prophets needn't send us to a place also waiting for God, because it would just be equally barren. We could just stay home and assume our place is as likely to be visited as the next."

"I need to show you guys 'The Great Pumpkin' by Charles Schulz," I said reflectively.

Jane gave a quizzical look and asked Alta, "Is he helping or joking with that suggestion?"

"I believe he's just using his great understanding of literature to show that he understands you, Jane," said Alta in a somewhat sardonic tone. Her comment was a cross between humor and an attempt to shame me for my joke. Jane offered her own explanation:

"So, by elimination, the remaining contenders are all the various branches of Christianity. The Jews still await their savior, and the Muslims don't believe that God Himself came here, only that he sent a prophet. Therefore, we can only conclude that Jesus really is God, as Christians claim. This is not enough for us, though. We need to know what the next step for our race is. Did Jesus die for us as well? If so, is there something we need to do? Do we just make a verbal act of faith, as some would have it? Do we need to be baptized? Do we need to join a church, and if so, does it matter which one? Are non-Earthlings even eligible to join a church? In order to get a proper grasp of the next step, we need to know which of the Christian denominations has the full truth, or at least the fullest truth." Jane paused for a second to allow us to process the whole idea.

She continued, "We have managed to narrow it down a bit further. We are working on the assumption that the true religion God instituted is still being practiced, because God would not let it fail. Also, He presumably wouldn't have told us to come looking for it here if it was already gone. This eliminated all archaic faiths that have been extinct for hundreds of years."

"There are slightly more than 33,000 branches of Christianity that we know of today. Some were easy to eliminate, like one that was started by a King who wasn't allowed to divorce his wife," Jane said.

"Jane, I assume you're talking about the Anglicans," I interrupted. With a quizzical tone, I asked, "What about their beliefs taken on their own merit? Anglicans are very close to Catholic beliefs, I know, so it's not like the circumstances of their founding completely invalidate everything they believe."

"True," said Jane, "but when two groups teach mostly the same thing, with just a few significant differences, then the history around how those differences arose is a key part of evaluating who is more likely to be right.

"Also, we have reasoned that God wouldn't have come and preached a doctrine other than the correct faith. So, religions that started well after Jesus' death are suspect. For this reason, we have broken the Christian faiths into seminal historical milestones." Jane pointed at the screen again.

"Other branches of Christianity also hinge on the correctness or incorrectness of one or two triggering events. Like the Protestant Reformation, for one," Jane concluded.

I thought about all that Jane had said. "Let me sum up what you've said so far. You've essentially ruled out the non-Christian religions because none of them are compatible with the two things revealed by your prophets: that God has already visited Earth, and that you are to seek the God of Abraham. So, now you're combing through history for evidence that supports or damages the claims that each branch of Christianity makes. Is that right?" Jane replied with a serious nod.

"Well, in that case," I said, "Since you mention the Reformation, let me offer a reflection on that, which you can research later. This is just a starting point, but if you know how I and other Catholics view the Reformation, that might help focus your research. At the time of the Reformation, the Catholic Church was having serious issues with immoral abuses, many at the hands of the clergy. The reformers rightly intended to reform these abuses. But rather than just reform the MORALITY of the Church, they went further and changed the THEOLOGY of the Church. They didn't stick with attacking what the clergy was DOING, they also attacked the TEACHINGS that the Church had held. By way of contrast, the later counter-Reformation worked within the Church to reform the morals of the Church while remaining true to the theology that had been passed on through the ages. You can see this when you look at early church beliefs, which are not fully present in the Protestant reformers practices and creeds 500 years after the Reformation. This is a point for you to focus your research on. You need to know what actually trickled down into the pews and also what the original churches practiced 2,000 years ago. In other words, what were the beliefs of the firsthand witnesses of the early church?"

"Lutherans might well say that the Bible itself is the very proof of what the early church believed, so that we only need to compare a church's teaching to the Bible and can't rely on any other early writers," Jane said, playing devil's advocate.

"Sure, but that is a matter of interpretation. The group taking that interpretation seeks to glean meaning out of the Bible apart from the history and traditions in which it was forged. They claim the Bible is 100% correct, and they are right about that. But when deciding what it is that the Bible is saying, for it to be right about, they separate it from its context. That would be like me dropping my college calculus textbook into a room full of twelfth graders and telling them to use it to build me a jet engine on paper. Even though the textbook is completely accurate, I'd have to reasonably assume they'd fail, because they don't even have the full context that gives that textbook meaning," I said.

Jane looked thoughtful. "We'll look into that. For now, let me ask you this. We have studied the two main reformers, Luther and Calvin, at length, and it appears that the matter of 'justification' is central to their beliefs. They believe that people are justified—that is, saved—only by faith in Jesus, without any reference to your actions, your 'good works.'"

"Yes," I said, "but Luther's ideas are cast in an entirely new light after an alien visit. If one can be justified by faith alone, and everything necessary was done by God for salvation, why did

God require you all to come here? Why didn't He just tell you what you need to believe and let you believe it where you were at? If He was actually going to accomplish all the justification without any 'works,' wouldn't the first thing to be taken off the list of your people's obligations be a dangerous space flight to even hear the truth?"

Jane pondered with her hand on her chin. "Hmmm."

I persisted. "Let's face it. We have repeated examples of where God insists that people DO something to be right with Him. Christ had to go to the Cross, Moses and his people had to follow the Ten Commandments, we Christians are commanded to re-do the Last Supper in memory of him. Abraham was asked to sacrifice his son Isaac on an altar, before God sent an angel to stop him, and now you need to go across all of space for the truth."

"So, it would appear that justification is a two-step process then. God does His part, then we do ours," Jane said.

I continued my lesson on the Reformation with a broader brush. "There are three central figures in Protestantism, not two. You forgot Zwingli. But let me sum up what I believe your research will reveal. Luther was a Catholic priest who taught in Germany at Wittenberg. It was really he who started the whole matter, trying to correct a genuine moral wrong that was too common in the church. But in the process, he initiated a teaching on justification that didn't just challenge the people whose morals he was confronting; it also adopted a view that was never the understanding of the church that preceded him. His paradigm placed the full burden on God, making men's deeds useless in achieving salvation. Worst yet, if works didn't matter, the sins of selling indulgences wouldn't either. He ultimately forsook his priestly vows and took a wife, who was a former nun. Not the kind of morality I'd expect from a guy whose conclusions I would trust to change everything we believe, frankly. People can be immoral and still believe something true, as some of the Catholic clergy at the time were doing, but that truth didn't come from them. They were just passing it along. When you're talking about starting a new teaching or a new take on a teaching, I'd trust a more upright man over an inconstant one, any day."

I paused before continuing, "Zwingli operated in Switzerland and was also ordained a Catholic priest. Like Luther, he also left the faith and took a wife. But unlike Luther, who kept most Catholic beliefs and just changed a few, Zwingli challenged a large cross-section of the church's long held beliefs, from priestly celibacy to the Real Presence in the Eucharist. In the end, he was killed at the age of 47 in a battle with the Catholic Cantons, in an attempt to cut off their food. This is another guy whose theology doesn't match that of the church that was founded 1500 years prior to his theological departures. Moreover, he is another man I'd find it hard to trust based upon his lifestyle and actions."

"Calvin was a lawyer by trade and operated out of Geneva. Calvin created what some call a religious theocracy in Geneva, stronger than what we saw in medieval times. Also, he introduced the idea of dividing justification into two parts by adding sanctification. This implied that God justified men by His sacrifice, and the Holy Spirit worked to sanctify men afterwards. The early church had never separated these ideas, because of the central importance of clearly responding to God's call by personal action. In Calvin's theology, none of your efforts would ever matter in God's eyes. Calvin attempted to say that there was no real merit found by men responding to God in a positive way. Again, this understanding was never part of the teaching of the early church," I said.

Jane thought for a second, and said, "We will consider what you have said. Alta has recorded everything, and she can adjust our software models to look for the aberrations you identified."

I interjected with a question, "Jane, how do those software models work? How would you sort out the original doctrines of a church that is 2,000 years old, and compare them to those held by modern churches? And do it with enough accuracy to rule out some of the modern options as being incorrect?"

Jane responded, "It's actually not hard at all. I suppose an individual Earthling would need to read through some of the writings of early Christians to gauge whether their own theology matched that of the early followers of Christ, but we have the resources to do a much more complete job. Taking your Catholic faith as an example, we just draw on all data sources from plus or minus 100 years around Christ's life, including ancillary historical documents, like the works of Josephus, the Didache, and the Targums. Any credible source will do. We use those to make a computer model of their teachings, practices, creeds, history, tradition, and beliefs. Then the religious factions we encounter are parsed into various cohorts. The same is done for each modern faith, and comparisons are made with the original teachings and beliefs."

"So, Jane, let me ask again. Who's winning?"

Jane thought again for a second. "At present, Christianity in general. We do not have enough data yet to paint a definitive picture of the beliefs of early Christian groups. We do, however, have a special interest in the Eastern Orthodox and the Roman Catholics, since neither of those groups appears to have an unambiguous founder in the era after Jesus' time; they appear to stretch back the furthest. That is why you are here obviously. It further appears that the split between the Orthodox and Roman Catholics occurred on seven occasions, of which, five were repaired."

Even though I knew the answer very well myself, I asked Jane, "Do you know what issue remains outstanding, that keeps the two groups from reuniting?"

"It appears to be the status of the pope," she said. She looked at me, waiting expectantly.

I responded, "I bet I can help you with this one. Many of the objections we are now getting for the pope being the head of the church seem to be arguments the Protestant reformers used. But those reasons are coming hundreds of years after the Orthodox actually split. In other words, objections to the papacy that are used by the Orthodox of today are those of the reformers circa 1517 A.D. or so. Those objections were completely unknown to the Orthodox who split in 1054 A.D., prior to Luther and the reformers. The last and final split was in A.D. 1472 A.D., also before Luther's 95 Theses. It's almost like if the South today started saying that the Civil War was over an argument about whether to build a mosque at the 9-11 site in New York."

"Furthermore," I said, "the pope's position was an issue that the Eastern Orthodox scholars resolved to their complete satisfaction on five of the seven splits. This leaves us to believe that the factors now separating the groups may be political or historical, but basically without substantial theological foundation.

"In truth, Jane, you folks will have to do the leg work and come to your own conclusions, but I can certainly continue to point out areas of interest," I said.

Jane pondered, then said, nodding, "It did catch our eye that the demons bristled when we contacted you. That also supports the case for the Catholic Church having the truth we seek."

I thought of one more thing that I wanted to mention, just because it had made a big difference in my life and was an issue close to my heart. "Jane, Catholics believe in something most other religions don't, what we call the Real Presence of Christ in the Eucharist. At the Last Supper, Jesus passed around the bread and wine of the Passover feast to His disciples and told them that the bread was His Body and the wine was His Blood. He told them to repeat this, in memory of Him. Most Christian denominations hold some sort of reenactment of this ritual now and then, but they believe that whatever they do and use is just symbolic, a ritual that connects us to Jesus only through the way it keeps our memory of Him alive. Catholics, on the other hand, believe Jesus meant it literally when He said the bread and wine were His Flesh and Blood. This is what we mean by the Eucharist. It is during our Mass services, when the priest consecrates the bread and wine, that this change to the Body and Blood of Jesus happens. We call the change 'transubstantiation' to indicate that it is no longer bread and wine, even though it still looks and tastes like bread and wine. We believe that it is only through the power of God that we do not actually see the Flesh and Blood as such after the transubstantiation in the Mass."

Jane looked at me with wide eyes. Clearly this was a lot to absorb at once. She paused to think and then looked back at me with an expression of realization.

"I'll bet Alta could see this transformation," she said. "Since Alta has the ability to see spiritual realities to a greater degree than any of us, if there is some substantial change, she would see it immediately."

Jane asked, "Would you help us with this? If you could take Alta to your church to look at the Eucharist and see if she can see a substantial difference after the priest does the consecration, that would help us verify this. If anything changes in the spiritual realm, I'm confident Alta will know. So, if you please, tomorrow, take her to your church first thing in the morning. We'll be heading over to the Library of Congress while you two are at Mass."

"Well, gosh, why not? I believe it is 'bring an alien robot to Mass day,' anyway," I joked. I wasn't worried about testing my beliefs this way; I was confident in the Real Presence. I didn't know enough about Alta's "spiritual realm" to be 100% sure that it was the same level or realm in which the Eucharistic change was happening, but it seemed likely enough. I did have a few quivers of nervous concern about just how well Alta would fit in at Mass, though. I squashed down firmly on the picture in my head of a horde of parishioners descending on us while shouting about aliens and calling for the cops.

Alta, however, bristled at my comment. I looked at her, wondering what I had said that bothered her. I called her an alien robot, but she WAS one. Was my humor just that bad?

Now that we had gotten plans for tomorrow settled, Jane walked us back out of her quarters into the hallway. "So, tonight if you like, Tom, you and Alta can relax and enjoy yourselves on the ship. We have every worthy distraction here. There's lots of techno stuff on board, but I'm thinking you'd probably like the water park or the observatory," she said.

"Observatory?" I asked. I was excited at Jane's invitation to enjoy her ship. This luxury-liner spaceship was about the most awesome thing I had ever seen. I felt like a kid in a candy store.

"We have a good link to satellites all over the galaxy. It's sort of like your own version of Google Sky, but all over space.

Our ship has a subscription to cameras all across this part of the galaxy. This even includes some rovers you can steer and a couple of submarines with cameras. You can study life all over the universe," Jane said.

"There is one techno game that you might like, knowing you," Alta put in.

"What game?" I asked.

"Fast Track," she said. "You ride in a game console that makes a virtual trip to any point or time on your planet. We have created detailed 3D maps of every inch of your planet from light leaving it over the last 1,000 of your years. So, you can sit in a console, dial in any time and any place, and see that place as it was at that time, accurate to the millisecond."

I stared at Alta with amazement and after a moment's reflection, I asked, "So, I could find out who shot Kennedy?"

"Yes," Alta said, and then added in a tone of fake excitement, "In fact, you could even go back to Roswell to see if there really were aliens in 1947!" Jane snickered at Alta's attempt at irony.

"In our world, Fast Track evolved out of a law enforcement tool, so that we COULD find out who shot our equivalents to Kennedy, and later into a tool for resolving property rights," Jane commented.

"So, what you're saying is that there is no need for a jury trial, when you can just dial up a virtual view of the past and see who did what," I said. That sure would simplify things.

"There are limits, obviously. You can't use it to invade someone's legitimate privacy. You have to have our equivalent of a court order to use it in legal matters," Jane responded.

"Well, Jane, since Alta can traverse time, can't you just ask her?" I asked.

Jane replied, "At the core of it, Alta is a military asset, not a research tool. We do the research, Alta protects us. But more importantly, we all need to cooperate on this goal, because the team effort will return data to our world that some will accept, and others may not. To be fair, we can't delegate a job of this importance."

"Well, you've ruined my fun, Jane. But none the less, I'm going to take the military asset here and give your high tech amusement park a try," I said.

After that, Alta headed off with me towards the games.

Alta and I found amazing game machines in dozens of arcade rooms along a mall grouped for recreation and sorted by type. There were more choices than I could imagine. Rows and rows of toys, consoles, and studios for music, sports, and a water park that made Six Flags seem small. It even had a kayak tour through a water course on which you could control the speed of the water to adjust the challenge level. There was also a beautiful waterfall. We got to Fast Track after a ten minute walk up the main thoroughfare through the arcades. We got into the game console, and Alta asked me for a date range and place. I gave her the data and took her back to my senior prom from high school.

"Remember, Tom, on Fast Track you are just seeing light, not current events. This is a completely accurate movie of the past, not the past itself," Alta said.

I didn't care. Anyone would want to go back to see their own senior prom. Hard to believe I was ever that thin. After hours of fun in the past, we went back up the hall from the arcades.

Alta looked at a door on the hall and said, "Guest room."

"So, you weren't kidding about having a guest room on the ship?" I wondered aloud.

"We didn't, but we do now." Alta said as she waved me into a room with a giant window overlooking Earth below. The window filled the whole opposite wall. The rest of the room appeared empty at first glance, with just a spongy floor decorated in a dark fractal pattern, a table, and a door on the left side wall.

"Here's the remote I promised." She handed me a small control that looked like it was for a TV. But I didn't see a TV anywhere.

"Alta, I don't see a TV, or a bed for that matter." Alta pointed to the ceiling above the big window facing Earth. I looked up and saw that on the ceiling was a large cushy mattress with red velvet blankets.

"There it is," she said.

"How do I use that bed on the ceiling?" I asked sarcastically.

Alta pointed to a button on the remote. It was labeled "Gravity."

"Hit gravity off," she instructed. "And, the window is also the TV. See this other switch?" I nodded to indicate I understood, and Alta left the room, leaving me to settle myself in.

Clearly, the plan was to hit the gravity off switch, push off the floor weightless to the bed, and then watch the TV or Earth from the ceiling. I started playing with the remote.

I was worried that if I hit the gravity button back on in the morning without paying attention, I'd fall twenty feet to the floor. I guessed they'd be too smart to have me drop like a stone. Orbiting at this altitude, any gravity in this ship is artificial anyway, I figured. But I thought I should test this to be sure. So, I hit the switch, and rather than float up, I just floated where I was. I wasn't falling in any direction. Then I switched it off while still on the ground. Gravity came back on. I switched the gravity off again, moved myself to hover about a foot off the floor, and then switched the gravity back on again. After some practice, it was clear that gravity returned at a rate that depended on my height from the floor. The higher up I was, the more slowly the gravity came on, drawing me gently to the floor before hitting full force.

I hit the switch again and pushed off the floor, up to the bed on the ceiling. As I closed in on it, I was magnetically adhered to its surface with a light force that prevented drifting. Without actual gravity to orient myself, the magnetic force felt much like gravity, and the bed now felt like it was "down". I was facing the big view port. The remote had lots of other features. The view port could shade over. It could become a TV, or even a video phone. The sound system in the room was to die for. Speakers seemed to be everywhere. At one point in a movie, I thought I heard a woman whisper in my left ear, and it startled me. I eventually found their video library, and all the videos were in 3D. They had all our stuff plus movies from their own world. I was amazed by their historical tapes, their nature shows, and even live video of their early space explorations around the galaxy. They had a complete medical tape library that covered any conceivable circumstance. This was a real treat.

Chapter 7

The Watchers

The following morning I had breakfast in one of the ship's galleys, which was the one thing about this ship that did remind me of Star Trek. The room itself was a fairly normal eating room, with three or four tables over a smooth white floor, but along the wall were several square indentations where the food appeared after you spoke your order. I would be hard pressed to come up with something that looked more like an Enterprise replicator than that. You could order anything, any way you wanted. I ordered filet mignon, medium rare, with fried eggs on top. It was delicious.

Every plate came with a data card next to it. These data cards had the dish name and type, how it was cooked and even the calorie, carbohydrate and vitamin counts, plus the percentages of protein and fat. I asked Alta about the cards, and she said the ship's computer kept absolute track of all food inventory, what we need to get at a port, the rate of consumption by the crew, and even what might go bad. Moreover, the same data was being kept on us. Even what I threw away was measured and applied to what I didn't eat. Every time I went to my room I was weighed and measured fifteen different ways without my even knowing it. The ship's computer knew where we were, how we were doing, and even when we were up to no good, Alta said. I hadn't planned on doing anything nefarious on board, but I filed that information away anyway, just in case.

When Alta and I were finished with breakfast, Jane came over and said, "Alta if you please … ". With a wave of Alta's arm we were back on Earth, but Jane and the crew weren't with us.

"Alta, did Jane and company stay on the ship?" I asked.

"No, Tom, they are at the Library. I split-transferred us, so we are here and they are where they should be," Alta replied.

I glanced at her with amazement. "Scotty would have loved you, Alta."

"Tom, if I were on Star Trek, there wouldn't have been much of a show," Alta said conversationally. "I never break down at critical moments, and I would have just vaporized the Klingon ships light-years away. Who would have paid to see that?"

"Good point," I said, shrugging.

As we walked up the drive leading to my church, I saw a bright flash that seemed to travel along the entire horizon just over the curve of Earth beyond our view. I had never seen anything quite like it. There was no sound, just an intense flash, like a meteorite of light struck Earth just over the horizon.

Alta looked concerned. She leaned over to me and whispered, "I suspect we may be attending a later Mass today."

"How's that?" I asked. In a flash, a wispy vaporous image began to take shape right in front of us. Five other shapes began to materialize as well, one next to the first, and four more behind them.

Alta whispered to me, "That first one is Azazel, Hell's weapons master and a top twenty leader of The Watchers. That one next to him is Sariel; the others are probably lower-ranking but in the tow hundred or so that make up their group."

They first appeared as dark wispy figures whose outlines changed as though trying to contain the dark storm that made up their bodies. As their presence stabilized, I could see that they were larger than a man, perhaps eight feet tall and proportionately wider. It even seemed to me that they were kind of dirty from whatever environment they had left. The immediate outline of their shapes continuously shifted before us. As they came closer, I could see that they had long hair and black eyes and were covered with long flowing robes. All six appeared to be male and made of some sort of living stone.

"Azazel, what do you want?" Alta asked fiercely.

The demon looked at us and said, "I suspect that you're not going to make it to Mass at all today." He snickered as if he was a school bully who expected his posse to laugh at his joke.

Obviously, he had overheard Alta's words before he appeared to us. Alta flicked her wrist and a sword appeared in her hand, but its blade was not metal. It looked like a light, but the light had a certain life to it as it shone. It wasn't a laser. There was something else at work here. Alta's stance changed entirely, like an angry dog getting ready to fight a bear. She held the sword in front of her arm, outstretched with the blade faced diagonally to the ground. Her face radiated a cool confidence. Azazel raised a hand and everything that was moving around us stopped. He had frozen time, so no one would see this fight but us. The entire battle would happen in between the seconds.

Then he held a hand to his ear as though getting a radio call. The cliche of this position was an odd contrast for the frightful figure, like watching a lion talking on a cell phone.

He spoke to two of his followers, saying, "We are being called elsewhere." Turning to Sariel, he added, "This problem is all yours." Azazel and two of the demons disappeared just as they had come.

As it turned out, Sariel was the captain of the two that remained with him. He was also one of the twenty Watchers under Samyaza. Alta later said he was one of the fallen Dominions, which are ranked four choirs down from the top-ranked Seraphim. He was a leader in Heaven and now is a leader in Hell.

He looked at us, pointing our way, and said, "I guess I am going to be tearing you two apart." He said this as calmly as if he was talking about what he ordered for lunch. His own sword appeared in his hand, and he swiped it at Alta. A bright flash of energy left the blade as it streaked towards us. As the wave of energy crossed near us, Alta's invisible shield temporarily appeared and deflected the attack. The shield completely covered

Alta, almost like a glass dome was placed over her; it even appeared to have more than one layer. The shield recoiled and shimmered from the strike. Incredibly, there was no sound from the impact whatsoever. Alta slashed back and Sariel met the strike with his own blade. The two were wrist to wrist, staring into each other's eyes. Now that he was very close, he reacted with surprise.

"You are a machine!" he exclaimed.

"Yes, and you're an insane demon from Hell who's just been abandoned by the rest of your team, so I can destroy you all." Alta glanced at his lieutenants as she made her threat. "Remember Custer … moron?" she added.

Using a martial-arts-type parrying move, she used the downward resistance of his sword to step under his blow and propel her around him, where she neatly cut one of his team in half. She then blocked his next strike and made a downward hammering fist movement; a huge unseen weight crushed the other demon into dust instantly. Sariel launched forward and Alta quickly wounded him with one more pass of her sword. By now, the remains of the other two demons had disappeared completely.

Sariel shrieked in rage and screamed, "Incompetent fools!"

He then came at Alta with the sword over his head, slashing down with both hands. Alta blocked with her own sword from the left and elbowed Sariel with her right in one smooth move. Sariel was knocked off his feet and quickly got back up, slashing at Alta again. This time he took Alta off her feet.

Just then, the horizon flashed again, and both Alta and Sariel stopped fighting. Sariel pointed his sword at Alta.

"I'll be back with a better team for the next go round, robot, and we'll mount your head on a pole in Hell. We have the perfect spot already waiting for it on my mantle," he snarled.

Alta angrily shouted back at him, "I might be there in a week or a month, but you're in Hell forever, right where you belong!" Sariel disappeared with a snarl. Some small part in the back of my brain—the only part that wasn't frozen stiff and gibbering in mind-numbing fear—thought that, while Alta's parting words may or may not sound like much of a comeback, no one could help but be impressed by this beautiful robot when she was in a fight. I had not moved a muscle since the demons first appeared. I was so glad that Alta was there, I could have kissed her, if only I had been capable of moving.

Time around us did not resume. Another presence appeared before us, and Alta kneeled. There were five or six other angels standing behind an imposing figure who was clearly their leader. These seemed like the same caliber of creature I had just seen, but they were glowing white. Even though they were larger than humans, they appeared far more familiar than Azazel's crew. The largest angel hailed her.

"I am Michael, and you must not kneel before me, for I am a creation, just like you. I have come to bring you very unfortunate news and to help you. We were sent by God Himself."

Alta stood up and asked matter-of-factly, "What is this news?" She was still amped up from the fight with Sariel and had not really absorbed Michael's grave tone when he said he had "very unfortunate news."

Michael paused a moment and then said softly, "Alta, Jane and your entire crew were killed by Azazel and two demons in front of the Library of Congress, just minutes ago." Alta's face went blank, and she put her arms across her stomach, the way someone might if they had been punched in the gut. I tried to picture Jane, who had come to our breakfast table in what was surely less than an hour ago, dead. I couldn't quite do it. It didn't seem real.

Michael continued, "You are the last emissary from your world here on Earth. It is the will of God that you complete their mission. We shall help you, within the constraints that bind all transcendental beings in this creation, whether they are angels like me, or robots like you."

Alta looked puzzled. "I am alone?" she asked.

Michael said, "Yes, Alta, but now you have our assistance. Also, because Ostara's demons went over the line, you may now travel to any place previously forbidden to you, to gather whatever answers you need to find the truth."

"Ostara?" I inquired, having finally found my voice. That name, pulling at my memory, poked through the fog of residual terror from the attack and shock at the news of Jane's death. "Alta mentioned her before, the demon who could travel between Heaven and Hell?"

"Ostara is not a demon," Michael responded. "She is the queen of Hell, and she controls the actions of the demons you face."

"Oh, is that all?" I said in shock, shooting a quick look of terror towards Alta. "There's a queen of Hell?" I didn't want to think about something that was even more powerful than the demons we had just faced, so powerful it could control them, in fact.

"Absolutely!" Michael responded. "And, I might add, you don't want to meet her, which is why we are here." To myself, I fervently agreed that I didn't want to meet her.

Alta asked in a concerned tone, "Michael, there are people back on my world who are now depending on me alone. Considering the circumstances, can't you just tell me the truths I seek? Then I can go home, and once the word is out, these demons won't need to keep killing people in the effort to keep it bottled up." A surge of fear ran up my arms and legs at the thought of Alta leaving me, with demons still out there. But I could see the sense in giving Alta and her people a shortcut to the truth.

"If things worked that way, Alta," Michael responded gently but firmly, "It certainly would have worked for Jesus Himself two thousand years ago. God would not have needed to actually go to the Cross; He could have just told people what they needed to know. But the very struggle for truth is part of the process of growing in holiness and merit. The Son of God Himself followed through to the Cross, and so must you endure this trial for your people."

"However," Michael added, "I can give you detailed knowledge of Heaven, Hell, Purgatory, and your adversaries, so that you can do a self-guided tour for the truth." Alta nodded and Michael touched her forehead. I could see from her reaction, the widened eyes and the head taken back slightly, that she now knew detail previously only known by Heaven's angelic protectors. Michael had instantly "educated" her in a big way.

Alta winced but said, "Thank you." I wondered if it was the process of absorbing knowledge that way that made her wince, or if it was something in the knowledge itself that he had passed along.

Half scared to death, I was nevertheless a theologian to my core. I mustered the courage to pipe up and ask a question.

"Michael, how could the actions of a robot possibly merit the support or favor of God? Isn't that like saying a fish gains in worth just by swimming, or a bear by eating berries?" Alta looked at me, and I thought I saw a brief flash of sadness or hurt or maybe even longing, but it was gone so quickly that I wondered if I had imagined it.

Michael turned to look at me, and I felt a sense of awe in the gaze of this magnificent being. He said, "It is the will of her people for her to be here and accomplish this very purpose. If she fails, the people of Gihon must try again and again until they succeed or give up. So, it is the conjunction of their desire and effort in this extragalactic pursuit of truth, represented here by Alta's presence and work, which pleases God. Alta is the agent for her world, much as parents act as their child's agent when a baby is baptized. They stand in for the baby, acting on the baby's behalf, but that action is effective, and the baby receives that baptism, with its benefits. In a similar way, the people of Gihon could not all be here, so they sent a suitable agent to seek out and find God. Her search is pleasing to God, because the people of Gihon did the best that they could, considering the distances and technical problems of getting here. It is their collective will to find God, and Alta is now their way to do it. So, we will help Alta do their will, thereby doing God's will."

Michael added on, "We'll be close at hand when you need us, and you WILL need us."

"I have not yet actually met Ostara," Alta said slowly. "Just exactly how powerful is she, and why did she send The Watchers to kill my crew on this outing?" Her voice was hollow.

"She was once human in life, thousands of years ago, and has since become the acting Queen of Hell. She travels with twenty other demons called The Watchers, some of whom you have already met. She also leads a very nasty expeditionary group called the Knights in Satan's Service. They move between Heaven and Hell doing Satan's bidding. They are Hell's very worst. My team is their antithesis, opposing them in every way. Ostara is very dangerous and one of Hell's most powerful and influential agents.

You will need every feature of your design to defend against her, including all the capabilities that had been previously forbidden to you. Azazel is going back to Hell to line up an elite team to destroy you, and Ostara will recruit many of Hell's very worst this next time around. Remember that if you cast out one demon, as you did with two today, each demon returns with seven more, worse than himself. I assure you Ostara will do precisely that," Michael said.

"Luke 11:26," Alta said mechanically. I knew she was giving the Bible reference that Michael's words had referred to, although I thought it seemed like she was saying it more out of a habit or reflex than from any particular need to point it out. Michael nodded and continued to explain, mostly for my benefit.

"Our team is Heaven's perimeter guard, and we have dealt with her before. She is borderline insane and has even been known to destroy her own troops in fits of rage. She will not stop until you are destroyed. You will need to work very quickly from this point on," he said.

I raised my hand just like a kid in school, to ask a second question. "Are you actually Michael the Archangel, from the earliest stories of the Bible?"

"Yes, I am that Michael from the Bible." I thought I detected a hint of humor in his tone, but then I decided I had imagined it.

"So," I said, "you threw Satan out of Heaven because border patrol was your specific job at the time?"

"Yes," Michael responded, "and that has never changed. Ostara has likewise confronted us and been repelled. We also disallow any others who might enter, for it is not in God's design. Essentially, Heaven is a gated community. We would not have allowed Alta in, because she did not have the invitation. At this point, that has changed. She already had the native ability to go to Heaven; now she has the permission, as well."

Now more confident, I asked, "So, can Alta bring me too?"

"We suspected that you'd ask," Michael said, and this time I was sure that there was a grin on his face. "Already got the okay for you to go anywhere Alta does. Moreover, it is the will of God that you assist her, for your actions will help in his greatest commandment to the faithful, 'Go and make for Me disciples of all men.' Recall that a man helped Jesus carry the Cross at one point, and he was whipped for his trouble. Sadly, you are taking a greater risk here, Tom. You will be subjected to terrors beyond your imagination if you accept this task. Many of the attacks on you will be from this world and some from beyond. All the powers of Hell are now aligned against you two. For if you succeed, Alta's advanced civilization will use star travel to spread the word of God throughout the entire universe."

Michael paused for emphasis, "This is the greatest of battles," he said. "If you two fail, the remainder of the universe will remain in darkness for a very long time."

Michael left us as quickly as he had come. Time around us resumed. I sat down abruptly on the sidewalk. When I felt I could walk without shaking and say the words of the Mass without making my fellow Mass-goers look at me funny, I got up and said, looking over at the church door, "Well, Alta, we may as well go in." Alta agreed. We started walking over toward the entrance, which wasn't far, talking as we proceeded toward the door.

"Well," I tried to joke, "At least Azazel was nice enough to stop time so we wouldn't be late." Even I thought it sounded feeble, though, and Alta just looked at me.

"So, I guess I can check the 'conversation with an angel' off my bucket list. Did Michael seem a little 'preachy' or 'stilted' to you?" I asked.

"Really, Tom? Preachy? He's an angel. What do you think his day job is anyway? I know you're very devout and all, but it surprises me that you're surprised," Alta said.

"Why?" I asked.

"How long has it been since you read Daniel 10? Angels are messengers, not people you sit down with at a bar for idle banter. If we are visited by one, generally speaking, God sent him to us for a necessary information dump," she said sounding disappointed with me. It occurred to me at that point, in all probability Alta's comment extended to her also, as she had great infused knowledge, just like the angels. I needed to get used to being taught, it appeared, as I would be the most ignorant one in any conversation with any robot or alien.

"Preachy," Alta repeated with frustration.

"Why does that bother you, Alta?" I asked.

"Tom, preachy is a word I might expect from a person who isn't going to church anywhere weekly, which you are. It is a word I might expect from a person who ISN'T looking for God in their own life. Again, you are. As for me, when I get home … I'll become the preacher. But only those who ARE searching themselves for the alien God will hear me without thinking I'm 'preachy.' Any others will reject me, or you and this entire mission to your world, just as people here on Earth rejected and crucified Our Lord two thousand years ago. In that case, He gave His all for creation. Remember that most people are comfortable with a god concept that requires nothing of them. In those cases, their nothing god has also done nothing for them," she said with emphasis. "So, there's no need to preach … nothing," she concluded.

We reached the door and attended Mass. I was very interested in seeing how Alta would react at the point when the priest lifts the Eucharist, during the consecration. She didn't show any visible reaction, so at the conclusion of the service, I asked her for the results.

"So, Alta, what did you see?"

"There is a supernatural change," Alta said slowly, "but I cannot know what the significance is. You mentioned that other Protestant denominations practice similar memorial rituals, but they don't all believe exactly as you do about what happens during that ritual. I still need more information, or at the very least to do this same thing in some other churches, not of this faith, to compare."

"And if we run into Ostara's thugs?" I said nervously.

"Then, I will destroy her followers and engage her myself." Alta said this with what I interpreted as complete confidence.

She paused for a moment, hands at her side, looking despondent. I could see that everything was beginning to sink in.

"All my friends are dead. I am alone on an alien world and being hunted by demons," she said. The depths of anguish in her tone moved me. I felt awkward and uncomfortable, because it was because of me that Alta hadn't been around to protect the others.

"Yeah, Alta," I spit out awkwardly. "I'm sorry about that. I know that Jane's giving you to me left her team unprotected. I am very grateful to you and to Jane." It didn't seem like enough to say, but it was all I could think of.

"Sure, Tom. Protecting you is the least we could do. It's not your fault that demons are after us. But looking at our odds … this is truly the worst," she said. She looked down at her hands. I sheepishly nodded my head in agreement as she persisted with the thought.

"Michael explained the rewards that lie ahead for my world if I succeed, and possibly for your world because of your efforts to help me. He did not include me in any of those rewards, I noticed." There was again hollowness in her voice.

"Every saint in the Bible was an unlikely hero," I commented, "whose reward wasn't given till he left this world."

"That's fine," she said despondently, "because I have a life expectancy of 10,000 years. Although the demons seek to shorten it." She looked glum again.

"Wow," was all I could get out in reacting to her huge lifespan. She didn't say anything more, so after a moment, I decided to get off awkward topics and asked something a little lighter.

"What was that sword you had?" I asked.

"It was a gift from an angel I once rescued from some demons. His name was Raphael. It was made by the angels for this very sort of mission," she responded.

"Is it a lightsaber?" I asked.

"No!" Alta said. She looked like she was tempted to laugh. "This is very different from Star Wars. It has two settings; a superheated plasma setting, or a stronger setting amped up with some of my transcendental features. In the lesser plasma-only setting, it has nearly unlimited wattage, because it draws its power directly from me. It could slice your world into rubble if properly applied."

"How is that?" I asked.

Alta explained, waving her hand at the sky. "Simple. See the Sun? It's a super-heated plasma. But MY sword can get MUCH hotter. In the higher setting, the sword can throw energy just like you might throw a baseball. The energy flies off the sword itself."

"So, it's not like a light saber?" I asked, torn between disappointment and awe.

Alta looked at me as if she couldn't believe I was real and said, "You have a very one track mind regarding all of this, don't you. Frankly, it's more like that crossed with a Power Ranger sword." Alta still had a sense of humor.

Undaunted, I continued my interrogation, "And, about your name? Are you gonna tell me you're called Alta in your world? Alta sounds very familiar. How'd you get Alta for a name?"

Alta said, "Well, you got me there. I saw 'Forbidden Planet' and liked Dr. Morbius's daughter. Certainly, you must realize that any civilization coming to visit you here is going to receive all your radio and television years before arriving. All your habits, language, and traditions are embedded in those transmissions. Even all of your military codes, master card numbers, and everything you think is secure is easily cracked by our far greater computers. Imagine taking today's computer power back to the code breakers of World War II, just for instance. And that's only fifty years. We have way more than that on you."

"So, what is your real name in your world, Alta?" I asked.

She replied, "Robots traditionally have no names in my world until attached to a human crew for a mission, hence, my name, Alta. But that's changing for combat teams. At inception we have … well, the tech-savvy on your world would call it a point of presence, sort of like an internet address. We meet, greet, and communicate point to point, so a name is redundant. You are your

105

point of presence, and your mind, being, and worth are tied to your identity. Imagine if a website of a person could actually become that person. That's a little like what it's like for us. We don't typically call others of our kind names, we call to an address, which is also their very self. We have machines you can't imagine, doing every function conceivable. It would be as pointless for us to name every machine like me as it would be for you to name each breath. Just as a suggestion, watch the original 'Astro Boy' anime cartoon in black and white. It has odd similarities to our world at a veneer level."

"Okay, how would you plan a surprise party for a robot friend then?" I asked. The way she described it, it sounded like the only way to refer to a robot would be to do the equivalent of having them there and pointing at them.

Alta responded, "That would be what your computer science folks refer to as a call by reference to his or her identity or address. The advantage is every conversation, letter, phone call, and transaction of worth all apply to that single addressed Point of Presence (POP). We have made your POP the same thing as your phone number, master card number and what you call a name. You can even open a locked car door with your key, which is also tied to your POP."

"You could probably hail someone as their address, right?" I said. "Like 'Hi there, 42 Metro City!'?"

Alta gave me that look of unbelief again and said, "You really do have a one track mind." She shook her head, as if she couldn't see the point in my questions and stopped the alien history lesson to reconnect with the task at hand.

"Well, now, it's just us, so what do you think I should do?" she asked resolutely.

"If you and I have an invite to Heaven, Hell or, whatever, from Michael the Archangel, I'd say we ought to move Heaven to the front of the list. Let's face it, that's where your support is right now, and if you have one friend there who gave you an invitation, and another who gave you a sword, we'd better go see your friends. Not to mention, it IS Heaven," I said with purposeful emphasis.

She squinched her face at me doubtfully. I hadn't known that whatever she had for face muscles could do that.

"While it sounds fun there," she said, "we need to stay on task and accomplish our mission. After all, we are still seeking the alien God."

"That God, in my opinion, is best understood by the Roman Catholic Church. Frankly, I would have been very interested to see what would have happened if a group of you advanced aliens actually did walk into the Library of Congress as impartial judges, and exited being Catholic," I responded.

"Well," Alta said, "they did get the data and it is back waiting for us on my ship's computer, so you will still get to see your thought experiment carried out after all. Moreover, if what the crew gathered was worth dying for, we need to see what it was immediately. It's gonna take a while to plow through all that information and make sense of it. Maybe we'll make our trip to Heaven tomorrow. Right now, the safest place for us is back on the ship."

"Okay," I said, as I suddenly remembered something, "but it's still barely noon, and believe it or not, besides saving the universe, I have a couple things I need to do. I need to make a stop at the store and I have a meeting at a club in Baltimore for a dance teaching job."

Alta scratched her chin, weighing the risk.

"Well, I guess life has gone on despite everything that's happened in the spiritual world so far, so what's one more little risk?" It was pretty clear from Alta's facetious humor that she didn't like our chances.

Chapter 8
The Dance Club

We decided to go back home to my place first, because despite all the demons, angels, and extra-galactic excitement, I still had a life. I was tired and hungry and Alta had just gotten the news that her crew was dead. We drove back towards Laurel, and as we passed the Best Buy, I decided to stop to pick up a couple HDMI cables for the TV in my living room. Alta came in and shuffled right over to the music shop in the back of the store. Unbeknownst to me, while I was in the Audio/Video section, Alta was sizing up the guitars. She walked back into the closed practice room, took an expensive Fender off the wall, plugged it in, and started to play Lenny Kravitz, "Are You Gonna Go My Way." Ordinarily that sort of thing was a usual occurrence in the store, but Alta was the best guitar player anyone had ever heard. While I was talking to a clerk about HDMI cables, the music store staff and some customers were going over to hear Alta play "Rage Against the Machine" and Michael Jackson's "Beat It." A customer who was a drummer even sat down on the electronic set next to Alta and started to accompany her. By the time I got back to looking for her, people were flocking over to the practice room from the video and appliance sections. I pressed in behind them, looking through the glass to hear Alta play Def Lepard's "Pour Some Sugar on Me," as an audience request.

When I actually got in the practice room, I was as amazed as everyone else. I decided that with all Alta had been through, I'd let her have some fun. She saw me and offered to do something special.

"The last one is for you, Tom," she said.

She played "Burn it to the Ground" by Nickelback. It was amazing. Wow! Alta looked like a blond Joan Jett and played like Eddie Van Halen. She thanked the clapping onlookers and rehung the guitar.

"Got what you need?" she asked.

I said, "Yup, and by the way, you're real good." Belatedly, it occurred to me to wonder why she had picked that particular song to dedicate to me.

She whispered, "I'm the best on this end of the galaxy, in actual fact. But you should hear me with my own guitar."

"So, this is a regular habit for you?" I asked.

"Absolutely!" Alta exclaimed with confidence. The whole crowd clapped for her as she left. Even the drummer was trying to get her to join his band. Once we got home, I told Alta that I needed to meet the new manager of the Havana club about starting a dance class there on Fridays. We had planned the meeting weeks ago, and tonight was the night.

After seeing angels, demons, and a guitar demo all in one day, I began to consider the fact that I was at the focal point of something that would be considered historically significant to later onlookers. I was now exclusively partnered with Alta, who also had no one else but me. The ramifications were sinking in a bit deeper.

Alta herself was quite a mystery. Either she was a soulless modern version of Pinocchio seeking to solve a mystery, or a dangerous alien robot created to destroy the demons who killed her crew, plus any others she encountered along the way. Judging from the story of the gift sword, it was clear that Alta was very connected. Michael and his crew of angels clearly respected her and never questioned her ability. She traveled in both the physical and spiritual realms with equal alacrity. It seemed to me that she saw demons, angels, and perhaps even God on a fairly regular basis. Oddly, she didn't seek out special relationships with any but a very few of these spiritual entities. Being with her was almost like getting the cosmic equivalent of a back stage tour from Madonna, except Alta could crush the Sun between any two fingers. It occurred to me that if Alta went off the rails, nothing on Earth could even delay her wrath. Fortunately, she seemed to have some sort of higher ethical code. She was courteous to people. She was thoughtful and kind. She seemed to understand the weaknesses of others, though she had none that were apparent herself. She didn't even have any bad habits that I could detect, unless you wanted to count watching wedding shows, which didn't really count, despite my low opinion of them.

Alta was also beautiful. She seemed to even care about me more than just for the theological work I was doing. I just had to get into her head, and find out what made her tick. Alta had grown on me. I decided there was no better way to find out more about her than to take her out clubbing, and I was sure I had a place she'd like.

"Alta," I said, "We've had too much demon killing for one day; we need to have a little fun tonight. And, after all, it is dance night at the Havana Club on the Baltimore Waterfront. I'm meeting the manager there tonight to talk. Can you dance?" I asked.

Alta looked at me incredulously and said "First Heaven and now dancing?! With all that's happening, do we really have time for this?" The strain in her voice reminded me of the pressure she was under; her entire world, and more besides, were depending on her.

"Hmm," I said thoughtfully, "I guess it would be nice if we could stop time the way the demon and Michael did. Then we could take a break without worrying so much about time." My brow furrowed as I wondered whether we could get ahold of someone in Heaven who might stop time for us if we needed it.

"Oh," Alta said, looking almost … was she looking guilty? That couldn't be.

"I can control time, and travel back and forth in it," she said self-consciously. My jaw dropped.

"You're just telling me this NOW?!"

"I can travel forward and back through time," she continued to explain. "But, I cannot change past events. And, Tom, the demons haven't given up because of this last meeting. I can stop people time, but not demon time. They'll be back at the time and place of their choosing. Worse yet, they may use other humans against us, whom I can't just vanquish with impunity."

I tried to take these concerns seriously, but I still thought we should go dancing, so Alta reluctantly agreed.

About 8:30 PM, I was ready to go, and I looked at Alta and asked her if she had a suitable dress for the occasion. Just like Samantha from "Bewitched," Alta snapped her fingers and changed into something that made her look like a Bond girl going out to the seminal meeting at Goldfinger's multimillion dollar estate. Alta seemed to know what I was thinking.

"I didn't have to snap my fingers, but I figured you'd appreciate the effect," she said.

She even had a separate shoe bag for her dance shoes. I asked her how she knew the dress code and to bring shoes like that.

She responded, "I have complete knowledge of every facet of human history, from the club's building code to the boss's review of the last five or six managers of the place. I even know with high probability what discs the DJ is bringing tonight."

"So, Alta, you have all knowledge like the angels?" I asked.

"No, I have vast knowledge, not all knowledge. Angels know more than I, but much of their knowledge does not matter in the performance of my regular tasks. I don't need to know which angel makes the best spaghetti in Heaven. I do need to know how to travel faster than light within the universe," she said.

"Well, Alta, you do travel faster than light, right?" I asked.

She replied, "Yes, but not by bending space. I reduce my mass to zero to leave the universe and re-enter at the point most convenient to my destination. Same as the angels do."

Once again, I felt a little stupid after talking to Alta about her credentials.

We took my Acura to the club and had it parked by the valets. We went in at about 9 PM and saw that we were nearly the first ones there. After a while, the DJ started up and we saw more folks came in, so I figured we'd see if Alta could dance.

Alta seemed willing, but oddly nervous about who else was in the room. We started to dance a little, and it was clear that Alta was an expert at this also. I had been teaching the Hustle for years, and she was as good as anyone I had ever danced with. Having been humbled a bit, I figured I'd get her off the floor. Fifteen minutes later, the DJ started to play something familiar. Nickleback's "Burn It to the Ground." It was the song from Alta's afternoon guitar solo at Best Buy's music room, but now the CD was being played in the club. This was just too cool, and sounded like the perfect song for a dance with a smoking hot alien robot. Alta seemed to connect with the song, so I figured I'd try some of my dance tricks. Everyone's first hustle trick is a simple death drop. Alta liked it. Then I tried the illusion step, which is a move that has us holding onto each other's right wrists at arm's length, and her falling face first towards the ground with straight legs, till I deftly step over her swinging body and bring her back to her feet. I explained the move and Alta just executed it without a second thought. I was amazed by her trust in me, till I realized that she had no fear because it was impossible for me to injure her. So, I turned her quickly twenty times, and she looked like an ex-ballerina. We went through the standard basic figures of hustle. People close to the floor watched with interest. I was amazed by Alta, who quietly walked off the floor with me now for the second time.

I left Alta at our table and headed over to the bathroom. As I returned to our seats, I saw two big guys who had come over to see Alta in my absence. Alta seemed very cool towards them. One grabbed Alta by the wrist, and Alta didn't resist. She just looked at him, and she waved her free hand in a short sweeping motion with her palm facing the floor. As she did, every glass within 50 feet broke, in a wave that followed the motion of her hand. This included the ones the two guys were holding, which broke first. Fear took over, and the men let her go quickly, retreating back to where they had come from.

I returned to our seats; Alta got there just a step ahead of me.

"Making friends?" I asked sardonically.

"Tom, I think we've had enough dancing for one night," she said.

"Who were those guys, Alta?" I was wondering what was up. Normal overbearing louts would hardly spook Alta into wanting to leave.

She said, "They are regular people like you, who are easily manipulated by Kokabiel. After their death, they may ultimately end up as surrogate spirits of his if they stay on their current path. Many of the current surrogate spirits already have 'relationships' with these people through temptations and other sins. These men wanted to do us harm, but because they are just humans, I decided it'd be better to scare them off rather than fight with them."

"Kokabiel?" I asked.

She replied, "Another top tier Watcher, Tom. He is a very powerful demon who manipulates people here on Earth. They then become weapons against us. I know of him because of what Michael shared with me, but fortunately we have never crossed paths."

It was pretty clear that Alta was singly focused on her mission. Not that the demons would let her off the hook. At this point, with me in tow, and a dead crew, she had nothing else to do except to follow the angel Michael's suggestion. She now had to sort out the truth of God, creation, and the complete eschatology for her world. I suppose she had the supernatural power to retreat home to Gihon, but then she'd have had both angels and demons mad at her. As I looked over at her and saw the face of a late twenty-something girl, I wondered if she was just an alien doll disguising "beyond physics" superpowers that let her play us all like puppets. After all, for her quest, why do you need to ask what the right belief is when you already know nearly everything? Truth was apparently different than mere fact collection. Truth was the correct assembly, the right understanding, of the properly chosen facts. Still, Alta seemed benevolent in all things except her dealings with the demons. They hated the very fiber of her being, and she returned the sentiment in the cool manner of a hired killer. It seemed almost impossible to believe she had the job she did, to look at her. But little things she let out now and then let me know just how completely alien her experiences from beyond this world actually were. There were times when I wondered if we could just take some time off to talk of her world, and space travel, and the realm of the angels that she obviously had to know. Perhaps she even knew MY guardian angel. She had mentioned his recommendation, but I didn't know if that was all she knew of him or not.

Alta looked ready to leave and grabbed her stuff from the table. I stopped her and said, "Alta, whether here, or in the car ride back, or even at home, we're equally unsafe. We may as well make the best of it and hang a while."

Alta stopped and said, "Surprising wisdom from you, Tom. But my ship is the safest of our choices. In fact, we could do this whole club thing in a Fast Track console, if it means that much to you."

Looking back, every pit was equally deep for the two of us. I bought Alta a New York Iced Tea and a White Russian for myself. I finally just asked her why the truth was a mystery to her. "Alta, if you have such vast knowledge, and the ability to communicate with angels and demons, why is religious truth a mystery to you?" I inquired.

Alta responded, "I suppose for the same reason Satan tempted Christ before He went to the Cross. Surely, Satan must have known Jesus couldn't yield to his temptation. Or perhaps he didn't realize Christ was God. But the demons know all of men's failings and can recount them in detail without a computer. They must have known this man 'Jesus' was utterly without fault. So, then they had to recognize Him as extraordinary."

"Moreover, Satan may have lived with God for eons prior to the fall. He must have known God like a brother, and realized no temptation could work. Yet he persisted. Why, Tom?" Alta asked. I scratched my head, and Alta filled in the answer.

"It appears that there are levels to knowing God completely, that the pre-fall angels had not achieved. As it is with all on Gihon, and countless other worlds. This life is a test, which doesn't work if civilizations are allowed to stick their nose under the creator's tent. Imperfect knowledge and figuring things out over time is part of the test. Even if I discovered the truth by cheating, my ability to recall and share it one second later is dependent on the will of God. I can only remember something if God lets me, and if I try to use my knowledge to get around His test, He doesn't have to let me keep my knowledge. This is clearly a cardinal rule of the universe and the larger framework in which everything is embedded. It's like the speed of light. You can never exceed it. Neither can I ever abrogate God's testing of creation," she said.

I corrected Alta and said, "But you DO go faster than the speed of light, employing a technicality and therefore effectively DO control time."

Alta was flustered and said, "We're back on this? When I have any mass greater than zero, I do not go faster than light within this universe. EVER! I have to drop my mass to nothing, and then I just leave the universe by one exit and re-enter at another spot closer to my destination. This isn't a wormhole through space and time, it's an exit route out of this universe. The path to Heaven can never be found by even the most thorough search of the universe we are in now. We exist in a fantastically sophisticated simulation, embedded in a game console on a marble altar in Heaven! Yet the actions of the human players here have real consequences in eternity."

"So, Alta, if you've never been allowed into Heaven, and this universe is a simulation in Heaven, how do you leave the simulation? Aren't you then in Heaven?" I asked.

Alta said, "Not really. Imagine an orange floating in a lake. A bug walks out one hole, across the top, and down another hole back into the orange. He never got wet, yet the sea is all around. Had he gotten wet, the water would have carried him off and he'd have been lost."

I followed up, "So, you travel like a surface charge then?"

"Yes, Tom, essentially that's about it." Alta smiled, suggesting that my understanding showed promise.

I was just beginning to understand how truly weird and vast the universe I was about to explore might actually be. Having heard enough about space for one day, I decided to ask Alta more about her home. After all, we could both be dead tomorrow. I wanted to know, specifically, did they invent the bicycle? Apparently, they did and so did many other worlds. The wheel, the bow, and the bike were common features everywhere in the universe. But not surprisingly, all three had flavors that lent themselves to denser air, water, and other conditions that human-powered travel or hunting might want to effectively negotiate. Alta was always pleased to talk about day to day life on her world. Obviously, she missed her home. I hadn't even been to France, much less outer space. The stories she told me were riveting.

I was back in my stateroom on her ship later that night and Alta came by to say good night. The absence of Jane and her crew aboard the ship really drove home the reality of their death. I was depressed, and I wondered if it was hitting Alta pretty hard, too.

When she came in, though, she had a pleasant surprise. "There are several angels guarding our ship," she said.

"No kidding," I said, "you can see them?"

"Absolutely! I suspect we'll be safe here tonight," Alta said very matter-of-factly. I was just glad to see someone was trying to help us for the first time since this all started.

Chapter 9

Heaven

The next morning, I thought about being on the ship. I felt safer there, but considering the fact that we were being hunted by demons that could walk through walls, my confidence was probably unfounded.

"Alta, can the demons reach us here in orbit?" I asked her over a breakfast of ham and eggs. The meal was delicious, but my mind wasn't on the food.

Alta responded, "If I can travel anywhere by the same means, it stands to reason that some or all of the demons can too. But the ship can defend itself, now that we know what we're up against. We should not waste any time in getting on with our task, though; because once Ostara gathers up a mob of demons, we're gonna have trouble."

She added in a determined tone, "She's the one who's going to have trouble!"

Alta had undergone a change in personality after the loss of her crew. She was now very focused on the task, and very serious-minded in all matters. It was clear that she felt the weight of her duty upon her.

"Alta, are you going to bring us to Heaven today?" I asked after finishing a bite of ham. Alta was not eating this morning. I thought she was too focused on her task to bother with something that wasn't strictly necessary. Yesterday she had sounded reluctant to take time off to go to Heaven, but I still thought it was our best bet.

She responded, "Based upon the information Michael transferred to me, I can bring us to a specific part of Heaven. It can be any part you choose, but only one part at a time." She still didn't sound enthusiastic about the idea, but I guess she was willing to go along with it.

I gave Alta a baffled look, wondering what she meant by "only one part at a time," so she tried to explain.

"We have not been transformed into the state that occupants of Heaven are in, which allows them to better appreciate the realm. So, before we do this, I need to tell you some things. I must then ask you a question or two, after you understand the first part," she said.

"Huh?" I said.

Alta reeled back, pondering the scale of the divide she needed to cross to get my human mind to understand Heaven.

Finally she began, "First off, Heaven isn't one place. And, the collection of places we call Heaven isn't marked by our worldly time. There are countless different regions of Heaven. Each of these regions has a different theme. Let's call each region a separate mansion in Heaven. There are many mansions. Each mansion is an entire realm, like our current universe. Our universe is like just one more mansion, but outside of Heaven. The mansions have rooms, or sub-shells, that are your own personal experience of the region you are in. All the rooms are clocked differently; the time in one doesn't have to match the time in another. There is no master time in Heaven. Heaven is truly timeless. Your experience of time could be moved forward or backwards in that mansion's time. So, I guess part of what I'm getting at is that Heaven is really big. It's as vast to the angels as this universe is to man."

"I presume this is to give every person their own unique experience with God?" I said, pausing with the fork halfway to my mouth.

Alta responded, "Yes, I think so. Moreover, it might make numbers greater than ONE meaningless, since the singular experience of God trumps all other experiences."

"Numbers greater than one?" I asked. She had put an odd emphasis on that "one."

"When you arrive in Heaven, you get a number that is, well, your reward position, I guess we could call it. A ONE is the most common, but extremely good people might get a THREE and a saint might get a SIX. The Virgin Mary has the highest number, but I don't know what her number is," she said.

"What's the number do?" I asked curiously.

Alta said, "The number means a lot. Each mansion in Heaven is a unique, made to a different theme, right? One mansion is the entry concourse, where you welcome incoming friends or relatives; that is the only house that every human passes through. Another mansion is the throne of God, and still another is like Disney World. Some mansions are journeys into your earthly past, and others are geared for the angels. Your number tells you how many places you can be in at a time. If you had a SIX as your heavenly reward number, you could be in six places at one time. So, everyone in Heaven is completely happy, but some have a greater capacity for happiness than others."

Alta looked at me sternly and asked, "Are you sure you understand this?"

"Sure, why?" I ate another bite of ham.

"Since you are not dead, nor glorified in understanding or vision, you would see Heaven with less than a ONE. You can only be in one place, and then your experience of that place will in every way be dimmer compared to the souls who have died. So, I need to know exactly what we seek and why, to get us to the exact right place that meets the mission goal," Alta said.

"You see," Alta continued in a curiously uncertain tone, "I am the creation of man, not God. I should not even enter Heaven on my own. I can only go in to assist those created by God and then only with the special permission that we received from Michael. So, we really need to narrow down what we aim to do in Heaven, because I don't want to overstay my welcome."

I responded, "Alta, our goal is your people's quest. We want to zero in on the right faith, so you can spread the word. Since Heaven isn't handing you the answer on a silver plate, we'll have to do that the old-fashioned way, with some research and discussion and thinking. But to accomplish that, you first need to survive. Ostara is gathering a demon army to destroy you, which means that you need to counter her efforts by recruiting assistance in Heaven. You need allies. Heaven offers you support, and that's what we need to seek when we get there."

"Well, yes, I'm not going to succeed if I'm dead," Alta said, but she sounded like she wanted to argue with me about it.

"Though you may just see yourself as a robot," I said as I continued to press my point, "you are an emissary of an entire world, and every other world your people touch in the course of space travel. All those people WERE made by God. Obviously He wants you to succeed in this, so He's not going to be sitting over your shoulder casting disapproving glances while you get what you need from Heaven. He gave you permission. Use it!"

I continued, "We need to go there to get our own team and our search for the truth might also be helped if you experience as much of the framework of creation as possible, including Heaven. My first best guess for a location is to find the angel who gave you that sword. Heaven is where the angels live, and Michael has already suggested they might choose to help us. We need to work the streets there and make some powerful friends to counter Ostara's gang. If I had the connections you do, I would go to Heaven and do precisely that. Find a dozen of the biggest, baddest angels who already have a problem with Ostara and her Watchers. We can't be the first good people she has pissed off. Frankly, if we don't go to Heaven, the alternative is being torn in half and I find that troubling."

With all that settled, I looked at Alta, and just asked her point blank. "So, are we okay with your 'I'm just a robot' concerns then?"

She said, "Yes, except the part about where we start."

I could clearly tell that Alta hadn't let the robot thing go. She was very self-conscious about not being a creature of God, especially after her hand-to-forehead interface with Michael. I could only guess what he showed her, but it wouldn't take much to assume that she now better understood how much God loved men and placed them beyond all other things.

"How about we just start at that mansion you mentioned, the entry one for newcomers, and we'll ask around till we get some traction," I suggested. Alta realized that I was just as lost as she was, but then shrugged and nodded. I didn't think she really look convinced about the plan.

"Okay, Alta," I said, standing up. "What do I have to do?" I had finished my ham and eggs, and I was eager to go. Eager and also intimidated by the thought of seeing the reality of my beliefs in concrete form. I couldn't help but experience a shiver of concern that what I believed was going to be proved wrong by the hard facts in Heaven, even though I was confident in those beliefs.

"Just stand close and let me do my stuff," she replied.

Alta took a step back from me and raised her arms above herself, pointing her index fingers into the air, straight above her head. Her pointed index fingers just touched over her head. She closed her eyes and began to lower her arms in a slow arc towards the ground. As she did so, everything around her became dark, and this darkness enveloped me too. There was a terrific engine sound like a diesel locomotive's rumble as things went dark. In a moment, I felt an odd sense of vertigo, and the daylight reappeared. From a distance, the approach to Heaven appeared to be a close flyby of the Sun . I recalled all of the earthly folklore about telling the dead to go towards the light. Well, apparently our Sun back home was a metaphor for this heavenly phenomenon in the afterlife. We appeared to be headed right for what looked like the Sun and its surrounding corona. The corona was littered with thousands of souls suspended at high altitude above the surface, all moving at different speeds towards the ground. Angels passed right through the corona unaffected. Different souls had different degrees of brightness, where apparently the brightest whitest was the highest order of merit. So, the most righteous and worthy also passed right through the corona. Those who were worthy, but less righteous, took longer but still got to Heaven's surface, eventually. Some souls seemed almost stuck and might take centuries to complete the trip. Those who were unworthy bounced off in a fiery torrent, just like a spaceship skipping off Earth's atmosphere due to an improper approach angle. I realized that this corona was Purgatory. So, then, Purgatory was a localized effect that surrounded Heaven, rather than a completely separate place. How fascinating, I thought, enthralled. I recalled a passage from Corinthians 3:15:

> If anyone's work is burned up, he will suffer loss, though he himself will be saved, but only as through fire.

Purgatory was real, but it wasn't what I expected. I had been sure it was a sad, dark place of waiting. Rather, people in this corona seemed eager to do whatever was needed to complete the transit. They could see Heaven in the distance, they could see each other, and they could see the angels passing by.

Alta and I were not prevented from entering Heaven. We flew through the fiery tendrils just as the angels did, with not a hint of discomfort. As we got closer to Heaven's surface, I could see a visible difference in the souls closest to the ground, compared to those high above it. Clearly, this experience in the corona changed them for the better; they were glowing brighter and seemed even happier than the farther souls. Alta and I were now flying about 1,000 feet over what appeared to be a combination of an amusement park and the Garden of Eden. Green grass and trees with delicate pink flowers were on one side. It was clear, however, that this was just an entry concourse to something far greater that lay beyond. There was a tremendous bustle of activity below in what appeared to be a pre-staging area for Heaven. As we descended, we saw other souls entering Heaven by the same means as I was, carried by what must have been angels. I was amazed at the sheer size of the operation that we flew over. It looked like Six Flags or the opening ceremony at the Olympics had taken over a place as big as Rhode Island. People below didn't seem to be in a hurry.

As I got closer to the ground, I struggled to see what lay ahead. Then I discovered that I could see even when I blinked. I was seeing without my eyes. When I tested this further, I discovered I also had infinite magnification, to any resolution. This was better than the Hubble space telescope. I could even see through any obstacles in my way. My ears followed suit, and I found I had the ability to resolve sound from wherever I looked, and at any wave length, even those above and below the normal human hearing range. This was cool. Except for one deeply concerning thing; my heart wasn't beating. Then I remembered where I was. Another Scripture quote came to mind, 1 Corinthians 2:9:

Eye hath not seen, nor ear heard, neither have entered into the heart of man, the things which God hath prepared for them that love Him.

This made my mind reel back to those in the corona still being purged before entry into Heaven. Perhaps if they had the vision and hearing that I now had, they could see firsthand what they were missing in Heaven—suspended away from participating. I should think that would be very troubling.

I was amazed by some of the basic differences between what we saw in Heaven and what I recalled from many years on Earth. It almost appeared as if a renewed pseudo-Earth had been constructed and placed here specifically for mankind. This pseudo Earth was the very ground on which we'd stand. After transiting the surrounding corona, everyone wasn't just floating. There was no Sun above us, but there was plenty of light. At least it's what I took for light; after all, my eyes weren't needed. There was no population of celestial objects in the sky. There were no street lamps, so I had to assume therefore that this place also had no night time. Heaven was a place of eternal daylight. Neither was there any wind in this place. It was persistently fascinating to me that there was a sky but nothing was in it other than the falling daylight. I kept looking up to check if something was flying over, or if I was missing something. There was gravity, because I could see people walking down below. But I sensed that at a whim, I could fly even without Alta's help. Still, in all, I realized that we were just in one mansion, and others could be completely different.

After a moment more of flight time, Alta brought us to a point just inside the first main concourse. It was closer to what I'd call the Garden of Eden side. We passed over it, and into an archway that led to a second concourse. I knew this wasn't the Garden of Eden of course, but it looked just like I would have imagined it to be. We passed tons of people who all seemed very focused on meeting their relatives who were waiting there to greet them. People were just happy to be there. Everyone was so young. It reminded me of the athletes in the 2012 Olympic village footage I had seen on Earth. All these folks were in great shape and the scale of the operation was immense.

I also felt different than I did on Earth. I had no fear or anxiety. I had what appeared to be a supernaturally heightened sense of everything. And, moreover, there was a certain excitement to the place. In fact, the best way to describe the whole thing would be to say people here were like people on Earth two days before Christmas, but without the rush. The spirit between people was amazing to observe. Apparently, the process of getting through this corona, that I assumed was Purgatory, changed people in a united experience. It was like the survivors of a plane crash, re-uniting, years later. That purgative experience and the one here in Heaven obviously trumped every other consideration from their past life.

But the best part was the overwhelming sense of the presence of God. The feeling was oddly familiar. I felt like a child walking out on Christmas morning realizing Santa had been there. I wondered for a moment if I was having the Beatific Vision, but I quickly decided that could not be. Strong as this presence of God was, I didn't feel like I was looking at Him face-to-face. I even felt a twinge of nervousness at the thought of seeing Him that way.

After leaving the entry concourse, we moved into another adjoining area that appeared to be completely tropical, but it was improved with paths and amenities. After walking some of the paths within this tropical realm, I was standing on a pretty island surrounded by what looked like a cypress swamp and a lake. The whole thing looked like a post card. The surroundings were absolutely manicured. The water was as clear as I can ever remember, and the trees were lovely, but not of any type I had ever seen before. We walked over to the edge of the island, where we approached a young woman from behind, who was sitting and looking out over the water. I felt sure I knew this woman. As we approached, I could tell she knew we were coming, from a little voice within me. Though she didn't move a muscle and still had her back to us. As we got closer, she rose and faced me. It was Tina, whom I vaguely knew in life, but we had never been friends. In life, she really didn't like me at all. In fact, I recall praying for her, quite a lot. Tina was tall, with dirty blonde hair and blue eyes. She hailed us first.

"Tom, I am so glad to see you here," she said. "If it wasn't for the assistance of your many prayers, I would not be here at all." She surprised me by hugging me.

"Where exactly IS here, Tina?" I asked.

She said, "'When' is more the question. You have the distinction of visiting the lowest place in Heaven, reserved for

133

those who were saved by the narrowest of margins. I'm so grateful to you because except for the prayers that YOU said for me, I wouldn't be here at all. When you return to Earth back in your time, you will see me being angry and hateful towards you, as ever. Remember the reward you will gain here for your selflessness towards me and others here, whose places have also been secured by things YOU did for them in life."

"What do you mean, 'my time?'" I asked.

Tina said, "You are fifty years into your future, and all that you see here is after our lives have passed. You see, Heaven's time is ahead of Earth's, so there is no apparent wait when you arrive here to meet other family members."

I thought for a moment and realized I couldn't even imagine how that could work. We walked together while Alta followed. I had lots of questions for Tina.

"Why is this the lowest place in Heaven Tina? Because it looks too beautiful for that."

"All of the places here look beautiful, but the higher places are like those of the higher angels, closer to God. We are all close, but some are closer than others." I was a little surprised that Tina did not sound resentful at this, but then I realized no one could be resentful in this beautiful and happy place.

"Though my station here is lowly," Tina continued, smiling, "I shall always welcome you as a visiting dignitary anytime you return. Except for your actions, my fate would have been black. I know why you are here, and shall return the favor your prayers did for me. Seek out Raphael, for he is already assembling a group to assist you and Alta. In fact, seeing the urgency of your need, Tom, I brought that matter to him myself days ago."

I guess that solves the "intercession of the dead" question, I thought. Clearly, those in Heaven see it as just returning a favor to help those on Earth who had helped them get to Heaven. At the time, I didn't realize the extent of what Tina had done to help us. She had organized an entire campaign to get angelic assistance funneled our way.

I thanked her and hugged her again. Then I walked off her little island home and started out to a field that looked like a summertime "people in the park" scene. As we walked past, I sensed hello's from people. There were none that didn't know me, and I also sensed an implicit invitation to join them. Amazingly, every door was open to me. After a while, it was clear that there wasn't a person in Heaven who didn't know who we were. No one in all of Heaven was a stranger to anyone else. There was no identity, fact or historical detail about anything that was hidden, and, with each person I met, their "heavenly rank" was obvious. The crowd was completely populated with young people. But there were some oddities. A birthmark I had in life was gone, and I was 25 again. No one seemed to have any weight problems, or warts, or any external malady that they had in life. But more important was that the people exhibited symbols of faith I had seen often in life, I saw rosaries and other things uniquely Catholic. Even a girl whom

I knew and biked with, who was a very dedicated Mormon in life, now had a Catholic rosary! That really made me think.

As we travelled on what appeared to be a bike path through a public park, I also began to notice more subtleties that were unique to the heavenly experience. To start with, my sense of perception of people was greatly expanded. I was now surrounded with a perceptual aura emanating 30 to 40 feet out from wherever I stood that worked almost like the whiskers on a cat. Apparently, everyone had this same aura. When others came close and these auras overlapped, you connected with the totality of the person on a level exceeding any experience on Earth. I passed the aura of strangers whom I now knew intimately, and had cross-pollinated feelings, life histories, and even salutations without even a word. I had to ask Alta what this was all about.

"Alta, is this 'perceptual aura' that I feel—normal?"

Alta nodded yes and said, "Everyone here has it, as you no doubt can guess. It's an enhanced version of what we use in my world. So, you can see why no names are necessary, rather just tradition. Little is hidden in my world, but absolutely nothing is hidden here. But obviously people DO have names here in Heaven. Go figure."

The holier people had greater aural reach, some covering most of Heaven. God's aura is the only one that permeates everything in creation simultaneously. Perhaps it was the cause of what we took for light. It occurred to me then that since God obviously knew I was there, he must be allowing it for some greater purpose. My aura even had an extended capability that applied regionally, well beyond the place I stood. I quickly realized that I could search for others in Heaven using this new ability. Alta saw my quizzical expression and offered some explanation.

"What you are encountering is a manifestation of your soul, which you now perceive for the first time. Every thought, deed, and intention here registers within the soul's fabric, and so you can make a spiritual connection beyond any physically possible on Earth. On Earth, your soul was always with you, but your five earthly senses overshadowed its signals," she said.

As we walked, I realized that I was transitioning into an area of Heaven that must have constituted a city. There were buildings and roads, but oddly, no cars. There were also no huge bridges, at least not for automotive travel here. There were no signs or billboards, yet oddly, I knew every street and address as I passed it. Just to test the theory, because, hey, I'm still me, I went further and discovered I knew every address and the way to get there through the entire region.

Alta and I had been walking for some time, when she surprised me by asking, with what I would have described as a sly grin on her face, if I didn't know any better, "Would you like to see the island with Tina again?"

Not sure what she had in mind, I replied offhand, "Sure, but later, since it would bring us all the way back to where we started our walk."

Alta gave me a "wait till you see this" kind of look and just said, "Watch." She waved her hand, and we walked through a gateway of some sort that brought us right back into the middle of the conversation I just had with Tina, but in progress. I stopped speaking, and Alta waved again, returning us to the path at the entry to the city. I realized the significance of this immediately. Alta was showing me that I could go forward or back in time, to any point of reference in the vast heavenly address book. She looked pleased with herself for being able to show me something so cool. I decided to skip to the chase.

"Alta, just how vast is the territory and associated timelines which we can visit here?" I asked.

"Vast beyond your dreams," she said knowingly. "It includes all of space, in this dimension and the earthly one from which we came. Heaven is the same for all who attend here, but the amount one can take in at one time is a function of your status here. Recall that there are some who can literally be in two places at once, and there are others who can be in more places than that. The possibilities of God's reward to the faithful cannot be limited by your ability to receive only one reward at a time, if you have sufficient earthly merit."

She continued, "To understand this place, you need to realize that as earth is a product of the industry of man, this place is a product of the industry of the angels. Except that they are far greater in number than man and have far greater capability and creativity. They have been at work on this place far longer than all of human existence. In part, they were created first to assemble this vast reward for those of your people who attained Heaven. You'll note that unlike man, angels cannot reproduce and have never had a savior die for them. Their purpose is here."

Alta had made a subtle point in the middle of this that I just realized as she said it. There were far more angels in Heaven than men, and by a significant ratio. Moreover, I suspected that even this observation was underestimating the difference, because I was still in the receiving concourse where all of humanity entered Heaven, so there were more humans around than there would be in other parts of Heaven. I recall once asking a teacher how many angels there were, and she responded that they were as numerous as the stars. The idea had come from Isaiah 40:26 among other passages as I recall.

Alta's instruction on Heaven was a lot to absorb in one sitting. After thinking about it a bit, I said, "The vastness of Heaven makes sense, considering that it is for the angels, who can travel anywhere at great speeds. But back on Earth, what possible purpose could there be for OUR universe to be so vast? After all; men can barely get out of their own driveways."

"To hold all of what you call aliens, of course," Alta said, in an "isn't it obvious" tone, and looking at me as if I should have figured this out already. "As you can guess, from meeting me, God has other planetary projects that are both ahead of and behind the one on your Earth, technologically."

"But your world is special," Alta went on, musing. "It alone was the one visited by God, 2,000 years ago. The good souls of those who died from your world already fill the ranks left empty by fallen angels here, and some are assigned to Earth, or other projects beyond Earth. Remember, that time here is not as it is on Earth. Time is an artifact of gravity and mass. All that is different here. You'll notice that people can fly in Heaven, but as a rule they don't. Having infused knowledge already, they already have a complete aerial view of everything here. They can travel to any point as you and I just did a moment ago to see Tina again, without assistance. They also know everything about every earthly event, person, sin, or good deed. There are no surprises of that sort here, though there are unexpected pleasantries."

"So, why are there roads here?" I asked.

Alta shrugged and said, "Among other things, people here have bike races. Some have custom cars, others just like to walk or run. They are for pleasure, not need."

"Alta," I asked, "Is this first concourse the only central staging area where all new heavenly arrivals go? How does this place work, evaluating and placing people? Where is final judgment? Here, near here, or someplace we've yet to see?"

"Great question!" Alta said, in the same tone my high school teachers had used when a student appeared interested in the lesson. "I'll try to take you by to see for yourself if we have time, but it's a little hard to take in all at once."

She took my hand and we ascended Peter-Pan-style above the ground. We returned to the first entry concourse, which still amazed me in its sheer vastness. After a short time, we arrived over what looked like a huge staging area that might almost pass for a concourse outside of a major airport. This was the actual point of entry for new arrivals into the larger concourse we had been flying over. New arrivals were entering from what appeared to be a portal in space. They were guided by the same angels that had protected them in life; so it was clear that the relationship between men and angels was to continue into this existence. Once here, people were preoccupied with their new residence and meeting relatives who were already here and there was a party just for the angels whose charges made it to this perfect place. It appeared to be a welcome-home and job-well-done celebration all rolled into one, but angels-only. The angels peeled off to their party while human arrivals chatted with relatives sent to meet them.

Interestingly, the staging area also contained meet-ups by people who were clearly not relatives. I asked Alta why they came to this spot.

She responded, "They are people who have come to say thanks to the new arrival, because some action of his helped save their souls from Hell. Everything here is connected. It's what Tina would have done with you, had you died before you got here, rather than coming in as we did."

I had understood the Tina thing, taken by itself, but now I knew thanking those who helped you get to Heaven was commonplace here. I suppose logically, just the opposite would be true in Hell; people might come up and spit on you for helping damn them. Over time, we passed a number of teams of people and angels who were obviously working together. I paused for a second, and asked Alta if we could speak to them.

"Why not?" she replied, so we walked over and hailed them. They spoke to us openly and without any reservation, clearly understanding why we were there before we needed to explain. I asked one of the young men what their team did.

"We are one of Heaven's many expeditionary teams, dedicated to a world in a star system not far from Earth," he said.

I asked him what they did there, and he said, "It's basically Earth minus 2500 years in theology, but plus 500 years in technology. So, our ultimate goal is getting them ready for what you guys are working on."

"You've got to be kidding," I said, surprised. "You know what Alta and I are working on?" What were the chances that we just happened to walk up to a group that had something to do with our mission?

The man changed over to a very serious demeanor and answered us with great conviction.

"We sure do. And, we all hope you win. Everything is hinged on spreading the truth throughout the universe, and you two are on point. Failure is not an option. But mind you, we all expect to support you in this," he said.

"We all?" I said. Just how much of Heaven was involved in our mission?

He responded, "There are over 2500 more teams just like ours on other planets. But all that goes nowhere fast if you two fail. Do I even need to explain why?"

Alta and I got the point. This was a very high stakes game.

Finally, we moved just beyond the staging area to see where people arrived on their first full day in Heaven. Relatives already in Heaven tried to share some of the critical changes in time and physics, and reveal who else was there to see the newcomers. Interestingly, everyone here also seemed the same age, uniformly about perhaps twenty-five years old. Alta realized that I was having trouble understanding how Heaven connected to Earth and the world we knew, so she decided to bring me to the place that had been the subject of the tennis racket analogy from before.

She said, "Tom, you can better understand Heaven when you understand the 'Heaven's eye view' of creation, as known by the angels and saints."

She whisked me off to another place that looked like a public park. There was a large marble altar that had a large, dark, glowing, saucer-shaped sphere on its surface. It was guarded by the third highest order of angels, the Thrones. Alta explained that this border between what we are, and what Heaven is, was the Throne's domain. Taller than the tallest humans, they stood unmoving. Sharp golden weapons poked out from their belts and from behind their backs, between their wings. Their images shifted like a flame; instead of making them seem less real, this just increased their threatening aura, as if they might turn invisible and cut your head off if you weren't looking. They encircled the altar and strongly reminded me of the British palace guard.

"Alta, will they mind us being here?" I asked.

"No, they already know why we're here, and they know God okay'd it," she said.

The dark object was about seven feet across and two feet thick, almost like a pair of pie plates pressed together. The object was a swirling mass of what appeared to be star stuff. I looked at Alta and then back at the glowing starry mass with complete shock.

"No way!" My eyes must have been wide saucers.

Alta grinned triumphantly and said, "I told you so. Yep, this is your entire universe. It is a live action simulation. It's a lot like if the player's bodies were avatars with the souls of real men attached. Your entire world is a game; one that has eternal consequences for the winners and losers, but nothing you do there gets beyond the borders of the simulation. In fact, the rules of the simulation's physics prevent the inhabitants from ever escaping, by definition. The speed of light for instance, is limited for precisely that purpose and no other. So, every great discovery of your earthly science is nothing more than uncovering one more underlying rule of the game's inherent programming. Your universe, in its totality, is right there in front of you. 13.73 billion light years across, if you could travel end to end from the inside, or 7 seconds, if you walked around its border behind the Thrones."

"My reality is a game console in Heaven?" I said with disbelief.

Alta conceded, "Your world on Earth is fully real, Tom, but it isn't comparable to the spiritual reality, which is the larger framework in which your entire universe is embedded."

Alta made her point with a broad sweeping gesture of both arms. "All angels, demons, and even transcendent robots, like me, can operate from outside of the simulation, by influence. My true home is in the simulation, so I have more power than someone operating from outside. Angels are in Heaven, demons in Hell, and all still have the ability to influence outcomes in the 'simulation' that is your reality."

"Seeing this explains a lot," I said, peering into the depths of the smoky universe. "Remember the rich man begging for a dipper of water from deep within Hell?"

"Luke 16:26," Alta recited with raised eyebrows:

"And besides, there is a great chasm separating us. No one can cross over to you from here, and no one can cross over to us from there."

Alta knew the Bible in every flavor and quoted it anytime I couldn't recall the detail. But this time, the quote had a hidden meaning.

"Alta, do you realize the significance of this? The entire 'earth project' IS in Heaven. No demon could influence or tempt anyone without express permission from God. Moreover, it clearly shows that God loves us more than some might have suspected. We're like a prize jewel," I said.

Alta responded, "But this simulation is more than just a game, Tom, because real souls are the measure of whether the test that is executed here succeeds or fails. No achievement or victory won in this simulation we call 'life' matters beyond the saving of one's soul and the extent to which you assist in the saving of other's souls."

"So, when Mathew 6:19 says to build up your treasure in Heaven and not on Earth—they aren't kidding," I said.

"We'll come back to that idea later, Tom. Let's continue with the task at hand," Alta said.

Alta brought us back to the point we had last departed from and restarted without skipping a beat.

From there out, I just decided to try to take it all in. The wonders I saw were so numerous, I could not have listed them in detail. The first spot after the staging area was filled with people, and almost like a carnival, but of an unimaginable nature. Plants and animals were an odd mix of the familiar and the strange. The animals were tame in their interactions with humans, but still completely wild in every other respect. Lions were still lions. This next choice of paths appeared to branch out into several routes that could be taken by any traveler. There was the trek that led back into what appeared to be the Garden of Eden; another apparently allowed you to travel back into time and relive any past event of your life. There was another that routed travelers into the console containing our world and universe that we just left. Using it would lead to space and travel to other galaxies and the worlds therein. This last one obviously was a portal that worked just like the portal back to Tina. This whole experience was way past what even the best sci-fi writers could have imagined. Time and space were completely meaningless in an environment like this. There was even a route that led to the residence of the angels, and another to the throne of God Himself. This was truly the nexus of all creation, and the malleability of time was commonplace to heavenly residents. Heaven had the depth and breadth to encompass any desire in any place over any time period. Moreover, Heaven was the final destination of those rewarded; it was everything that was, and contained all the other domains. It was the expanse of all that was defined, and all that was yet to be defined, with the singular exception of Hell, which was quarantined off from Heaven by a great abyss.

Alta had previously explained that some who were closer to God could be rewarded in two or more places at once. All were completely happy, though some clearly had greater capacity for happiness than others. But we had a number less than ONE.

Alta said, "Despite all that you and I are seeing, we are just visitors here. We are like tourists outside on the airport walkway, looking in through the glass at the shops and people, wondering what lies within. Those who have earned their final destiny here in heaven have a view of all of this that is far more complex than is possible in our whirlwind tour."

For a moment, I felt guilty being here, because every other person here had earned their way in. I was the kid that snuck under the ballpark fence. I was also nervous about running into God, or family members. Now I knew God knew I was here, but like the dog that thinks he is invisible when he closes his eyes, I figured it'd be better not to have to explain why I was here, face to face. But even more oddly, I found myself praying, out of a combination of fear and habit. I almost laughed to picture my prayers doing a U-turn to God who was right there. It was odd being the only person in Heaven who had concerns about being here.

Upon reflection, I wasn't even sure of what I would say if I ran into Jesus Himself, but it still didn't change my feeling of being a kid sneaking into the ballpark. As a result of my soul's aural perception, I felt that God's love and presence was very strong everywhere we went. So, I supposed that all these angels, like Michael, Raphael, and the ones Tina lined up, were working for God, just to help us. Maybe the best thing I could have said to Jesus on a chance meeting was, "Thanks."

All the while that we were seeking allies in Heaven, Ostara's Watchers were rounding up the team from Hell that would seek to destroy us. Hell's very worst were lining up for a shot at Alta. To them, she was like the fastest gun in the West. Any demon who took her out would move to the front of the pack in Hell's pecking order.

Chapter 10
Raphael's Team

We had done enough sightseeing, and Alta wanted to get down to the business of finding Raphael so we could complete our mission. First, though, I asked Alta about the sword Raphael had given her, and how she had met him. Alta told me about Sarah and Tobit, and that Ostara had sent The Watchers to kill all seven of Sarah's husbands on her wedding night. This continued until Raphael intervened and helped Tobit and Sarah, preventing further folly from The Watchers. The problem was that after his mission with Tobit and Sarah was complete, Ostara ordered The Watchers to attack Raphael en-route back to Heaven. This was where Alta intervened. Seeing a group of fallen Powers and Principalities beating up on a lower Archangel offended Alta's sense of justice, so she stepped in and destroyed two of the attackers, and the others retreated.

Raphael, in gratitude, became friends with Alta and gave her the sword that she carries to this day. Alta's sheer power was apparently equaled by only the most powerful angels in Heaven or Hell. But Raphael had a lot of influence in Heaven, being one of only seven who stands before the throne of God. The Watchers have hated Raphael, ever since he healed the earth, after their tryst with humanity, before the great flood. I recalled reading the account in Enoch of how Raphael had bound Azazel's hands and feet in accordance with God's instruction. This was clearly an old fight, and now Alta had a very strong ally.

After sharing this story, Alta stopped for a moment and looked inward. She explained that she had called Raphael from wherever he was. He promptly appeared before us with two other angels behind him. When he saw Alta, he shed the standard stoic angelic pose and ran over to hug her, as though she was the fellow member of a winning baseball team.

Alta returned the hug enthusiastically and asked, "How are you, Raphael? It's been a long time."

"Well, Alta, that all depends on where you're standing, I suppose. But I'm very glad to see you and even gladder to share what good news I have for you," Raphael said.

"Good news?" she answered back. "We sure could use some."

"Michael's team is going to help you, in any situation involving the borders of Heaven or Hell that they protect. Better yet, I have been given my own team to help you everywhere else," he said.

Raphael waved his hand and now there were six angels behind him, who all had the same sword Alta did.

He continued, "Also, if we get in trouble, we can summon Michael's team to support us even outside his regular missions." This was good news indeed.

I could see Alta looking at a scar on Raphael's arm, and I asked her why she was looking at it.

Alta whispered, "It's a scar from when we first met. A claw mark from one of the Powers that had grabbed Raphael."

Powers are one step higher than Archangels, and Raphael had been in trouble till Alta stepped in.

Raphael said, "I can see you are concerned, but fear not. We are following the plan that was created for us by God Himself."

I looked over at Alta and decided to tell Raphael about her concerns.

"I realize you find that comforting, but Alta isn't yet convinced that God has any will, good or bad, for a machine like her."

Raphael responded, "We are ALL God's machines, Alta. Trust me; God even has you accounted for in this."

"Yes," Alta replied with a bit of sarcasm, "I can just hear God saying 'Go out and make for Me disciples of all robots.' But regardless, it won't stop me from killing the demons that murdered my crew. Raphael, your team is made up of angels and archangels. They will be up against Watchers who have far more power than your team."

Raphael looked back at his group and offered us assurances. "These were all handpicked by Michael. Some are the very same angels who fought Ostara's team before, and others were selected for their special abilities. Rank isn't everything, Alta. Remember, Michael expelled Satan and he is an Archangel, like me. We'll be fine."

Secretly, I was still worried. I knew that Alta had already rescued Raphael, and I had already seen her trash a couple of Powers in the fight in front of the church. If this group assisting us had been on the opposing side, I felt certain Alta could take them all by herself. How could they help us here? With my own life on the line, I decided to speak up.

"Raphael, we are grateful for your help. If your team should get into a bigger fight than they are ready for, what is plan B?" I asked.

Raphael responded, "Then we draw upon the power of God Himself. For our position here with you is His will. Remember, Moses parted the Red Sea, and he had no power of his own. Don't worry about it so much. The hard part for you now is to complete what Jane started. You should probably get to that. But I suspect we'll see you here again."

"Raphael, I AM worried. Alta is all by herself now. Huge demons from Hell are trying to kill her, the same ones who killed ALL of her crew. They are supernatural and immortal. How do you fight that?" I asked.

Raphael tried to calm me.

He said, "I still think you two are going to win this one. Alta 'all by herself' is more than you think. Her people planned ahead for precisely this kind of thing. Scientists from Gihon realized that anything made within a realm keeps that realm's physics. It's like, a man born on Krypton would still be superman on Earth. Something made in Heaven would have angelic power here or there. One of the big things that separate angels from men is that angels aren't limited by Earthly physics. Superman was strong, but of no consequence to an angel or demon. One very powerful angel or demon could crush a black hole out of existence.

So, these otherworldly scientists started a series of industries that could work within dimensions beyond the four you know." Raphael continued, "Anything created in these enclaves would possess the properties of THAT dimension and carry it over into their own world. It's the same principle as your attempts to make perfectly round ball bearings in space, where there is no gravity to impede their unblemished roundness. Scientists from Gihon assembled a small but elite team of super robots made in this extra dimensional way, who were not bound by conventional physics. Though intended for service on their world, these guardians could also defend against demonic assaults. If they were assigned to do so, they could even thwart assaults from Hell itself. Alta and her little sister Raven were two of these guardians. But only Alta was complete in time for this trip. The crew planned to finish Raven's programming after finding Earth, once they had some firsthand experience to determine the abilities they would need her to have."

"So, her people are building more of these on Alta's world?" I asked.

"Yes," Raphael assured. "There are many robots on Gihon. But not like Alta and Raven. These two are a new design, made with far greater capabilities, especially for this mission. Much of their design incorporated human engrams, appearance, and behavior. Alta was genuinely indistinguishable from her crew in all ways but her assigned tasks."

"Raphael, if you know all this, then so does Satan, right?" I asked.

He replied, "Yes, most definitely. The agents of Hell know very well what they are up against with this crew from Gihon. The demons are always eagerly upping the ante in the arms race to confront these most advanced robotic defenders of men. Because of the importance the demons place upon stopping this new transcendental society from succeeding on Earth, they assigned their most fierce emissary of Hell, Ostara."

"What can you tell us about Ostara?" I asked.

"I shall be sending you to an expert on that very matter in Berlin, Maryland. Her name is Jessie. You'll be meeting at her gravestone within a few days to get the entire story. But we'll need some time to set up what you need on Earth. Powerful demons like the Prince of Persia and the Prince of Greece will oppose us mightily," Raphael explained.

Those names rung some bells, and I suddenly remembered that they had been bad guys in the book of Daniel. And now, they were coming after us.

"Haniel will get you the details for the meeting. He is part of my team. I'll need to set some things up to make all this happen, however. Go back to your ship and we'll post a guard till we're ready on my end. I will call you back here very soon," Raphael said.

Raphael warned us sternly. "Once we get this meeting set up, you should expect to encounter some stern resistance on Earth, maybe even getting to your meeting. Even as we speak, The Watchers are spreading disinformation and unleashing surrogate spirits to turn Tom into a social leper, lose his job, traffic tickets, angry coworkers, mistakes on the cable bill, the works. You will find every door closed to you, Tom. It is their way. From this point on, nothing will be easy for you on Earth. We can't directly intervene in matters where there are struggles between humans, so Kokabiel will use his surrogates to make your life Hell. We can intervene when demons directly attack either of you, however, and will come as soon as you call us."

"Good luck and Godspeed," Raphael said to Alta, as he shook her hand. This was clearly the parting of two friends, despite Alta's inferiority complex regarding her place with God.

As we parted, I asked Alta again about the whole thing with Tobit, and her first meeting with Raphael. Alta said, "The account is in Tobit for you to read. The Azazel story is in Enoch, but you should ignore the part about The Watchers hooking up with human women and giving birth to giants. That didn't happen, although The Watchers did indeed cause all the mayhem, and more than, the book records."

"Is this why the book never made the Bible?" I asked.

"Probably," she responded, shrugging. "There was truth mixed in with spurious history. The account deserves respect in my opinion, but not at the level of scripture."

"Why do you think that?" I asked.

Alta said, "Simple. I have all the data from the Library of Congress, remember? I can statistically compare and cross-reference every critique ever written of every work that was considered for the Bible. Upon review, I can see that the early Christians knew of, and even quoted Enoch, but rightly removed it from the canon. Also, of the two choices I have for the Old Testament, that is, the Hebrew and Greek canons, I believe there is sufficient evidence to show that the early church used the larger Hebrew canon originating from Palestine. So, the Catholic Bible appears to be the most complete and accurate collection of the total writing attributed to early Christianity. But still Enoch didn't make that larger, more complete canon."

"So, you're okay with the New Testament, then?" I asked.

"Yes, except for the missing books," Alta replied.

"What missing books?" I asked.

Alta explained that first Corinthians mentions a letter that was sent prior to its writing, making our first Corinthians, actually second Corinthians. Our second then becomes third.

"Can you use your vast search capability to see if any of the missing books or original Aramaic are in your database, but just not identified?" I asked.

Alta said, "Good idea, and yes, I have found fragments of early Aramaic, and some other parts of the Bible that had been listed as lost. But the material in them does not apply to our questions directly."

With our meet-up with Raphael complete, I quickly asked Alta to bring us back to our home, and she precisely reversed the process that got us there.

Chapter 11

Visiting Angel

The following day, Raphael visited us at my home to tell us news of the actions taking place in Hell to oppose us. He told us of Ostara's campaign to gain support in Hell and to counter our success on Earth. I'm not sure why, but upon seeing Raphael on Earth, I was reflexively tempted to genuflect. I knew he would chastise me if I did so, so I stopped myself. Michael had already told us not to bow, because he was a creation of God, the same as us. Raphael spoke to Alta and me from the deck behind my house, just having appeared out of thin air.

"Greetings once again to you both," he said.

His voice had the classic ultra-deep angelic tone that no human could imitate. He asked us, concerned, why we weren't safely behind his posted guard at Alta's ship. I explained that the deviation in plan was my fault. After all, I had a life that went on here, with or without all of this intrigue.

"I have news from Michael, regarding Ostara and The Watchers," Raphael informed us.

"First," he said, "I have been assigned to drop every other duty to focus on you two. This is because of the importance that God places on your mission and to assure your protection, Tom. This includes my whole team. It is the will of God that no person from Earth should be harmed in the process of Alta's quest on behalf of Gihon or those other civilizations. But, you also need to understand that this does not make you invulnerable. We expect that it will help free Alta up for her task, to resolve the matters of truth to the best of her ability. Secondly, you should be aware that Ostara has gathered the most powerful demons in Hell to assist in your destruction. The Watchers who killed Jane and Alta's crew are now seeking others from various groups who specialize in this sort of challenge. Among them are the Knights in Satan's Service, and a large number of Samyaza's surrogate spirits whose job is inflicting Earthly mayhem."

"Specialize?" I asked.

Raphael said, "You need to understand what Hell is and how Hell works. Hell is a tremendous barren expanse. It contains massive tundra-like areas, utterly barren of creatures of any sort. Like Heaven, Hell has more than a billion-to-one demons to humans, by ratio."

I again mentioned the passage in the Bible that compared angels to stars in the sky.

"Well, it's true," Raphael answered. "But there are far more stars than you know of. The Bible also tells you that a third of them fell to Hell. But this was all intended metaphorically."

The numbers thing intrigued me, and I felt a little capricious.

"So, Alta, just for fun; carry the metaphor to its logical end. What ratio does that give us between humans and demons in Hell or humans and angels in Heaven?" I asked.

"Earth has produced 110 billion people over the last million years or so. The average galaxy has a billion stars and 300 billion galaxies are known. Your Earthly astronomers have found only 170 billion galaxies, so human star surveys are a little short of our number. Let us say that gives us 300 billion-billion angels. Let us further accept that one-third of the angels fell to Hell along with two-thirds of all humans after judgment. So, using those rough numbers, Hell has 1.36 billion demons to every human. The balance gives us Heaven's population at 5.45 billion angels to every human, just for fun," Alta said proudly.

Raphael bristled, "Very humorous, Alta."

It appeared that he didn't think we were taking this seriously, so I tried to rescue the situation.

"Well, Raphael, I guess I can conclude that humans are very, very rare in Heaven or Hell."

"If you look at it that way, yes, I suppose that's true. But the issue here isn't the headcount, it's for you to accurately understand how Hell works and what impact that has on you."

"Oh, sorry," I said. I was chastened ... a little.

Raphael continued, eyeing me to see if I would stay on topic this time. "Those in Hell are imprisoned there, and not free to leave. But there are a few exceptions among the demons. They are the ones you need to worry about. As a rule, angels and demons can act at a distance, so their presence is not completely necessary to feel their influence. They can do most of what they need to do without actually being at the spot. But, there are limits to this. A person can give a demon extra influence on Earth with a Ouija board, holding a séance, or the practice of witch craft. What's happening behind the scenes is that good angels guarding men open the gates of Hell for bad angels to come closer to Earth because now they have an 'invitation' from a human. Picture it this way. A pack of wild dogs waits outside the palace gate. The fence keeps them out. Then the guards at the gate get a signal to just open the gate and let some wolves in, because some kid with a Ouija board sent an invitation."

Raphael explained, "For a demon to get the opportunity to directly tempt a human and leave the depths of Hell, it's like winning the lottery. As Alta's calculation crudely demonstrates, at best, the odds are one in a billion, considering the sheer number of demons in Hell to start with, that any one demon will get the invitation and get out of Hell. Some demons have created cottage industries designed to ensnare humans, thus raising their status in Hell."

"What kind of cottage industries?" I asked blankly.

Raphael responded, "There are several which you should be familiar with. Like a demon called The Prince of Persia, referred to in Daniel 10:13. He restrained Gabriel himself from coming to the aid of Daniel for 21 days; Gabriel only got through with the help of Michael. The Prince of Persia is a very dangerous and powerful demon and has a particularly strong influence over the part of the world for which he is named. Now, he has a team of his own, like Ostara, and is from the very same group of demons who tempted Muhammad to write an alternate testimony of the Bible. You may recall that Muhammad took many wives, formed a small army near Medina, and questioned the divinity of Christ. The Prince of Persia then later did precisely the very same thing to Joseph Smith and the Mormons. Joseph Smith led the army of Nauvoo, had numerous wives, and re-defined the divinity of Christ in a way that caused the mainline Christians to squirm for almost two hundred years. Joseph Smith's writings even mentioned Muhammad. Both men claimed to have been visited by an angel in person, who was in fact the Prince of Persia. He disguised his true nature and instructed them himself. Five-hundred years from now, the Prince of Persia will use the same technique yet again, and so on till the end of time."

"Raphael, one of my Mormon girlfriends explicitly told me that there is no appropriate connection between Joseph Smith and Muhammad," I said.

"Tom, do you know Catholics who don't know their faith?" he asked.

"Sure," I said sheepishly.

"Do you think that only Catholics have this problem? You should be aware that this connection was made by Joseph Smith himself in a speech he gave in Missouri on October 14, 1838. We agree with his assessment, and have just offered the explanation of the forces behind the curtain," Raphael said.

"If you know the Prince of Persia does this, can't you head him off?" I asked.

"Sure," Raphael said, "but remember you are warned against it in the Bible, at Galatians 1:8: 'But even if we or an angel from Heaven should preach a gospel other than the one we preached to you, let him be eternally condemned.' "

"So, you are asserting that much of our history has been shaped by actions of the demons?" I asked.

Raphael responded, "Yes, but it's also been greatly shaped by the good angels too. Bad angels have favorite localities for temptation. For instance, after she became Queen of Hell, Ostara was a Germanic goddess of the Sun and fertility. Perhaps you also recall the demons that tempted Luther. These demons specialize in causing trouble in Germany. They tempted Luther, then Hitler in turn. Hitler was aware that Luther's writings railed against the Jews for crucifying Christ. Luther's book was called 'On the Jews and Their Lies' written in 1543. It was prominently displayed by the Nazis in Nuremburg rallies prior to the war. These demons will also recycle their negative influence every couple of hundred years in whatever land is their domain of influence."

Raphael added with emphasis, "Satan likes reversing the model used by God to save men. Whereas our Lord built a Church, Satan has constructed anti-religions, meant to gather and deceive thousands of people. Now you see why your success is so very critical. Everything in Heaven has its corollary in Hell. Ostara is to Hell, as the Virgin Mary is to Heaven. As the queen of Hell, she will not tolerate being embarrassed by your meddling."

"So, what put Joseph Smith on the Prince of Persia's radar?" I asked.

Raphael said, "For the most part it was his susceptibility to the temptation, which is always out there, but the big thing was his decision to translate a document that originated from Egypt to create 'The Pearl of Great Price.' The Prince of Persia controls the whole area north of the rain forest in Africa, while we have equal teams from our side. But any cartouche, papyri or other artifact used in a religious ritual carries a blessing from the forces of darkness. It's really the same as using an Ouija board."

Raphael made his next statement with grave emphasis, even pressing his palms towards the ground as he spoke.

"What you believe and practice DOES matter to God, to history, and to all other men. You could never be close to a wife you didn't understand, and so it is true with God. Alta's success on this trip would save the need for Gihon to send another team. They could then very easily spread their findings throughout all of space. Even if her result here on Earth is flawless, all those people who hear of it in any distant world then must still choose whether to believe her testimony. But if she succeeds, they at least have a choice they may never have if she fails."

Raphael paused, then said, "Let's cut to the chase here. You have now got my team focused on your mission at the expense of every other priority. Michael put a guard around your ship, but it only helps you if you are there. Haniel is setting things up with Jessie to get her team here on Earth to assist you in dealing with Kokabiel's surrogate spirits. But you'll need to return to Heaven to meet with Haniel before you get Jessie's help."

I responded, "We're already ON Earth now, Raphael, and since you've already okay'd this whole thing and set it up through Michael, why not just get us over to Jessie directly?"

"Everything we do is according to a hierarchy," Raphael answered. "We angels follow that hierarchy. Except for Satan, he didn't. So, I guess you could technically skip all the protocol."

Alta snickered. I realized that this angel was either being humorous, or sarcastic, or both. I never figured they had it in them.

"It's not that simple," Michael went on, presumably serious now. "Just as the demons oppose you in this, they also oppose good angels even more so. Humans get good stuff done sometimes, but angels from Heaven ALWAYS move with the will of God. Demons put more effort into stopping us first. Prayer can move our armies of good angels faster, but you all don't have much of that working for you either at the moment, since no one on Earth knows to pray for you for this, beyond the daily masses of the church that cover ALL intentions. So, we have to fight our way back to Earth to get all this stuff done for you. It might take some time."

"Okay then, we must thank you in advance. I guess you all will call us when you're ready." I said gratefully.

I realized these angels helping us were going into this whole thing knowing they were in for a beating every bit as bad as what we had coming. Still, they never displayed a moment of fear or doubt. I could barely understand them or the world they called normal. But I now truly respected them. They had moxie.

With our meeting concluded, Raphael left as he came.

But there was another meeting on this same matter taking place in Hell. At the very same time as our meeting with Raphael, Ostara and her closest lieutenant Samyaza discussed the problem of Alta's crew on Earth.

Chapter 12
The Queen of Hell

Meetings with Ostara always took place in her home court, which was really a separate city in Hell. Her palace was near the center of the city and most of her business was conducted there. The usual misery and disarray found in Hell was absent within the city limits, but no one would consider its streets safe. After all, this was still very much a place in Hell. Her palace was distinctive. It was a huge domed building surrounded by Roman columns. Its vast proportions could house nearly 200 thousand visitors. It was clearly modeled after Albert Speer's design for the Great Hall Germania. This wasn't all that surprising; Ostara was German, as was Speer. What Speer had designed for Hitler just got finished here in Hell for Ostara. Still, it was hard to determine whether the hall was actually built by Speer, or, more likely, just demons acting in his absence. Ostara's decorators drew from traditions and symbols that came from the Celts, the Gauls, and Germania. The boar's head was a prominent standard in her great hall. Even her legions of angels looked like storm troopers readied for battle. The great hall had at its center a large throne room and space for a very large number of guests. Rows of her palace guard stood in the wings awaiting any command. Her huge throne was made of dark marble. She sat upon it like a Babylonian queen waiting to grant an audience to her visitors.

Samyaza, Azazel, and Sariel stood before her. They were discussing the "Alta" matter, and clearly tempers were short. Ostara fumed over Azazel's limited success in the attack on Jane and the others. She was beside herself that Michael had intervened before they could deal with Alta. Ostara questioned Sariel angrily.

"Why didn't you just destroy her before Michael got there?" Ostara asked.

Sariel responded defensively, "This one is different. She has extraordinary power, and I was probably lucky to get out of there in one piece. She destroyed my team without even getting scratched. It was like getting a fighting lesson from a master. She moves in a way that we do not. I even suspect that she was just toying with us."

Samyaza looked at Ostara in amazement. "You're kidding, right? You are one of the most powerful demons in all of Hell."

He was referring to Sariel, but speaking directly to Ostara, who was now beginning to figure out what was going on.

"It is obvious that her people made her specifically to counter this sort of threat. But if we really want to know exactly what we're dealing with, we should consult those demons charged to tempt and destroy her home planet. Summon them before me, and we'll find out everything we need," Ostara commanded.

A short time later, several demons from the group targeting Gihon were brought before Ostara.

As they approached, they cowered in fear, because they knew Ostara's reputation well. She might have them tortured for giving incorrect or incompetent answers. Or they could just as likely be abused for no reason at all. No visit to Ostara's court was ever a good thing. Many of the demons in Hell had already lost their mental faculties in a way that made them useless even to Satan, but Ostara had a unique mix of madness and rage, that still found a place in Satan's purpose.

Madness was more common in Hell than earthly theologians suspected. The description of guilt in Mark 9:48 hints at what happens to the damned after countless eons:

> Where their worm does not die and the fire is not quenched.

Eventually every entity in Hell would lose their normal mental faculties because of the magnitude of their own guilt, separation from God, and self-loathing. Guilt and shame became the loudest mental voice, once every other distraction was removed. With even the purpose of tempting men lost after the end of the world, nothing but guilt would remain to incapacitate its victims in Hell. Even the demons that don't need to think because they have infused knowledge, have no other thought but guilt to comfort their consciousness. Satan alone bore the curse of an

170

utterly incorruptible mind, so he alone would spend eternity without a single rational companion in all of Hell. But this fate was still eons in his future.

As the three visiting demons entered Ostara's court, they were announced by name and rank, in accordance with the angelic positions they held before the fall. These three were all of lower rank. They were archangels prior to the fall, and sentenced to tempt Alta's world until one of three things happened: they themselves went mad, everyone on Gihon turned to Satan, or time itself ended.

Ostara hailed them as she hailed all other lower demons in Hell. "Worthless servants of evil, what can you share with us of your progress in your assigned tasks?"

One demon stepped forward and said, "I am Merihim, formerly an archangel. We are the demons assigned to Alta's world, known as Gihon by the inhabitants. We have been in place for more than 10,000 of their years. Their year is about 66.8 days in Earth time. During those years, we have won many to the cause of Satan."

Ostara stopped the cowering demon and said, "I didn't call you here for a press release. I want specific information regarding their technology, in particular, those things meant to thwart what we do. Tell me about their robots."

Merihim said, "In this regard, no other known world is their equal. The people of Gihon maintain a group of robots made by micro-climatizing environments containing extra-dimensionality. Properties of that extra-dimensionality are inherited by any product created within those industrial frameworks. They are made of hylomorphic matter and can operate in both the physical and spiritual realms with equal ease. This new breed of robots have power equal to the greatest angels in Heaven or Hell, because they have the ability to localize their power at the very point of conflict, rather than attempt to act at a distance as we do from Hell. If you are confronted by one of these machines, we have found it wise to leave."

Merihim paused.

He continued, saying, "They can do anything we can do and with more force at the point of impact. Fortunately, they are very few in number, less than six in total at the current state of production, but we believe they now have the ability to generate gigantic numbers with the throw of a switch. We also suspect that it is their ultimate purpose to create a vast expeditionary army. That army could potentially be sent to destroy us."

Otsara stood up and lashed out at the demon in a screaming rage. "So, they're going to come to the shores of Hell then, to expel us? Ridiculous! I don't want excuses. I want to know how to destroy them!" she raged.

The demon consulted with his two peers and turned back to her with an answer he knew that she didn't want to hear.

He said, "This is a battle of force against force. We do not know the extent of their power, but we believe that they could be overcome with sheer weight of numbers. Even if they have a thousand times our power individually, we still outnumber them by more than a billion to one. We have calculated that if they converted the entire mass of their solar system to the creation of this new breed of robots, by literally grinding up the planets they stood upon, we'd still outnumber them gigantically, having thousands to one advantage."

The demon continued, "However, mathematically, the scales tip their way if they can gain the assistance of other civilizations, and share the technology they have now. There are simply too many planets for us to overwhelm, if the humans everywhere in the universe unite. They retain the advantage of localized force where as we operate at a distance in most cases."

Ostara pondered for a moment and glanced over at her team, who were quite interested in this report.

Merihim said, "Though there are no more than six of these super robots to oppose the legions here in Hell, numbering in the hundreds of billions, we do have one concern. We believe that the later generations of these robots, the ones made after Alta, may be far more powerful. We have seen plans for a far more capable warrior class that has not been released yet. This new group could be thousands of times more powerful than what they are fielding today. In that case, the tipping point of force against force comes far sooner. We have calculated that an increase in capability of about three orders of magnitude is possible from their designs, and that would enable them to match Hell in a toe-to-toe challenge without recruiting the assistance of other worlds."

Merihim added one last thought, saying, "But most importantly, these robots have no soul, no fear of death, and operate completely autonomously. They have gigantic knowledge bases and have the same clairvoyant ability to see us as the people of Gihon themselves. We cannot hide from them. They cannot be threatened or bribed because they cannot be damned or rewarded. They just act."

Ostara considered Merihim's words without her characteristic rage. She whispered to Samyaza that they now had a threat warranting the intervention of Satan himself. Over the next several days, they would carry their request for assistance to the highest power that is resident in Hell. For surely, Satan himself would see the need to kill Alta before she could spread the message of God throughout the entire universe.

The following day Ostara and Samyaza approached the throne of Satan, which was quite distant from Ostara's home region. The journey required them to pass over many thousands of suffering souls and their demons who suffered even more. Occasionally, throughout the journey, others could be seen falling into Hell. They entered from different vantage points, because each was sent directly to the spot of their eternal judgment. Rarely did any of the damned ever migrate from those spots where they first arrived. As you looked up, you could see that it was a team of angels from Heaven itself that had the task of these deliveries. They were one of only two teams of heavenly visitors in the region. The other team of good angels was Lahatiel and his crew of 12 high-ranking angels, serving as border guards. They are called Powers in the angelic choirs and are higher than Archangels. They never wandered far from Hell's border and regularly repelled the efforts of demons who sought to escape.

The flight over to the throne of Satan looked like the old World War II newsreels of the bombing of Dresden. There were human body parts strewn about indiscriminately. The damned souls looked shell-shocked. The demons attacked them and each other with no perceptible pattern. A blazing hot wind passed through and helped further ignite fires already in progress. One could discern cremated remains of adults, now shrunk to the volume of a child. Other than the fact that the landscape was more wild than bombed-out city, Hell was the spitting image of the last days of Hitler's reign. The landscape was like the barren Canadian tundra, except much of it was smoldering. This was a place of misery, but even more so of utter and complete chaos. Looking at all of this, it is incredible that Hell had the capacity to muster enough stable troops to even tempt mankind at all. The level of noncooperation was off the charts, and this impacted both demon and human souls equally. Only the threat of still greater pain caused people or demons to act coherently. Ruthlessness dominated all of Hell. The population of the damned ranged from the constant victims to the hardened criminals. Many sought to just hide from the terrors, worst of which was just the sight of God. Shame ruled every inch of Hell.

Ostara and Samyaza approached Pergamos, the city that contained the throne of Satan. At a distance you could see a choir of demon guards at the city gate. The entire border was protected by these demon guards, who allowed Ostara and Samyaza to pass without incident, since they were expected.

Within the city walls was the throne of a king. Pergamos was a complete departure from the rest of Hell. This was the one spot where you might think you were in Heaven, except for the occupants and activities within. If you moved a mix of the households of Hugh Hefner and Saddam Hussein into the Forbidden City in China, you might have a pretty good reproduction of Pergamos's place and position in Hell. The architecture was more Roman than Chinese, and there was gold in the basic construction of the buildings. The palace floors were of impressive marble and granite. Even the court had a certain arrogant air about it. The impression was of both importance and disregard for any rules, other than fear of the boss. Satan himself was hearing pleas from other demons, over the distribution of Hell's resources or various struggles in their war on creation. When Ostara and Samyaza finally got called forward they came before Satan himself, who was surrounded by a group of highly placed onlookers, functionaries or soldiers in his cabinet. Satan was a very large demon, bigger than any others encountered so far. His swagger and way of communicating seemed more like a Columbian drug lord than the king of Hell. This was because people's sinful manifestations on Earth were directly connected to the sinful habits and behaviors of the same demons that tempted them. A sinful man on Earth would feel right at home here. It was clear that, on some level, many of the occupants of Hell actually wanted to be there.

Ostara stepped forward and began to make her case. "Lucifer, we appreciate your seeing us on this grave matter on which we seek your assistance," she said. Politeness was always called for when talking to someone more powerful. "A human civilization from a planet called Gihon is creating an army of robots with transcendental powers. These new machines pose a threat to our ability to influence the population of both their world and Earth, whose souls we seek to damn. One of these robots, named Alta, has travelled to Earth from her home world on a mission to search for the history of the humans and teachings of God. It was the mission of her human crew to get details of

Christ's teachings back to their own world and from there spread the news by star travel. Worst yet, they started talking to the Catholics. We have therefore killed her crew, but Alta has retaliated and destroyed several of my team, The Watchers. Demons from Gihon have told us that this type of robot can only be destroyed with overwhelming force, which you alone control. We believe they are now building even more combat troops that may have far greater powers than Alta. So, therefore we have come to ask your assistance in this gravest matter," she said.

Satan leaned back into his throne and, hand on his chin, said, "Can this Alta be turned against her creators? Better that we have them destroy themselves, than engage in a protracted battle that would only further reveal our existence. You know how this works, Ostara; first, we seek to get them to do our work, only stepping in when all else fails."

Ostara responded quickly, "We have evidence that these robots cannot be bribed because they have no soul." She did not want Lucifer to think she might have missed something. Lucifer pondered this new development.

"I suspect this means the transaction will have different currency, but still could be done. If this turns out to be true, we could level the playing field with a distraction," Satan said.

Ostara asked, "What sort of distraction?"

"Why, the Three Days of Darkness should just about do it," Lucifer responded.

He was referring to an apocalyptic Catholic prophecy, sanctioned by Padre Pio and other Catholic mystics for hundreds of years. Essentially, it is the Passover of Moses redone in modern times, on a Thursday through Saturday. Every demon in Hell is released to roam the earth and destroy the unfaithful. It will be preceded by lightning strikes, and a terrible storm. Total darkness envelopes the earth, and power is out everywhere. Anyone not at home praying around a blessed candle will be struck down by the demons.

Upon hearing this, Ostara said "This will take the approval of God Himself to allow."

Lucifer said, waving his hand vaguely, "Yes, if it were the real deal, but we can certainly pull off a good counterfeit for one night, and localize it to your area of concern. But this is a measure of last resort. First, we try to reason with our adversary. Keep me posted on the progress of this matter and report back to me in one week with your status. In the meantime, I shall replace your fallen troops. Return next time with better news, or it will be a more unpleasant visit."

Chapter 13

More Like the Angels Than Men

Later that same afternoon, we returned to Alta's ship to gather up some of her things. We knew Raphael preferred for us to wait there for the return summons to Heaven. As usual, Alta herself transported both of us. So, after a moment and a little vertigo, I was back at Alta's ship and I returned to my quarters.

Having been there before, I kind of knew my way around. I threw my stuff down on a table. The table had a magnetic lock that I switched on so my stuff wouldn't float around if I turned off the room's gravity. I realized the little metal coin-shaped objects on the table were to put over any of your things that couldn't be magnetized, for when the juice was on and the gravity off. How convenient!

I walked back out to find Alta. She was in her own room kneeling by her bed, almost like she was praying. Her music was playing. It was always the same Boston song; "More Than a Feeling," I believe. Apparently she just loved that song.

As I came closer, I could see that she was crying. This surprised me, because I knew Alta was a machine. I didn't know what to say, but I wanted to comfort her. She looked at me teary-eyed as I spoke to her.

"Alta, I guess I hadn't really thought about how hard it is for you to have your crew die and now be alone. I know they were your friends and having to complete their mission by yourself has got to be difficult," I said.

"That is sad of course, but it is not why I am crying," Alta replied.

"Then why ARE you crying?" I asked.

Sobbing as she spoke, Alta responded, "I'm crying because of our visit to Heaven. You see, I have no soul, and thus no eternal destiny. I will never get to live in Heaven OR Hell. God does not want me, but the success of this mission for his sake still lies with me. I must defeat all that Hell throws at me, I must protect you, and I must return to share the truth of your God with my own world and others. You, Tom, ARE part of God's creation. You can look forward to being rewarded in Heaven for the risks and troubles you're taking. But I don't get to have the final reward of the just, even though I have been the champion of the just. Even to the demons, I am just a 'thing.'" A fresh burst of sobs broke out.

I decided to think before I spoke, for once, and with my hand on my chin, I looked over at Alta and realized that crying or not, she was still a very dangerous alien robot. But, apart from knowing this to be the case, I could just be staring at one of the prettiest girls I had ever had an adventure with. She was sitting on the side of the bed now, head in her hands, with tears dripping on her bare knees. Her long, light hair fell down the sides of her face and brushed the sides of her knees. I had to admit that anyone would be attracted to her. But she was still a soulless machine, no matter what else, right?

"Alta, what did Jane whisper into your ear at the pitcher's mound when you first materialized there?" I don't know why this question popped into my head right then, but I felt it important to ask.

Alta looked up, hair hanging down and still teary-eyed.

"Well, Tom, it wasn't meant for anyone else to know, but I guess it doesn't matter now. Jane told me, 'You love this man, and must even give your life to protect him if needed.' Of course, that man is you, Tom." She glanced at me and looked down, not sure if she wanted to see my reaction to this.

I swallowed hard. This explained a lot about my future with Alta that otherwise would have worried me greatly. The fear of her turning on me was no longer in the back of my mind.

"Alta, you are beautiful, good, heroic, and completely self-sacrificing. But you carry more burden than belongs to you. On top of everything else, the capacity to love isn't a property of ordinary machines," I said.

"So?" she said, breaking out into fresh tears.

I responded, "You are clearly something more. Even if you don't have a soul, you still have what you need for your mission. You're capable of doing this. Besides, the success of God's mission lies ultimately with Him alone," I said. "We are judged by the battles we choose to fight, but the victory of those battles is the domain of God alone. What you are doing is VERY important to God and to all men. I should add that the God I know has never been in debt to anyone. Though you are just a machine, you are a magnificent one. History has never seen anything that claims to be your equal. I, too, am a machine but one made of flesh and blood."

She replied, "But God died for all of you men, that you might have a chance at Heaven."

"The angels have no savior. Neither can they reproduce, yet they have the very highest places in Heaven. You are more like an angel than a man," I said.

Then, deciding to make my point a little differently, I asked, "You are aware of the entire Bible right?"

"Yes, of course, in every known version," Alta said, rather proudly, despite reddened eyes.

"Well, then, doesn't the Bible say that 'God could raise up descendants from Abraham out of these stones?'" I asked.

Alta reflected. Putting a finger against her lower lip, she said, "Sure, Matthew 3:9. I suppose you're saying that if God could give a soul to a stone and make him be of the family of Abraham, then why couldn't He give a soul to me, too?"

This was progress, but, to be fair, I didn't want to give her false hope.

"Alta, what God CAN do and what God DOES do are a mystery to all men here on Earth. But yes, God CAN give you a soul, it seems. But soul or no soul, think about Hans Christian Andersen's story of 'The Ugly Duckling,'" I said.

I sat down next to her on the edge of the bed, and rendered my best regaling of the story to her, as though sharing the tale with an eight-year-old daughter. Of course, Alta already knew every work of human literature across all of history, but she sat and listened with great fascination and joy. The Ugly Duckling story made a connection for her with the Matthew passage that she had not seen, despite her great mind. Then I told her about Pinocchio. Alta was like him in a way, I figured. She didn't want to be human; she just wanted an eternal destiny like humans had. Alta wanted a soul. After fifteen minutes of storytelling, her tears were replaced with fascination, and then a certain unexplainable optimism.

At the end of my story, Alta made a rather childlike statement. "I suppose I can see that I am like Pinocchio. But first, I'm going to kill the demons that murdered my crew!" She said this with a gleam in her eye, and I decided this counted as being cheered up. Or close enough.

My other problem now was that despite all this excitement, life was going on back on Earth. I still had a job and commitments to people who would never believe me if I tried to explain my excuse. Oddly, I felt safe with Alta despite the external threats. I knew I couldn't just wait up here in orbit forever. I told Alta that I needed to deal with my life on the ground, despite the risks. So, the following morning we returned to Earth and were back at my home. James came over, and I filled him in on some of the events that had transpired.

The police's discovery of her crew's deaths in a mall outside the Library of Congress had hit the news services and was even in the paper on my kitchen table. As it turns out, the police couldn't identify any of the people that were killed. They had a first-class mystery on their hands, considering how the execution was performed. Witnesses said the body parts "just appeared." Obviously, the demons had stopped or slowed time. Even security cameras had no explanation for the gruesome instantaneous appearance of shredded human remains on the mall.

To take Alta's mind off the news reports, and because we had been traveling so much, I asked Alta, "How did we actually make that last trip to Heaven?"

Alta shrugged and said, "We traveled outside the constraints of this universe, which means beyond gravity and time. We were still constrained by other factors, though. Only God is completely unrestrained."

"Does everyone from Heaven have immortality and powers like yours and the angels we've met?" I asked.

"Yes, but remember, I am not immortal. All of the heavenly hosts and the departed humans are in the Heaven that we saw. But there is another realm of sorts, which is as far beyond that Heaven as Heaven is beyond Earth," she responded.

"Who lives there, Alta?" I said, surprised. No one had mentioned a realm beyond Heaven before.

185

"Only God Himself. So, it really isn't a place, but a 'Whom.' There is no limit to HIS power, within any of the levels of creation, and He has no equal from His realm nor is there any other realm to match Him. Hence, there are three Persons to the creator, with one component most prominently visible in each of the three domains we discussed. The Father is from the superlative dimension that contains all others. The next is the spiritual realm you know of, from whence angels and demons reside, lastly, this earthly existence which was the domain of the Son, Jesus. But God's presence radiates through all at once," Alta said.

James looked at me and puzzled, "If God is from a superlative dimension, who or what made that dimension?" he asked. "How could God have made a dimension that He comes from?"

Alta responded, "God could not have come from a place, or that place would have been a creation that came before God. There WAS no 'before God,' for God even made what we perceive as time. You can't have a 'before' before time itself exists. So, even Heaven was made by God; He's not really 'from' there. That's why I said that the realm beyond Heaven isn't really a place; it's a Whom." Alta's heart didn't seem to be in the conversation, and I was not surprised when she directed it more towards her mission.

"What we don't know, in detail, is what God expects of those who are to be saved. That story is told here on Earth and nowhere else," she said.

I whispered to James, "It appears that their eschatological picture is incomplete. They need to know more about how life moves towards the final things: death, judgment, Heaven, and Hell. This must be why they need our help. In fact, in all of this, those things are the real players, more important than you, me, OR Alta. Given a choice, would you rather meet a cool alien robot, or see Heaven? Heaven wins in my book and obviously has already won in theirs. After all, they MADE those robots. We think of the Trinity, where Heaven and Hell are part of the spiritual realm. You know about the Father and the Son already. The third person of the Trinity is the Holy Spirit. The Bible tells us that the Son 'proceeds' from the Father, so, the other dimensions might also proceed from God's creative force," I said.

There was a pile of mail at the end of the kitchen counter. I pulled out a piece of junk mail to demonstrate my idea.

"Think of it like this." I drew three concentric rings on the back of the white envelope on my kitchen table. "The outer ring is God the Father, the point from which all other things come; the next ring inside is the spiritual realm, where the Spirit dominates; and the innermost ring is the earthly physical realm, where the Son came and died."

"That matches what we know so far, if your church's teaching is right," Alta said.

"Alta," I said, sighing, "I'm not sure this IS the belief of my church. Frankly, I'm struggling with this one too. But I know

187

the three are one, and anyone who has seen one, has seen all three."

James looked at me, and then at Alta, pondering silently. I looked down at my hands. We three sat around the kitchen table in silence for a moment. I realized that I was too worried about our fate in general to discuss any more philosophy for now.

"So, Alta, what's next in our battle plan?" I asked.

Alta looked a little disconcerted.

"Well, I expect things will get worse before they get better. And, for his own safety, you'd better invite your friend to head home and wait for a call from you before re-visiting," she said.

James said, "I think that's a very smart idea," and stood up to leave. I looked at him in surprise that he would hurry to leave on Alta's warning alone. I saw that he was more spooked than I had realized by the story of Jane's crew being torn apart by demons. He must have been just waiting for a good chance to leave, and Alta's warning had given him the excuse he needed. He didn't have a powerful robot protecting him at every step, so the farther away from me he stayed, the better.

James grabbed his stuff to make a rapid exit. We walked him to the door. After a quick good-bye, I sat with Alta on the front steps. James's situation had made me think of something.

I asked, "Alta, what happens if the demons show up, and you are not with me? Like what happened to Jane and your crew."

"That would be catastrophically bad," she answered in a forceful tone. "This is not like the movies. We are dealing with things that are already damned, things that can manipulate physics. Men are protected by their guardian angels, and yours is listening as we speak. But their powers have limits. The demons have limits to a point, but you have seen plenty enough evil in the world to know just how much harm they can do before they hit those limits."

"So, is there anything I can do besides just keep you with me all the time?" I asked.

"I can help you," she said, nodding.

"What do you mean?" I inquired.

Alta stood up, raised her fingers over her head again, and gave another willowy imprecation as she lowered them in a big circle.

"Give him great speed, and clairvoyance into the supernatural realm," she said.

Well, that should be useful! I waited a moment to see how this would work. Nothing happened.

"I don't feel any different," I complained.

"Yes, that is by design, but what I gave you will definitely be there when you need it," Alta responded.

Chapter 14
Clairvoyant

The next morning, I was talking to Alta and cleaning mud off of the bike from the ride I had taken yesterday. I had just gotten to the re-lubing part of the operation, when I realized my concerns about Jane's demise were making my hand shake. I had assumed that Alta's imprecation from the night before would cause some change that I could feel. But even the next day I didn't feel any different. Despite her assurances, I was still worried. I was still looking for that disembodied floating head.

Alta's gift to me was sort of like someone snapping their fingers and saying, "Now, you can fly." Yeah … right. Realizing the stakes here, and nervous as a cat, I persisted with Alta.

"Alta, should I test the stuff you gave me?" I inquired.

Alta looked at me with patience and said, "No need to, Tom. Remember how I make things happen; your words will control the action of this gift, and with it, you can outrun any foe."

"All righty then! So, what is this clairvoyance you gave me?" I asked.

Alta said, "In your world, others would consider it to be clairvoyance. In reality, you are just seeing what they cannot. Call it night vision for angels and demons. But it only applies to threats."

"So, that's why I can't see my guardian angel?" I asked.

"Yep," Alta said leisurely.

By the time I finally finished repairs on my bike's drive train, I figured we'd fix dinner.

"What would you like for dinner?" I asked Alta.

"Whatever you're having," she said.

"Okay, that's easy, shrimp and noodles," I replied.

After a quick preparation, we sat down to eat. Alta seemed to want to pray. This will be interesting, I thought.

She thanked God, and followed up with, "And may all the little animals have something to eat."

I looked at her incredulously. It was a surprising thing to pray for, and I pointed out the conflict inherent in it.

"You realize that in many cases, that means each other, right?" I asked.

Alta grimaced and looked down at the table sadly.

"Alta, are you SURE you're still up to this demon fighting gig? Honestly, if I had just met you on the street, I would never suspect you could kill anything. At least till I saw the fight with Sariel in front of the church. But a lot has happened since then, and your self-doubts have got me worried," I said.

"Self doubts?" Alta said it as a question.

"The other night you were crying, and honestly, you've been through a lot. Not to mention, if you lose even one fight, I'm dead too," I responded.

"You will be very happy with what I do, Tom," she said in a lifeless tone that was less that reassuring, but which I couldn't argue with.

Alta had great power and responsibility, but she clearly wasn't just a ruthless killer. She seemed to have a stripe of humanity in her. She had been made too well. She was charitable and kind, patient, and even had courage in the face of great adversity. But she felt every blow that was sent her way. Her robotic character didn't seem to spare her any pain whatsoever, and she did her level best to hide it. Moreover, she was never motivated by a sense of personal gain, or concern for her own safety. I could tell from the reaction of the angels and demons to her that she had far more capability than I had witnessed up till now. But with the challenge in facing the new tougher wave of demons who were hunting us, we wouldn't have to wait long to see Alta exceed my expectations.

After clearing dinner, I looked out the back window, and saw a storm approaching. It was as black as I can ever recall, and moving towards us very quickly.

I said, "Hey, Alta, look at this storm charging in."

Alta rose from the table and looked out the back window.

"That's no storm," she said with great seriousness.

She quickly ran out to the back porch and raised her fingers above her head and looked straight at the tempest facing her. The storm stopped, so she lowered her arms. What appeared before us was something terrifying and clearly supernatural, a black tempest foaming in furious confusion stood before us. Apparitions of body parts appeared, but clearly of more than one being, or perhaps one with numerous manifestations, foaming out from the deep black cloud. We could see lightning inside its boundaries. There were white cloud fronts followed by the blackest black. It looked like a super-cell, the kind that that drops hail just before a tornado, then gobbles up a town and shreds all the people.

After a moment, one image prevailed in the center. I guessed it was a demon. Its power and rage were evident, as was its fallen nature. As the image became clearer, I saw at the same time what seemed to be extra-dimensional secondary images of the same being. I got the feeling that this dark warrior was probably both here and somewhere else at the same time. Its face was not clearly recognizable in the tempest. As it stood before us, I wondered if we were sitting next to a nuclear reactor going critical. Let's face it, that would be a great way to kill us both.

A voice came from the dark cloud.

"Robot, give us this man that we may destroy him."

The voice had depth like it came from a canyon. Alta looked angrily at the swirling dark cloud mass.

"Leave here, because I will do no such thing," she answered.

193

At that moment, I saw Alta change her form. I had not known she could do that. She shifted into something that was similar to our adversary, almost delocalizing her appearance, but Alta was as light as her adversary was dark. She started to glow white hot. I was worried she'd melt my deck, which was made of that new plastic fake-wood, but then I felt that there was no heat coming off of her. They two were polar opposites. The voice from the storm boomed out another command that began with an echo of some sort.

"Then you shall share his fate."

Alta replied with great confidence.

"So say you. I am far stronger than you are, and have no soul. I cannot be rewarded or damned and have no eternal destiny. The worst you could do is destroy me. My role is merely to stand between you and your goal. All I have to lose is myself, but you will lose the universe, and Lucifer will deal with you as a failure even after I tear you apart."

"You already know you are overmatched—leave here before I destroy you!" she commanded confidently.

The incongruous image popped into my head of Alta as the good witch Glinda threatening the evil witch who came for Dorothy's slippers. Alta certainly could have dropped a house on this bunch of demons, not that it would have helped. The storm roiled and then fired some sort of high-energy charge at Alta that was terrifically bright, but completely silent. Instantly, Alta raised a transparent shield that sprung up between them. She recoiled behind its shimmering layers. I remembered how it had sprung up around her like a glass bell jar during Sariel's attack. Stray energy splattered in every direction.

She drew her sword and switched it on. With a quick sweep of her sword, a sheet of energy left the blade, cutting right through the offending presence. The cloud disassociated then vaporized completely. Alta spun back down from her intense white glow, till she looked normal again.

"Do you really think it was a good idea to tell them that they'll lose the entire universe?" I asked. Somehow, making the demons MORE desperate to stop us didn't sit well with me. And, I thought Alta had only mentioned spreading the good news to several star systems in their range—a far cry from the whole universe.

Alta looked unfazed by the attack, and she removed the shield with a wave, then shut down her sword. She wheeled to answer.

"Tom, they have infused knowledge; there are no secrets to keep from them. It's only here on Earth that people don't know the stakes. Obviously the universe is the prize. A civilization like ours could easily spread the truth faster-than-light speed to more than 2,000 galaxies in the Virgo cluster in a couple of weeks. All have people seeking what we found here. This galaxy is 100,000 light years across, and more than a billion stars in total; but we know of many other civilizations here. We are just the first star travelers to find the answer here on Earth. Despite your being aliens to us, your God is also our God," Alta said.

I asked, "So, are you gonna tell me what that was that attacked us?"

We walked back inside, and Alta said, "That was an agent from Hell, but not from Ostara's group. It was a fallen angel from one of the lower choirs."

"Lower choir?" I echoed.

Alta looked at me for an instant and then shared a thought that gave me my first real sense of the scale of the threat against us.

"Yes, a lower choir is in the bottom three. But make no mistake, that one demon could have easily fried this entire planet in less than a second. Angels have utterly fantastic power over physics. In fact, they control and even guarantee the operation of physics," Alta said.

"Then, why weren't you terrified?" I asked. The confrontation we just had with the demon was beginning to sink in. I sat down at the kitchen table, and Alta joined me.

Alta gave a one-shoulder shrug and said, "I'm not worried because I have far greater power than that one demon. In fact, he wasn't even actually here, which meant he was afraid of me. Given half a chance, I would have torn him into pieces for what his associates in Hell have done to Jane and my crew." She said this in a casual tone that gave a touch of cold to my bones.

This whole experience was impossible to comprehend all at once. I was on a back stage tour of the supernatural with what may as well be an angel. Or maybe I should say I was being protected by a dangerous alien robot on a vendetta to destroy the demons that killed her crew, while praying for the welfare of hungry little animals. That's in between her guitar playing and crying over Pinocchio issues. Still, the demon in the storm that could vaporize the planet in less than a second was a lightweight compared to her. The problem was that very soon there would be thousands just like him thrown at us. And, this demon had asked Alta to turn me over to him.

The next day, I got up early. We still hadn't been summoned by Haniel to hook up with Jessie, so I had some time to kill. I was very nervous about leaving Alta after last night's demon encounter, but I was also going stir crazy. I just had to get out of the house. I decided to go for a run out around the park and then around in back behind the retirement home. It was my usual course, and about three miles total. I was about half way into the usual run, when I came to the back parking lot of the retirement home that was the return route home. At a point just short of the main road and up ahead of me to the right, I saw a glowing golden figure. It was crouched down but rising, slowly. It was a featureless man of some sort, but not clothed or naked. It had an almost liquid look to it. I got a streak of fear, as it was now at full height, and moving to intercept me ahead. Just then, I remembered the speed Alta gave me, and I decided this was a great time to run faster, much faster.

I said, "Give me great speed in running!"

With that I took off and found myself running at probably 30-40 miles per hour. The wind just sailed by, like biking down a mountainside. I was amazed at how well this worked. But my golden adversary was also running, and he was only about twenty yards behind me and closing the distance. He was apparently faster than I was, even though I was now running at 40 mph. I was scared past the point of reason, when an image of Alta giving her verbal commands popped into my head. I tried a new command.

"Increase my speed such that the distance between me and my adversary gets larger," I said.

That was all it took, and in a short time, I was in the clear. I returned home and told Alta about the encounter. She surprised me by grabbing me in a tight hug. I think she was relieved that I was okay, and joyful over my success.

Chapter 15
Powers and Principalities

Between the fight in front of the church, the thugs in the bar, and the storm on my back porch, I had seen enough to know that Ostara's gang would come at us by any means available. Demons were just fine with using Earthly means to attack us, if supernatural means were unavailable. This was just the battlefront we could see. It was clear from my discussions with our angelic visitors that even they had to fight through demons just to get to Earth. In fact, it had been that way at least since the book of Daniel 2500 years ago. This meant that everything Alta and the angels warned me about was already in the pipeline against us. I figured my Earthly life would start to get rough. But, despite all the threats, I also knew I was sitting on top of an incredible opportunity. Like a juror on the murder trial of the century, I knew that surviving this would mean a dramatic change to the rest of my life. When they found out, the whole world would want to know every detail about what happened, and I had a front row seat. I was privileged to be here, if I survived the danger. But then, I would have been happy just to have a conversation with my own cat if it were possible. All these superpowers, the beyond-physics events, didn't faze me anymore after a couple of days of having my mind blown. But there was another opportunity here I hadn't considered in all the rush. Here in my own living room was an incredible alien machine that would answer ANY question I could dream up.

WOW!

So, if you could ask anything, what would it be? There were so many options. Perhaps ask Alta what she thought about being a dangerous-alien robot. Or, perhaps just a plain ole supernatural robot at the very least. Then again, she was already upset and crying about that back on her ship. Gosh, now I'm worrying about a robot's feelings, which I guess is appropriate, because she clearly HAS feelings. An insensitive question by me right now might be a mistake. She could just split and leave me to the demons. But her motivation for doing this task or any other is still mysterious. I could see that her best bet would be to save herself by cutting and running.

Still, I just have to know what, and how, she thinks. I sort of had the feeling a kid has when he asks a childhood friend what it's like to be adopted. I have to admit there was a bit of mischievous pleasure in messing with Alta's head, because despite her ability to flatten a trash truck between two fingers, her mission was to protect me.

"Alta, exactly how powerful are you? Are you as powerful as the Sun—or even more powerful than that?" I asked.

Alta looked at me with disappointment as though I had asked the star character of "I Dream of Jeannie" if she could ride a flying carpet or give three wishes. Obviously this was too easy. So, I tried again.

"How about as powerful as a black hole?" I asked.

Alta could see the dilemma of scale, so she decided to work on explaining this.

"Tom, did you know that there is a supermassive black hole in the center of Andromeda that is 200 million solar masses in size? It is far larger than the one here in our galaxy," she explained, and then added, "I am more powerful than both together."

"Okay, Alta, how much more powerful?" I asked.

"I can show you with a simple demonstration of scale," Alta responded.

I suspected this was going to be interesting.

She handed me a piece of paper and ordered, "Draw a big number 2 on this sheet of paper. Make the toughest, meanest 2 you can draw."

I curtly etched a 2 of no great stature. Alta graded my work.

"Well, that is a pretty mean looking 2," she said.

She picked up my little scrap of paper with the 2 on it and said, "Grrrrr" while she shook the mean 2 at eye level. She looked just like a really young kid.

"This 2 has as much power over you as that black hole has over me in a head-to-head struggle," she explained. She tore my paper in half and the 2 disappeared in a flash of flame at her fingertips.

"Okay, Alta, this is clearly useless, so let's try something more descriptive. How does it feel to be a robot?" I asked.

Alta pondered. "Good question! I see myself as the pilot of a spaceship that is this body. It has virtual reality that is so good, I share its presence."

She reached out with one finger and poked me lightly on the arm.

"When I touch you, my eyes see you near, and my finger reports a tactile sensation that alerts me to the realness of your image before me," she said.

"That's how people feel, too. So, I guess I am a robot like you, sort of, but just made of other stuff." I admit I was hoping for a more exciting description.

"Carbon, mostly," Alta replied. "I was beautifully designed with the greatest care, but if you are a robot, you are a far better one than me."

"Why?" I asked.

"You were made by God and have a soul. Though we both share will, intellect, and have bodies … you have an immortal component that is actually the greater part of your true essence."

I realized then, that Alta truly was like Pinocchio, but rather than wanting to be a real person, or even wanting a soul, she missed out on not having been created by God. Her lack of that eternal destiny had a component that I hadn't considered. By not having real membership in either tribe, destined for Heaven OR Hell, she had no eternal purpose, even if she had a soul. She seemed to have purpose for the moment, but once that purpose ended, hundreds of years from now, she was back to just being a thing--assuming we survived this challenge. Perhaps Alta didn't mind not being like me. She minded not being from God. And, not being from God meant not having a soul, which was just a by-product of having no eternal purpose. I was God's creation, and thus belonged to Him FOREVER, so I had purpose and reward forever. Alta did not share that distinction and knew it keenly.

"Alta … do you pray?" I asked. I had been wondering ever since I had walked in on her crying that day.

Alta nodded, "Yes, but it is like communicating with the landlord of a neighboring housing complex that I don't live in. I don't belong to God, or have anything He needs, wants, or cares about."

"Well, He wants something from you now. You're protecting me; you're like the soldier that is protecting the king's favorite pet. The king DOES care, by definition," I said.

I left Alta to ponder that and decided that perhaps it was time to pray for my own welfare, since so much was at stake. Little did I know that after leaving Alta, curiosity caused her to spy on me. Alta didn't offer much detail on her ability to become invisible, extremely small, large, or monitor anything at extremely remote locations. All these things were now on the menu because Ostara killed her crew. After their death, Michael had told us that her prohibitions in travel or manipulation of physics were conditionally removed. So, she disappeared without my knowledge and watched me. She wanted to see how I prayed, and moreover, she wanted to see how God answered, which she might hear because of her transcendental nature. Alta wanted to see what humans had as a connection with God that she did not.

For whatever reason, I always pray aloud, usually while on long walks outside alone. This time I just found an empty room to walk around in, because I didn't feel like getting too far from Alta so soon after my encounter with the golden man. Like many prayer walks before, I always take stock of my situation first, and demons aside, it hadn't been particularly good lately. My engagement to a lovely girl had just ended in April, and I was laid off from my engineering firm in July. I was now doing a little contracting work, but it was just a stopgap solution. I still had a sense of purpose, doing some young adult ministry in the church, but I got a call from the Archdiocesan coordinator asking me to not attend any more of their events, because I was over their age limit. This left me the dance business, but my new talented little partner just split, for greener pastures. Honestly, things were bad, but things had never really been very good prior to now. I was like a creature in the Sahara that had just gotten used to heat and lack of rain.

Today was a new low, because the one area in which I really was succeeding had made some changes. A friend of mine had been throwing a series of very small dances at a local church, in hopes of attracting interest to the facility, and for charity. He called me in to help promote some events there, which I did, but with not much more results than he got. That was until our holiday party, which was huge success. Honestly, this was a great party, with two bands, two DJs, dance lessons, and food. Even though I was unemployed, I was responsible to pay everybody, win or lose on the event. Well, we won on this gamble. Absolutely everyone came, and it was a real blowout that finally put that little church on the map. Two months later, my "friend" ended our partnership to carry on by himself, based upon the momentum we had from the holiday party. With a success in the hall just behind us, he no longer needed me around, because now the secret of how nice the place actually was had gotten out. Although this hurt me a little, I realized that in the end, it all belonged to God. So, I prayed and said precisely that.

"God, in the end, it all belongs to You."

There just isn't any sense in fighting over that which is all God's anyway.

I prayed aloud, "God, with all this in mind, I should tell You that I now have nothing left but my health. I don't have any sense of purpose. Not only am I utterly alone, I don't even have anyone else who needs my help any more. I realize there are always strangers to help, but I mean none of my friends and fellow churchgoers need me. This connection always used to give me a reason to exist. Beyond this pain, and loneliness, I have the challenge now of facing destruction for what I believe. The demons fear that I might share the truth of God with Gihon.

Despite the danger, I have to thank You for at least that sense of purpose, though the price might be my life."

Alta heard every word and secretly sat thinking about it all after I left the room. She then stood up in the middle of the room, and looked to Heaven, with one arm raised, bent at the elbow so she could see her palm like a mirror. Her fingers were pressed together as she lifted the mirror-like hand between her and God and appealed with the greatest sincerity.

"God, I am not truly yours, but rather just a lowly thing made by others. I am not as beautiful or permanent as even the lowest angels. But even a machine like me knows that You are all good and kind. I love and protect what You love and protect, so we must be allies in this struggle. With all respect I realize that You are God and, being all powerful, don't require my help to achieve Your will. But if You would allow me to do so, I shall willingly risk my life to bring the truth of Your death and sacrifice here on Earth back to my world, even if I might forfeit my life in the process. I realize the greater good that will come from that and for a time, that will give me the purpose that I seek. I do not have a soul, but, almighty God, for a short time, I can have a purpose." Alta paused and then went forward with a request.

"Almighty God, although I have no eternal destiny; please allow my actions in this struggle to earn Your favor and assistance in furthering Your mission here on Earth. Those who despise You are also my enemies. I seek to prevent them from destroying my friend Tom. Send Your angels to help me, so that I can help You and all of my people on my world and elsewhere. I realize You don't need anyone's help, but still, we struggle through this life till You evaluate our final destiny. Please remember all that I do in Your service when deciding my final fate here or in the next world," Alta said.

Finally, Alta asked for something for me, that I didn't find out about till much later.

"God, may I ask a request on behalf of Tom? Though he cannot see his own future, or what the demons see that makes him such a great threat to them, I can. I see the Powers and Principalities aligned against him that want to isolate and persecute him in this world. They use people against him, falsely accuse him, and punish him without a trial. He has remained faithful to You through it all, and shown the patience of Job, from the Old Testament. If we succeed in this mission of spreading Your word throughout the universe, would You consider rewarding his faithfulness to You as You did with Job?" Alta asked.

Shortly thereafter, an angel came to visit us with news that we were being invited back to Heaven to see Haniel in two days. Perhaps it was Alta's prayer that got us our second invitation to Heaven. Or perhaps it was mine. Either way, the angel told us to see Haniel and invited us to a part of Heaven that few of Earth's heavenly residents had ever seen. Our meeting was set for the following day.

Alta felt guilty for spying and found me later that day. She told me she had heard my prayer. We spoke about the angel's invitation. She asked if the situation depressed me, as it surely would any other person. I decided to set her fears at ease by sharing my feelings and trying to see if pain was something she felt as I did.

"Alta, my pain comes from lack of a sense of purpose. Not just loss of a job, a girl, or ministry. You see, without any of those things, I myself have no idea why God tolerates me here for yet another day," I said.

At that time, I didn't yet realize that Alta was feeling exactly the same way as I did, because of her lack of an eternal purpose. I didn't understand till much later just how complete her empathy with me on this matter was.

"Why do you say 'tolerate,' Tom?" Alta asked in a concerned tone.

"When I was younger, I did lots of youth ministry and evangelism and I told myself that God saw me as useful. I no longer have that excuse, so for the life of me, I have no idea why God keeps me around. I'm sure you've heard that we all live as long as God has purpose for us. I have yet to figure out what my purpose is. Right now, I'm alone and separated from any task related to job, family, or church ministry. I have no purpose that is known to me. In fact, not that long ago, I was out on a very long bike ride that took me past Old Line avenue in Laurel. This was the return half of a twenty-five mile loop that I ride periodically. I was westbound on Leslie Way when I arrived at the intersection of Old Line avenue. I slammed on my brakes and narrowly missed being hit by a car. You see, I wasn't looking left when I tried to cross. Had any combination of events over the last twenty-five miles caused me to arrive there even a second sooner, I'd be dead now. No one really knows how long that period is, between the time you have fulfilled your purpose in life, and your actual death. It might be a second, or it might be a year. It might well vary from person to person. You could be in that 'waiting for an anvil to drop on you' phase for weeks. I have the strongest feeling that that's exactly where I am. I'm not all depressed about it, mind you. I'm a triathlete; mental toughness is in my genes. Frankly, life has never been that kind to start with, so I am unfortunately used to this sort of feeling. The best thing I can do is what I always do. Just soldier on. You see, Alta, I'm sort of alone like you are. We're a perfect pair, you and I," I said.

Alta reflected on this without a sound. Then she shared her thoughts on the matter of purpose.

"Tom, important or not, you have an eternal destiny, and I suspect a very good one. I am even more alone than you, because I am in an alien world alone, and when I pray, it is just to serve the greater good of those back home, or out of the memory of my dead crew, who were my friends. But they are all gone now too. I now realize that I am also 'temporarily' serving the purpose of God. But I don't even have the distinction of being able to claim him as my savior or creator. Let's face it, God never died for the robots," she said.

"God didn't die for the angels either, but their lot isn't bad. As I said last time, you are more like them than us. Alta, there isn't an ounce of malice in you. You are strangely perfect in your own way," I said.

At last, a new self-awareness flooded through me. The idea of having "purpose" was secondary to having a soul. Without belonging to God, there was no eternal destiny, and no lasting purpose. I suddenly realized how lucky I was, because here was Alta, nearly indistinguishable from me in loneliness and resolve, but without any heavenly inheritance. Purpose and destiny bound us together. I suppose even the demons had it better than Alta, because despite playing a losing hand, at least they got to play. All of the demons were residents of heaven previously. Alta could never win through merit, unless God intervened. But incredibly, her actions would serve to convey God's word to every other distant race in the cosmos. She would become a new Paul, who in his role as an apostle wrote two-thirds of the New Testament. With Jane and the others dead, Gihon's New Testament would have just one author, Alta. I have always wanted to meet Paul. I suppose, indirectly, by working with Alta, I have gotten my wish.

Chapter 16
The Girl on the Train

Alta was still concerned for my safety, especially after the demon in the storm had directly asked her to turn me over to him. The attack on her crew was like a gang hit that was meant to seem supernatural, and no other plausible explanation could be found at the crime scene by the police. But the demons clearly meant to advertise the fact that this wasn't a typical hit. Agents from Hell killed to feed an internal jealous rage. It was almost like watching a starving lion attack another lion over food.

Despite the promises of the good angels to us, Alta secretly harbored concerns that she might not be able to protect me, because she wasn't completely certain of the scale of the efforts mounting against us. I wondered why the good angels didn't step in sooner to save Jane till the thought occurred to me that maybe their people's contract with God was still an Old Testament type deal. I recall our Old Testament as being bloody and ruthless.

When the LORD your God brings you into the land you are entering to possess and drives out before you many nations; the Hittites, Girgashites, Amorites, Canaanites, Perizzites, Hivites and Jebusites, seven nations larger and stronger than you, and when the LORD your God has delivered them over to you and you have defeated them, then you must destroy them totally. Make no treaty with them, and show them no mercy.

This passage from Deuteronomy (7: 1-3) had always amazed me. It was a characteristic Old Testament ruthlessness that I could clearly see in the fight with Alta's people. But this fight was a two-way street. Neither the demons nor Alta showed any mercy in this struggle. So, one afternoon, Alta presented a strategy to hedge our bets a little.

"Tom," she said, "You should write down all that has happened with us; it would make a fascinating book."

"So, we're being hunted by an angry mob of murderous demons and you think this might be a nice time for me to start a writing project? First off, I'm not a writer, and second off, no one would believe a word of it. Who would even read it? I have a very mundane, anonymous life, Alta, not to mention that I've never been published in any other subject of interest. The genre would be what? Eschatological science? No one besides us even knows what that is," I said.

Alta responded, "Sure they do, it's just a description of the larger framework in which your world is embedded."

"Let me make this very clear," she persisted, with due emphasis. "My purpose for being here is to sort out the truth about who God really is and what He really taught on your world. I therefore need to know which faith is most accurate. I also need to know what God expects of me and my people back home in order for them attain the final reward, in case we are on different contracts for salvation. I have just accepted the fact that I will be taking a bullet for the team. But I have come to find so many flavors of truth that even an advanced civilization like mine would be confused if I just presented everything I found here. I now believe Satan quarantined your world on purpose. I also believe that manufacturing 33,000 different religions was Satan's fallback strategy in the event that others like us ever did get here to find the truth, as well as to mislead as many humans as possible. This plan allows the demons time to kill any curious meddlers from other worlds before the real matter of truth can be determined from all the choices. But somehow, I will muddle through. The stakes are very high. This obviously has riled the demons to the point of killing my whole crew, and now they've sicked Ostara on us which is REAL trouble."

I stopped Alta, "Hold it, Alta. There have always been demons roaming the earth, and they have never shredded people. I assumed it was against some sort of rule. They can only tempt us, right?"

Alta said, "Well, those were the rules for Earth people before yesterday, but I have no confidence that they are the rules today. Had I turned you over to the demon who asked for you, would an angel have stepped in to stop your destruction? That's a question I didn't want to test. But that gets to the point. If we were both killed, a written record of all this would be OUR second-tiered defense. We need a fallback plan. When you finish, or even before that, leave the book with James, or anybody. But write it all down."

Suddenly, as we spoke, I could see over Alta's shoulder a great lightning flash light up the entire distant horizon. It was a huge flash, but completely silent—almost like something was being let out of a box. Alta sensed its presence and wheeled to face it. I saw her concern and asked her what it was.

"A demon, more powerful than the last, is coming to test me in battle. The flash is light's reaction to something breaking the speed of light as it enters our universe, just like a sonic boom goes off when you break the speed of sound," she said.

While watching Alta ready her sword, I noticed a symbol on her belt buckle that I had never seen on Earth. An ellipse bisected at the bottom by a triangle. I figured that it was significant to her order back in her world. I didn't know why I hadn't noticed it before.

The new threat swirled before us with no discernible shape. Alta took its measure and seemed unimpressed. Before it could strike at us, she snapped up a shield over me and slashed her sword at the demon. What looked like a flat sheet of super-heated plasma left the blade and hurtled toward the demon, vaporizing the attacker completely.

"Alta, didn't you want to see what it wanted?" I asked.

"By now, everyone knows what it wants, Tom ... US!" she replied.

"So, if we're still under the old rules, the demons can go toe to toe with you, but not just outright kill me?" I asked.

"Tom ... I just don't know. Possibly that is still the rule, but it assures us of very little. Demons control many people, some totally, and some they only need to influence for a moment. That moment is usually a very critical moment, like getting some drunk to shoot you in an alley, or just to inspire fear in someone the demons think might be able to help you," Alta said.

"What do you mean?" I asked.

Alta said, "Do you remember the girl you met on the train? Maryann, I think it was?" Surprised, I wondered how Alta knew about that. Maryann had been a pretty girl who worked in DC. Every day she would get on the same red line train that I rode and get off a couple stops past me. She read from a NOOK every day, so I had once asked her if she could be a Beta reader of a book I was developing for that electronic format.

"Sure, I recall," I said.

Alta continued, "She was actually someone who could have been a great help to you. Recall that demons know every historical fact regarding every Earthly being. Ostara knew this and intervened when you initially asked Maryann for help, shortly after you first met."

"Well, you have your facts a little off; there was no 'us' with Maryann and me, because it never actually got started. I did ask her to be a Beta reader, but in fact I had no idea WHAT she could have done," I responded.

Alta said, "Let me tell you what you don't know. That NOOK she uses has links into NOOK publishing, and readers groups. She belongs to them and can download books there. It allows new writers like you to publish totally electronically. That might be an important way to insure the survival of our story, if you write it. You would have learned about this from her, and she could have helped you edit, being an avid reader of precisely the kind of stuff you will be writing. Ostara has influenced her to fear you, completely without reason. Just fear for fear's sake alone."

"Well, Alta, she's gone, and YOU just told me all that she might have told me, less the editing, so what's the loss?" I asked.

Alta said, "You are missing the point. This is about how demons work. Remember St. Patrick's Day? Coming in on the train?" Again I wondered how she knew about all this.

I said, "Sure, but I didn't see Maryann that day."

Alta said, "She saw you, but she had some help. Ostara said to her in a whisper, 'look up,' right as she came to the glass exiting the train concourse. She saw your reflection approaching her from behind, even though you never realized it was her from the back. She took a detour into the coffee shop in the mall so you would pass without seeing her. She has now put some action into her fear, which reinforces it. Just like waiting a whole year after falling off a horse before you ride again, which just heightens your fear of horses."

"Alta, that is so subtly manipulative, that no one could avoid being tricked," I said.

She agreed, but had more to say. "Tom, God gave you the guardian angels to thwart this advantage evil uses against you. A similar subtle influence, but for your good, is constantly exercised to assist you in remaining safe and completing the tasks God has given you. Right now, I suggest that one of those tasks is to write everything down that happens to us, because it is a good insurance policy if we need it. Think of the end of the movie Watchmen, when Rorschach's notes survived."

The next day I had to get to work, as always. I waited for the train, south bound to Union Station in DC. I climbed on board when it arrived, found a seat, and began my usual ritual of studying for my information security exam that was slated for later that month. As I left the train, Alta was there on the concourse waiting for me. She was standing right where I had apparently seen Maryann when she secretly ran away weeks before. I waved to her, wondering why she had come, and I glanced away for a moment. When I looked back, I saw Maryann standing in her place, but dressed like Alta. I realized it wasn't Maryann; it was still Alta. Obviously, Alta could appear in any form she chose. She greeted me and asked about my writing, as if she were Maryann. I wondered about the point of this masquerade, but I decided to just go with it. She skipped the first metro stop after Union Station that was Maryann's usual exit and walked the whole way with me to my work place. Our walk was along the route of the metro anyway. Had it really been Maryann, this would have allowed her to take the next metro down to her regular stop in the heart of the city.

We had a thoroughly enjoyable talk that never gave a hint of the pretense. It eventually dawned on me that Alta did this to make me feel better in a time of great stress. It was clear that she had imagination and creativity driven by an obvious sense of charity. Alta was also showing me by this stunt, the complete extent to which she truly understood the human psyche. I really appreciated her efforts. Her makers should be very proud.

Chapter 17
Resolving the Truth

The following day put us back at Alta's ship, where we were safer behind our angelic guard. One of those guards came inside the ship to notify us that the time to see Haniel had finally arrived. Haniel had sent an angelic messenger to the guards at our ship who brought us news about the second meeting, which we gladly accepted. I was impressed that it took a relay of three angels to get the message from Haniel to us. Obviously, the angels had a hierarchical way of passing information.

Alta began to tell me what she knew of Haniel. Much as she was friends with Raphael, she had recently made friends with the Archangel. She had even helped him in a fashion similar to the way she had helped Raphael long ago. Or, at least, helping Raphael was long ago in Earth time. Alta had a past history that was of unknown length to me. Beyond Earth and the universe we know, where Alta made these faster than light transits, time was different. I figured, though, that Alta had experiences that went back at least as far back as the book of Daniel.

Alta had rescued Haniel and a scientist from a larger group of demons who intended to do him harm, while Haniel was the guardian of a man working on a project for MIT. The project had started out in the math department. Over time it was reapplied to the Futures Markets. The mission was to enact thousands of micro-fast trades on the markets using tens of thousands of inputs from the commodities markets, plus local and national newspapers. Computer trades were so fast that they could turn a profit before human traders even had a chance to call their brokers after reading the morning news. The secret, of course, was to aggregate the biggest, most sophisticated collection of news items and then trade at staggering speed. When you could determine a pattern of behavior, you'd program the computer to search for it every day and respond accordingly, at great speed, when certain triggers were reached. The MIT team began to analyze the patterns that created both profit and chaos. Impressively, it seemed that chaos had a certain stripe that was becoming predictable. The demons took an interest in this project sometime after the MIT team temporarily moved their code over to the far larger, faster computer that had been part of a weather modeling project. They put the latest code and data into this faster machine for a twenty-four hour run. The weather modeling computers were the biggest available and enabled far more responsiveness and greater emphasis of the pattern analysis than was ever before possible. One member of the team began to see repeated evidence for an external negative influence that brought chaos to any process it touched. The team leader called this the "Satan" factor and initiated a coding project to highlight its negative influence on the world and markets specifically. This exposure was too much for the demons to tolerate, and they descended on the team leader, who was Haniel's charge.

Alta was made aware of the incident in the normal course of her business of absorbing all of Earth's computer traffic and radio intel prior to her team's mission here. She intercepted Haniel's call for assistance from Heaven, so she showed up, realizing the significance of the event. The demons foolishly attacked her, and she quickly destroyed them all. The end result was making a lifelong friend out of Haniel, who felt honor bound to return the favor. Alta never even felt that a debt existed, but Haniel became her greatest fan. Since Haniel was indebted to her for saving him, he was now especially glad to assist her in this time of her great need. It was Jane's death and sacrifice for us that got us the first invitation to Heaven and the selflessness of Alta's prayer that got us the second one so soon.

Had Alta been with Jane instead of with me that day at the church, Jane would still be alive. I had seen enough of what the demons could do to know that they were right on our heels, and that we were in mortal danger. Alta raised her arms again, and I braced for the trip. We ventured to a part of Heaven that was very different than the first place I saw. The first place had looked very much like Earth. This place was very different. It was a large open space, almost like a spaceport. We came, suspended in air, behind the audience of a large angelic proceeding, which was perhaps a half a mile across end to end. It was some sort of an administrative center where angels met or performed some function. Most of it was never designed with human foot traffic in mind.

Only the very center was suitable for human visitors who didn't want to just float like we were doing. The proceeding looked like a minor court hearing and the principles were at the center, testifying to something. I sensed that this place was very old, far older than creation, though nothing about its design betrayed any such passage of time, or wear. Angels were visible, and no two were identical, but there were clear differences in the nine choirs.

Alta said, "We are expected. We must wait here."

We stayed put, floating in place. Angels passed in front of us on duties of various sorts. They were larger than I thought, and not all shaped precisely like men, but similar. Some had wings for instance. Others didn't seem to need them, but none flapped. I had the overwhelming sense that that the wings were just for our benefit.

After a time, Haniel appeared and embraced Alta as a friend. He was very large, and dressed in white mostly, with features that appeared and disappeared as though extra-dimensionally present. He had a voice of the deepest baritone and looked me over as he addressed Alta. Due to this feature shifting ability, he was able to face us both simultaneously. It was clear that he had a lot of respect for Alta.

Alta came right to the point, "Haniel, how much can I ask of you in this matter of truth that I seek for my world?"

The Archangel looked just at her and said, "Alta, since you were expected, the will of God has already been consulted on the matter. We cannot violate man's free will or defy physical laws singularly in the pursuit of this truth. We also cannot abrogate the rules by which YOUR civilization is being tested. So, no shortcuts are allowed, but anything else is fair game. You must follow the chain of evidence to find the truth, the same as any mortal. You can bend physics to seek answers indirectly, like for travel. You can also visit any place or time in making your inquiry. By any place, I mean in any realm that you are capable of entering. But the demons also have similar license to prevent you. I have been assigned to help you sort this out."

Haniel continued, "Here's the plan. First, there is a school teacher you must find, now long dead, in a graveyard near Berlin, Maryland. She has considerable experience with the enemies you face, and her team controls forces on the ground. Her people have even fought the same demon that destroyed Jane, and they can assist you greatly in this matter of truth that you seek. Seek out Jessica G. who was born 1790. She is now at the Evergreen Cemetery. When you return to Earth, her team will assist you. They are all human beings who are long dead. They are now heavenly residents re-stationed on Earth, to serve God's purpose there. Some on Earth might call them ghosts, but they have great power to assist and teach you. Additionally, you have been given permission to traverse time, back to the Last Supper, itself. Between these two things all the questions you have about truth should be answered."

As our brief meeting came to a close, I was still impressed by the place and the courtroom activities near us.

I asked Haniel, "What is this going on behind us?"

Haniel said, "This is where I work. It is the Court of Life. It is one of many such final judgment points in Heaven. In this case, it is a trial of a mother, who aborted her child in life. She has just now met her daughter for the first time here in Heaven. Ordinarily, her daughter would be the principle witness against her. But in this case, the aborted child's prayers for her mother brought about her conversion."

From a distance, I could see the woman, racked in despair, sobbing at the feet of her child.

I asked Haniel, "Why was the child only eighteen years old, where all other people in Heaven appear mid-twenties?"

Haniel said, "All children killed in this way, who have never seen the world for which they were destined are re-united with bodies at age eighteen. It is the starting point in their unique process here with God. They have their own society like the angels, but all heavenly societies mix at points."

At this point, I saw the guardian angel who had been assigned to the aborted child come before the judgment seat of God, demanding justice.

I said, "Why is there no defense lawyer for the mother?"

Haniel said, "In all cases of eternal judgment no greater love, forgiveness or mercy could be possible than from God, Himself. In fact, what you are witnessing is one of many courts here in Heaven. This one relates to crimes against life of the unborn."

I was curious to see the outcome. I waited. After what seemed just an instant, I could tell the woman was spared. Before she died, but after killing this child, she had turned her life around, and her sorrow on earth made her an activist for numerous pro-life causes. What turned the tide were the child's prayers for the mother who had killed her.

I said, "Alta, I HAVE to see this eighteen year old girl before we leave."

I had forgotten that time wasn't really an issue here in Heaven. Alta glanced at Haniel, as if to seek permission. Haniel nodded his head yes to okay the visit. In an instant, the 18 year old girl appeared before us and introduced herself as Tallaris. She looked like a younger, blonder Alta and had a long white gown that was obviously a uniform for the court.

I thanked her for seeing us and said, "What an interesting and beautiful name you have. Forgive my boldness, but you have the most perfect and unblemished appearance I could ever think possible."

"I appreciate your compliment on my appearance, but you can thank my peers here for my name," Tallaris said.

"Really?" I asked in surprise.

"Yes," Tallaris answered. "In cases such as mine, where you died before birth without a name, the others in our society give you a name. I then become an instant part of the heavenly family, having been rejected by my original family on Earth. We all share the same bond, abortion. As far as my appearance, I have never known sin. My appearance is a hallmark of that fact, as it is with all of our group here."

It was readily apparent that Tallaris's group was huge. Their common experience was that they had NO Earthly experience. Not one of Tallaris's group of aborted children had ever LIVED on Earth. They had never seen a cat, or a flower, or known a mother's love. This made them different in many ways that were irreversible. The only companions they ever knew were each other, God of course, and the angels. Their entire family was here and here alone.

"Tallaris, I just have to ask. How could someone like you attain Heaven without baptism or even birth?" I queried.

Tallaris looked at me understandingly.

She said, "Oh, you mean the biblical prescription for sacraments. Remember Tom, God has given men the sacraments to save them, but is not bound by them Himself. Nothing binds God. At the instant of my death, which preceded my earthly birth, God gave my spirit a choice, Heaven or Hell. I chose Heaven. So, I was tested and judged within the framework that was possible, despite man's sin in preventing my actual birth. Just like the good thief on the cross, and the angels that were tested before the fall."

226

"What will happen to your mother, Tallaris? She had you killed and she abandoned you," I said.

"Tom, you don't understand this place yet. In this place, we realize that sin isn't always so personal. In reality, all sins are actually against God. Only on Earth is it personal. Here we realize, 'It ALL belongs to God.' So, in fact, sins are only registered with God. I had my full reward regardless of what was done to me on Earth because of God's great generosity. It was the least I could do, to pray for my mother, because saving her was so important to that same God who rewarded me with life here in Heaven. My prayers were answered and as God has wiped my mother's slate clean, so do I. Remember all the good things she did after my death. She started a pro-life group and saved many other lives from the same fate, due to her sorrow over my death with the help of our prayers for her from Heaven. So, after her conversion on Earth, in the eternal perspective, we were partners. I then prayed for her pro-life ministry's success many times while here in Heaven. Before she came here, we all could see that she was good, and I asked God to save her. But not all such women are saved after doing such a terrible thing," Tallaris responded.

"Tallaris, when you say 'partners' and 'we,' who do you mean?" I asked.

"Oh, permit me to explain. Everyone in Heaven has a job and a purpose. My group has a unique calling—to fight abortion. Almost all children killed by abortion, who chose God, have this same heavenly profession. Those still living on Earth who work in this capacity are our partners. We pray for God's assistance and intercession in their cause. On those occasions when mothers who have had abortions come to Heaven, having turned their lives around, we might even invite them to join our confraternity," Tallaris said.

"So, then, Tallaris, what will happen between you and your mother now? I mean, what kind of relationship will you have?" I asked.

She answered me very matter-of-factly with the serious and near emotionless way that seemed to be her style.

"I can tell you that I am nearly certain my group will ask me to invite her to join our ranks within hours. My mother has sinned, suffered, and repented. She has met the standard to be here and would fit into our cause with a great passion. No other purpose in Heaven would fit her as well. The invitation to join us is a rare honor that we shall bestow on her. You see, very few in our group were not killed by abortion," Tallaris said.

Alta interjected, "And, she'll get to know her daughter."

That comment amazed and impressed me. It again showed that Alta's understanding of human complexities went far deeper than I would have expected for even an intelligent robot. Tallaris responded with a correction in this otherwise pretty picture.

"Yes, but I am not who I would have been, had I lived a full life on Earth. You take for granted the extent to which your eyes, ears, and senses inform your soul. None of us here has ever stood out in the rain, or fallen off a bike, or felt a mother's love. These things change you," she reflected.

So, I was now having a discussion with someone in Heaven with whom I shared no common Earthly experience.

"Tallaris, things appear timeless here. How long do people retain their purpose? Do they change tasks after thousands of years?" I asked.

Tallaris responded with something I already kind of suspected.

"Events here are timeless. And, we're also timeless here. We don't tire, get bored or unsatisfied and need to move on. But people do change missions for other reasons," Tallaris said.

During our conversation, I saw a new woman arrive in judgment.

"Tallaris, what is her story?" I asked.

She replied, "Her story is actually a sad one. This woman did not abort anyone, but has been condemned to Hell, nonetheless. In fact, she never had children."

"Why is she here then, in this Court of Life for the unborn?" I asked.

"There are more women like her here than those who killed their children. You see, it was God's design for her life that she HAVE children. Four children in fact, that God would have loved and rewarded here for all eternity. She decided that her career was better or more important than God's will. So, she married, divorced twice, went to grad school, and made a lot of money. She was so-called 'spiritual,' but never had any real beliefs or religious practice. She never even attempted to save her soul and has lost it today," Tallaris said.

"And if she had had the four children?" I asked.

"All would have saved their souls and hers too. That woman's life would have been sent on a completely different trajectory, had she married when the numerous opportunities presented themselves," Tallaris responded.

I was stunned by the finality of this sentence.

I asked Alta, "Can we visit this woman, wherever she is bound?"

Alta said, "Where ... in Hell? Seriously? You realize who else lives there, right? Why in the world would you want to go there?" Then she shook her head and decided, "If for some reason we find ourselves already in Hell, and we can visit her safely, then maybe so."

She reminded me that my idle curiosity wasn't the mission. She said that we could see the woman at a later time. After all, the hot place for which she was bound had no end date. I realized that her fulfilling my request would probably only happen if we took a trip to Hell for her vengeance.

"Tallaris, how do you know all this about this woman who was just judged?" I asked.

Tallaris responded, "Everyone here knows everything about everyone else. That's the deal here, but it's also the deal in Hell."

"So, what are the biggest differences between Heaven and Earth that the newcomer sees?" I asked.

"If I had to sum up the heavenly experience, I'd say it like this: 'Adults in Heaven are like kids on Earth.' We have duties, which we take seriously. But there is always a sense of adventure, purpose, and fun. Mostly we have the desire to please God. By that I mean to say THAT goal replaces the ones we thought we'd have in Heaven when we were on Earth," Tallaris responded.

She continued, "Time here is akin to the digital VCR you have at home. You can address any matter now, later, or repeatedly. There is always enough time to complete any mission. So, you can never be marked late with an assignment because you don't deliver assignments that were not completed. What we have here that you do not have on Earth is flexibility with time."

Chapter 18

The Apple Hunt

Just when I suspected that Tallaris and her whole group were just a bunch of emotionless Vulcans who were permanently scarred by their failure to live on Earth, I saw something that truly reaffirmed my confidence in the power of God. The three of us walked a pretty trail toward a very large open meadow.

"Tallaris, life and things here seem amazingly familiar," I said.

Tallaris gave a knowing glance. She'd heard this before, obviously.

"So, you just assumed that in Heaven everyone would be floating in protoplasmic ooze looking at God with awe and utterly incapable of thinking of anything else. Right?" Tallaris asked.

"Well, the thought had crossed my mind," I said.

"Recall the Lord's Prayer that you often pray. The words, 'Thy will be done on Earth as it is in Heaven' speak volumes."

Just as she finished speaking, her little friend Suzy ran up in a frenzy and yelled, "Apple hunt!" to Tallaris and the others within ear shot. The whole group reacted like dogs that had just spotted a squirrel.

Tallaris said, "You guys come with us, this is fun."

She and the other kids from her group and those nearby broke into a run, following Suzy. Alta and I followed to find a group of about two dozen of the kids from Tallaris's group just inside a large apple orchard that was being tended by a group of angels. One of the taller boys was poking apples out of the tree with a very long stick; as they shook loose and hit the ground, the other kids dove for them. A couple kids gathered them up into bags.

So, there was gravity here now, and based upon this display, there probably had been for a long time. Obviously, the apples hung down from the trees, by design, just like on Earth. I was amused to think that Newton needed the falling apple on Earth to arrive at his famous gravity breakthrough, which I now experienced in Heaven because of this apple hunt.

The apple trees were set in rows of different varieties and there were types I had never seen before. Rather than using sunlight, the apples had ripened under the light of God's grace. Each was completely exquisite. The kids chased apples for an hour or more in a complete frenzy, till they had filled several bags. The tending angels seemed to tolerate all this abuse without concern. Once the bags were full, the group decided to stop.

"Tallaris, are you guys stealing apples from the angels?" I asked.

Tallaris laughed and said, "Those apples are for us, and so is everything else here. In fact, that's WHY it's all here. Remember where you are, Tom."

Across the way, I spotted another group of kids on the edge of the orchard, playing with a very young Border Collie who they called Scooter. Scooter was probably 4 months old, at most, and licked the kids profusely as they all reached in to pet him with eager fascination. His fur was very soft, and even I got to pet him once. Tallaris knew these kids, who were a clan that bordered her group, but all from the same larger confraternity she belonged to. The two groups exchanged hellos, after which Tallaris's group struck out for home with bags of apples in hand.

"Okay, so now I know there are animals in Heaven," I said in a whisper. Alta overheard.

"Tom, are you making a list of differences with Earth?" Alta asked.

"Well, yes, I suppose. Wouldn't anyone? I mean, I might end up here one day! Tallaris, whose dog was that?" I asked.

Tallaris said, "The angels breed them. In fact, one entire choir of angels exists for no purpose other than the infrastructure of Heaven."

"Where are those angels?" I asked.

"Each group has its own equivalent of a monastery, where some make bread, some brew beer, some make apples or even breed dogs," Tallaris said.

"Beer?" I asked in surprise. "I thought that 'In Heaven There Is No Beer.'"

Tallaris said, "Very funny. I know the song of course. But all these things are made for us, and all that was created. It is worth noting that angels outnumber humans by over a billion to one. We are in fact, very rare, which is why there was so much fuss over us throughout creation. You could assign a billion angels just to make beer and still have a billion more angels for every human who will ever set foot here."

"Tallaris," I said, "I'm not sure how you'll take this observation, but your group seems to be the social equivalent of Heaven's 'children' if there is such a thing."

Tallaris said, "You're not the first one to say that. But remember, we all have infused knowledge. And, any one of us could have snapped a finger and collected all the apples in one gesture. So, yes, we restrain our greater gifts for the sheer sake of fun. If that makes us kids, so be it! Remember, you and Alta have seen us at play, not at work. When you hook up with Jessie, you will learn much about what we in Heaven are like when we work. She will also help you resolve the theological questions. Learn all you can from her."

I acknowledged Tallaris's answer with a nod and thanked her for her kind assistance. Haniel told Alta where we needed to search next, after which Alta thanked Haniel and Tallaris. She then returned us to Earth, making the same grand arm gesture that got us to Heaven, only this hop was to my home. There was no angelic guard there. I knew that in short order Alta and I would be confronted again by forces trying to destroy us.

Alta shared my concern, and said, "You know, we might do better flying under the radar on this mission. It's not far from your home, and we could drive it in less than three hours."

"Why not just fly or transport?" I asked.

"The price for doing so is that we move beyond the protection of regular guardian angels here on Earth. Demons do not destroy humans on Earth, normally anyway," Alta said.

"Well, we both agree that the rules seem VERY flexible lately," I responded.

"Yeah, I'd like to go with every advantage we can bet on," Alta said.

"Alta, I have no idea what a good bet would be right now, honestly," I said.

Alta responded, "God has always shielded your world with guardian angels, but the extra-dimensional space around it that I travel through might not share that special distinction. So, I think it might be safer to drive. Our ship is protected, and, fortunately, that means Raven is safe."

"Well, why not get back there and finish her programming to get yourself some help?" I asked.

"She is my sister and designed as a combat model. She is considerably more powerful than I. But that greater power comes at the expense of characteristics I have in greater abundance. Those other characteristics enable me to solve the riddle of the truth that is the primary mission. Raven was made as a combat model with the understanding that if she was ever needed, it was because every other option had failed. Raven is a last resort option," Alta said.

"So, she is like Gort from 'The Day The Earth Stood Still?'" I asked.

"No, Raven is beautiful and brilliant. She can do everything I can do and then some. I am an A model, she is an R model. There have been a lot of changes since my model, and Raven has them all. She also has a different priority of design. Where I might let a transgression slide, she never would. I see our fact-finding mission as ninety percent of the challenge, and fighting with demons about ten percent. Raven is just the opposite. Her mission is to destroy any enemy stronghold that might seek to come back from here to attack our world. Raven is Gihon's projection of strength as a last resort," Alta said.

"I get it Alta, she's a last resort. Let's see, we have a dead crew, demons attacking the earth (plus your world) and beating up on the good angels, not to mention threatening me. We are at the point of LAST RESORT, now, don't you think?" I asked.

"Let's discuss this while we drive," Alta said.

Honestly, I was just fine with that.

Chapter 19

A Visit to the Dead

After a while of driving in my Acura, Alta heard a few beeps coming from the dash board.

"What is that beeping?" she asked.

"That's my radar detector beeping, and on the left, this little light is from the LIDAR jammer," I said.

"Oh. So, you speed?" Alta asked.

"Since the person asking that question exceeds light speed by leaving the universe, I find your concern fascinating," I said sardonically. "Actually, I just drive a lot. My favorite car toy is the CB radio. It's a throw back from the 70's. But loads of truckers still use them out here."

"So, let's see you do it," Alta said.

"Okay, but you have to remember, on the radio, I'm 'in character.' That character is my handle, 'Space Rabbit,'" I said.

"How appropriate," Alta quipped.

I looked at her quizzically. I powered up the radio and dialed to channel 19, the contact channel for truckers. My radio was a converted 10 meter rig, and thus more powerful than a standard CB. I clicked the mic switch and started my routine.

"Sweet trucker, this is Space Bun Bun, cosmic rabbit. Who would like to be the lucky, lucky trucker to tell the bunny where those bearzies are today?" I asked.

The truckers responded with righteous indignation, "Space Rabbit, I'm gonna give you a 12 gauge enema."

Alta leaned over to me from the passenger side.

"I assume this is a game you all play to fight boredom on the highway?" she asked.

I nodded, seeing she really didn't get the joke. What a great time for a change of subject, I thought and switched off the CB.

"Alta, you see guardian angels in THIS world too, right? I should think they could help us," I said.

"Yes, I can see them," Alta said. "In fact, you have several angels guarding you, which is quite unique."

"Really? Can we communicate with them?" I asked.

"Yes, certainly, but angels aren't given to frivolous discussions or demonstrations of power," Alta said.

"Okay, but will you ask them why I have a non-standard-sized group protecting me?" I asked.

"Sure," Alta said.

She knew they had already heard the question, so she just asked, "Can you please help us on this?" to the unseen angels.

She related to me the reply I had not heard.

"Each extra angel was assigned to you with the conversion of every person you brought to the faith. God gave you this extra help and protection to assist you in the task of converting others to the faith, which you have done three times now. So, you have a guardian angel and then three more assigned to assist and protect you. Two of them have greater power than I have and are from the higher choirs of angels not usually assigned to such tasks. You might note that this is also part of the reason we chose you for this task, because God had already chosen you for something that merited greater protection," she said.

We drove across the Chesapeake Bay Bridge and traveled towards Berlin. Alta listened to my Depeche Mode CD single, "Personal Jesus," and a series of other dance cuts my dance partner and I were considering for a performance. Her favorite was definitely that Depeche Mode song but it seemed anything they wrote was just fine with her. At times, Alta seemed almost human, and as I looked over at her little 125 pound frame, I realized that I had the full power of a black hole sitting in my car. But oddly, having dated several female lawyers, it was familiar feeling. As we approached Berlin's outskirts we saw Route 376 turn off from 113 out of Delaware. The cemetery was ahead on the left. We drove under a large stone entrance archway and parked. Alta led the way straight to the grave.

"Alta, how do you know where we're going?" I asked as I tagged along.

Alta looked back and said, "I don't, I'm just following the angel sent to guide us."

After a three minute walk, we were at the back of the cemetery, facing what appeared to be some of the first stones placed there. Alta came over to the stone we wanted and pointed.

"Okay, now what?" I asked.

"Call her!" Alta said.

"Seriously, you want me to holler to the occupant of this grave like I was knocking on a neighbor's door?" I asked.

"Jessie, Haniel sent us, we need you," Alta said in my place, impatient with my obtuseness.

I finally got the point and joined in, calling out, "Jessie! We need your help! We are facing a demon you know, named Ostara. We need your assistance. Tallaris recommended you and your team here on Earth."

Jessie came to our assistance very quickly when hailed. She rose from the earth as a beautiful translucent apparition.

She smiled at Alta, and said, "I have heard of you, Alta, even before Tallaris told me of your coming. I had hoped to meet you."

Alta said, "I'm flattered of course, but Haniel and Tallaris sent us to you and said you could help us. Haniel also said you could tell us how to fight this demon." Alta clearly wanted to get to the point, instead of dwelling on social niceties.

Jessie responded, "I will gladly help you, as we have many of the same goals in this matter. But first, may I meet your friend?" Jessie looked at Alta, then me in turn.

"Pleased to meet you Jessie, I'm Tom," I said. I resisted the urge to bow.

Jessie appeared as a young girl of mid-twenties or so. She was dressed in a white gown that might be taken as a heavenly uniform of sorts. She had first appeared to us as a flowing translucent apparition but was now standing firmly on the ground. She had dark hair and spoke with no hint of the Old English accent that was spoken at the time of her death. She seemed oddly radiant, and I realized that, like the demon who appeared in front of us before, she might not really be here where we saw her.

"Is everybody who is going to help us twenty-five or younger?" I complained. I did not really appreciate being the oldest one here.

Alta whispered, "Feeling old? Try to remember that Jessie died 220 years ago."

As we talked, we walked in the circle around the graveyard that joined her burial plot.

"Jessie, you've been dead for over 200 years?" I asked.

"Yes," she said calmly.

"Well, why are we meeting you at a gravesite, 200 years later?" I asked.

"You want to know why we didn't meet at your house, or out on the bay?" she said, pointing to the waterfront on the other side of the street, across from the Assateague State and National Parks.

"Well," she continued, "I wish I could say I got that question a lot. Try to remember that graveyards are sacred ground for a reason. This gravesite is my phone number for the rest of eternity. It's not where I am, just how I am reached. NEVER disrespect a gravesite!"

She shook her finger at me playfully. Jessie obviously added that last part as a serious but humorous warning.

"Still, your time on Earth was 200 years ago," I said.

"Before the Civil War, in fact. I lived in a time so different from today that it's unrecognizable. But this field remains as it was. Little has changed here in that regard," Jessie said.

"So, Jessie, what is your existence like now?" I asked.

"I now manage many of the efforts in the realm beyond, for which people on Earth petition with prayer. Many people in Heaven fill the roles of fallen angels and have jobs doing the very things the missing angels left. In other cases, as new worlds arise, we serve in the same arena angels do to protect, guide, and carry messages. But people and angels are not interchangeable. My specific talent is with one of the demons you face. His name is Azazel, and he is a high ranking demon in a group called The Watchers. He was one of the demons who split off to kill Alta's crew that day you two were at the church. The Watchers are the same group that has been killing or harming all the other people who have tried to come here from other worlds before now. I have been following this matter for many years," Jessie said.

Alta had been wandering around the graveyard loops while Jessie and I spoke. She was taking a slow, thoughtful tour. Hearing what Jessie said about her gravesite being her phone number, and knowing that Alta could see the supernatural, I realized that the tour she was on was one of deeper discovery. She could probably see beyond these graves. After a time, she reversed the route and began reviewing the gravestones on the other side of the graveyard that she had missed on her first lap.

Jessie saw this too and then looked at me seriously and asked, "Tom, what's it like working with her?"

"Jessie, you're a dead person standing three feet from your own headstone, and you're asking me that question?" I asked.

"Seriously, Tom, there have always been dead people. There has never been anything like Alta before. You are working with a completely automated demon killer of the highest order. Your own guardian angel couldn't protect you from her if she went nuts. Doesn't that concern you?" Jessie asked.

"First off, I apparently have several other guardians that Alta says are more powerful than she. But your greater concern is unwarranted. I see things in Alta that make me wonder why they gave her this duty in the first place. I see her great courage in battle one minute, and then the next minute she seems more like the park ranger who rescues wounded birds for the aviary," I responded.

Just as I said that, Alta lit up her sword and traced figure eights in front of her at hip level, which she had done before while walking. She was a complete master of the weapon, and a first-rate martial artist to boot. I figured Alta did this to release nervous energy.

Jessie said, "See what I mean, she's a killer."

So, I hailed Alta to make a point.

"Alta! Why do you do that with your sword? Can't you just raise your hand and flatten demons with your will?" I asked.

Alta came closer and switched off the sword before she answered. "Yes, I could just use my will, but the tradition of my kind is to associate a sign or gesture with an action. Just as your God applied visible signs to things that He could do with His will alone."

Then Alta started a "show and tell" for Jessie.

"The sword is a gift from Raphael for saving him from The Watchers, and he even had it monogrammed for me. See the bottom?" she said.

She showed us the symbol on the bottom that was Alta's sign, an ellipse bisected at the bottom with a triangle. The same symbol she wore on her belt buckle that I had noticed before.

"Okay, but why do you practice with the sword so much then?" I asked that purely for Jessie's sake. "You're already as good as you can ever get with it, by definition, seeing as you're a robot."

"Yes, but I'm not practicing with it. I just love to look at the pretty colors of the blade as they change while traveling through the air. The purple is my favorite," Alta said.

Her sword was indeed beautiful when waved through the air; its reddish beam glistened with other trace colors as it was twirled through Alta's routine.

I looked over at Jessie and said, "Pretty colors. See what I mean?"

Alta and I got our picnic lunch out of the car, and offered Jessie some chicken. I had decided to stop embarrassing myself with "So, do you eat?" questions every time I met someone supernatural. Jessie declined and the three of us started to walk towards the edge of the bay. She died more than 60 years before the Civil War, and this field was near her home at that time. Jessie looked at the bay and sighed. She pointed out long absent land marks.

"That was my neighbor's house, and over there was my place, and the edge of the bay was further off than it is now. I miss the times I had here," she said wistfully.

Alta said, "Funny, but I know many of the people who are buried in this graveyard. I may well have worked with your neighbors without realizing that this was their point of origin."

"Oh, you mean after their death they were tasked to Gihon somehow?" Jessie asked.

Alta said, "Yes, or they were couriers from here, just passing me on their duties."

"Jessie, apparently all of Alta's people can see the spiritual reality, because God elected not to be born at Gihon," I said.

Jessie gave an understanding look and said, "Tom, you do realize that after death, people have infused knowledge?"

I was frustrated yet again.

"I may never get used to all of this. How can you even have a conversation with anyone since you all know everything?" I asked.

Jessie said, "Infused knowledge is the fate of all men so they can appreciate the reward God offers, or appreciate the loss if they choose Hell. But we certainly can have a conversation; we just don't need to exchange facts that are already known. By the way, Alta doesn't have all knowledge. You can talk to her, right?"

"Alta was made by super smart aliens. What Alta doesn't know, doesn't matter, trust me on that." Whether Alta or Jessie knew the most, it was clear that I knew the least.

"So, Jessie," I said, "You are supposed to help us. What can you do to help?" I'd actually been wondering about that for a while now.

Jessie answered, "Quite a bit, but first I need to teach you some things."

I recalled how Michael touched Alta's head to give her knowledge. I stepped back and half-jokingly said, "Is this time for the Vulcan mind meld?"

Jessie rolled her eyes and said, "Very funny. I figured I'd just tell you."

She continued, "For starters you need to understand how Hell works, and the primary goals of its occupants. Next, you need to understand how angels are informed. Remember, having infused knowledge still doesn't mean the totality of everything that can be known, it just means knowledge of all material facts, measures, history and the complete deposit of faith. Some angels know more than others, and even those know less than God. Also, angels are immortal, but that just means they won't die if left to their own

248

devices, it does not mean that they cannot be taken out of service in this context."

"So, then, that would mean that higher angels can teach lower angels things?" I asked, trying to grasp how this worked.

"Yes, even if those facts are just the precise will of God on a matter. But here's the catch. God informs the highest angels, who pass that knowledge down to lower ones. This is ongoing. In Hell, the source is cut off. The most knowledgeable angel in Hell is Satan, and he has no longer has a pipeline to God. Also, Hell is a place without hope, so the incentive to progress in any way is removed. All actions there are out of fear of Satan," Jessie said.

"Jessie, if Hell is so bad, why wouldn't demons just ask to be put out of their misery, rather than suffer eternally?" I asked.

Jessie said, "They would, but God does not allow it. If He did, they would have wiped each other out long ago. However, God might not prevent Alta from flattening a few demons. But since she already knows they'd consider that a favor, I'm guessing she'd just make them suffer terribly, especially those who killed her crew."

"Jessie, I think you have the wrong girl here," I said.

Jessie gave me a stern look and said, "Who has infused knowledge here, me or you?"

"No matter, we'll both know in time. Jessie, we came a long way to meet you, how can you assist us with Alta's quest for truth?" I asked.

Jessie said, "Dealing with The Watchers is my chosen task, and I am part of a larger team, like Tallaris, whom you already met. I'm sort of a consultant if you will."

"Consultant? Okay, we'll get back to that later. For now, can you start by filling us in on whom and what we're up against?" I asked.

Jessie responded, "Well, yes, as I see it Tom, you need a quick course in the who's who in Heaven and Hell. We're not talking about The Holy Family and Satan, but rather, that next tier down where a lot of the business gets done. You certainly recall Satan's fall from Heaven, in which a third of the angels fell with him. Two thirds remained with God, but even so, the third that fell comprise a number that is greater than the human population times a billion. There were lots and lots of angels before the fall. The one third that is now in Hell has you and Alta in their crosshairs. Hell's highest authority is Satan, and the queen of Hell is Ostara. But in this association, Ostara works for Satan. She literally earned the position early in human history, back in druidic times. Within the next tier right below them are The Watchers. Remember, Hell mirrors everything in Heaven organizationally. Hell may be full of fire but we're still dealing with angels here."

"We've heard about Ostara several times now, but I know very little about her," I said.

Jessie paused. "Well, now is as good a time as any to tell you her story. Ostara was originally quite human and born around 1000 BC. She was of Germanic origin and lived a full life before graduating to join Satan in the afterlife. She had far more influence after her death, however, and ultimately became the driving force behind the Celtic ritual for spring. It occurred around March 21st every year and she named the event after herself. The ritual that bore Ostara's name was in its greatest prominence from about 275 BC until shortly after the time of Christ. At that point, Christian missionaries absorbed the holiday as Easter. With the vanquishing of her Celts, and destruction of her holiday, Ostara turned her rage against the Catholic Christians she blamed for influencing those changes."

She continued, "Thousands of years later, Ostara has become the equivalent of Hell's resident Queen. In the present age she rules by fear and ruthlessness. Her compound in Hell is an entire city that has nothing to do with where Satan's throne is. Among her many duties was command of The Knights in Satan's Service. The knights were Hell's Seal Team Six. This elite group is comprised of the very worst demons and had the capacity to travel beyond the borders of Hell to any point in creation. Several of the Knights are high-ranking demons in The Watchers, which is an older and larger group. Among the most famous and best known adversaries of Satan's Knights on Earth were the Knights Templar, which were later disbanded. But Satan's Knights continue to this day, unlike the Knights Templar. Archangel Michael and his expeditionary team carry the mantle to oppose Satan's Knights in the current era. Michael's team and Ostara's demons have clashed many times."

"Ostara is beautiful and ruthless. She is a complex, brilliant, and strangely inspiring leader. Despite the importance of her mission to Satan, she is among the most conflicted and tortured agents of Hell. She is an oddly wretched soul who would blow her own leg off just to splatter some blood on you. Watching her work is like watching a surgeon operate, while trying to ignore a self-inflicted dagger wound in one of his own arms. She is a wild mix of pain and precision, who seems to hate herself more than any target she is given. One might wonder if she sought her own destruction just to end her own misery. The demons that work on her team all fear her, with very good reason. After all, the only escape from the pain and shame of Hell is utter self annihilation. God prevents this easy way out for all those in Hell, but it doesn't stop the demons from trying. This only magnifies their misery," Jessie said.

"So, why does a former human lead a group of demons?" I asked.

Jessie responded, "Tom, the same could be true in Heaven, as humans fill the roles of fallen angels. The Virgin Mary was a human on Earth just the same as Ostara. The Watchers have a long history as the bad boy angels written about in the book of Enoch. They have been a thorn in the side of both good angels and mankind ever since. The Watchers have twenty high-ranking angels under the leadership of Samyaza who was a fallen Cherub. Most of these top twenty are fallen Thrones who ranked just below the Cherubs. It is worth noting that angels retain the same rank after the fall, but only have some of their duties changed. Their communications hierarchy and interdependencies are unaltered except that they now report to Satan instead of God. There are 200 more demons under The Watchers that comprise the entire group. That sub group of 200 is a mix of fallen Powers and Principalities, which are lesser ranking angels than the top twenty. Powers and Principalities are the same angelic ranks the Bible admonished men to watch out for in Ephesians 6:12. As a whole, this group of 200 could best be compared to Hitler's SS. These are Hell's front line combat troops of the highest order. The Watchers' other most prominent leader within the top twenty was one of Hell's teachers, Kokabiel."

"Kokabiel also was a fallen Cherub and had his own subgroup of 365,000 surrogate spirits. The surrogate spirits promote disinformation, astrology, and any other tasks Kokabiel assigns to them. They are Hell's regular army of earthly misery. The surrogate spirits are comprised of the very same human souls Kokabiel's efforts originally brought to Hell. After being deceived by things Kokabiel taught them in their earthly lives, these damned souls are now forever bound to him as slaves to do his bidding after death. It is an odd twist for these tortured human souls, to see God, at their judgment, and realize they have been fooled. When they realize all that they have lost, they become the indentured servants of the very demon who tricked them. They operate out of fear, because they hate Kokabiel, mankind, and most of all themselves," Jessie explained.

"And all these demons report to Ostara, their human queen?" I asked in amazement.

Jessie responded, "Absolutely! Ostara is the most powerful and interesting of them all. The highest demons around her fear her unstable rage, because at any moment in the pitch of a battle, Ostara might attempt to destroy her own team, and even herself, just to end the agonizing self-hate in her own mind. She doesn't seem to care that self-annihilation in Hell is prevented by God. Every demon who works with her knows this, and it spreads fear among all who see her."

"Ostara is the queen of evil herself, who has the same sway in Hell that the Virgin Mary has in Heaven. It is now her responsibility to destroy Alta, as the last remaining member of the team from Gihon. The stakes of this battle are unbelievably high. Failure to prevent Alta from spreading the truth would allow Christianity to arrive at every world the team from Gihon could reach upon their return home. Earth has therefore been quarantined by the demons for more than twenty centuries," Jessie said, while adding a caveat:

"In Hell, any industry that succeeds in luring many souls to be damned is rewarded. So, to sum up, under Ostara's banner are The Watchers, led by twenty high ranking demons. Samyaza is the captain of the twenty, and he is always near Ostara's side. Kokabiel is equal in rank to Samyaza but runs a large group of 365,000 surrogate spirits who inflict whatever mayhem Kokabiel instructs. These are the ones you want to avoid the most, but I suspect they'll find you, regardless." Well, gee, that was reassuring, I thought.

"Jessie, what do you know about OUR team?" I asked.

"On the plus side, Michael, Haniel, and Raphael are helping you and Alta. I'll tell you about their place in all of this in a moment, because they are not the problem here, obviously. Ostara, Samyaza ,and Kokabiel are your problem. By the measure of crude rank before the fall, they have more power than your angels, because Ostara alone is one of the highest figures in Hell. She has great influence, and can sway large groups of demons to focus on any task, without Satan's approval. She has more power than any angel in either group, but less than Satan or the Queen of Heaven, who has use of all of God's power if needed," Jessie said.

"You said Kokabiel is a teacher in Hell. What would he teach in Hell?" I asked.

Jessie responded, "He is responsible for counter-education. In fact, the phrase 'No church can save you' came from his group. They also get credit for substituting the terms 'gay' for homosexuality and 'pro-choice' for abortion. Their group of demons frames everything bad as something good, or uses misdirection to achieve their end."

"Their end? What IS their end?" I asked.

Jessie said, "That's hard to answer in a single sentence, but easy to frame with a thought experiment. For instance, Tom, what would you say was the greatest good thing that God ever did --at least that we know of?"

I scratched my head and said, "Well, I guess that He died for our sins, right?"

Jessie said, "Yeah sure, but a greater good preceded that good."

"Okay, what?" I asked.

"God created all of this! There would be no men to die for if there was no creation. His greatest good was to create everything," Jessie answered.

Alta chimed in, "The greatest evil would be to reverse that."

"Precisely!" Jessie said, with an eager smile.

"So, how would you reverse creation?" I asked.

"Well," Jessie said, "You could foster abortion, start wars, unravel the church, encourage murder. But there is one even better way than murder to rid the creation of men. Simply prevent them in the first place."

So, I said, "Birth control?"

"Sure," Jessie said, "The demons, not God, are the ones who benefit from promoting homosexuality, birth control, or anything that can prevent the creation of those God intended to be born here on Earth. We who have died before you have experience in these matters, and we have a simple method to determine whether any action done by men, politicians, or leaders is good or bad."

"And that is?" I asked a little skeptically.

"Follow the money!" Jessie exclaimed. "If Satan gets a payoff on his larger goals by the end of the transaction, the process is bad, otherwise it is good. Next time you see a politician running for office, skip past the flowery words and look at his prospective likelihood of meeting one of Satan's greater goals. That will tell you his true colors. You two are in a fight with major players in Hell: teachers, leaders, and the Queen of Hell herself. But enough of my overview of means and motives. Let me walk with Alta awhile, because for her, this is a theology lesson she already knows anyway."

Alta and Jessie walked the loops in the graveyard, talking for an hour. Alta finally came back to where I was sitting with a pronouncement.

"It looks like the best way to answer the question of TRUTH, is to go back to the Last Supper. If I see the same thing occur at the consecration that I saw in your church, I'll know that the validity of the chain of truth is unbroken. So far, I have not seen it in churches of other faiths," Alta said.

"We're going back in time? Sure, Alta, I guess by now, I'm used to hearing just about anything," I said.

Jessie hugged us both, because at this point, she had taken a liking to Alta.

"For now, let me leave you two to ponder all you've heard, till we meet again. But between now and then, if you require it, Alta can summon me at any time," Jessie said.

We circled back to the car, and we honestly enjoyed the ride back from the shore.

Chapter 20
Crashing the Last Supper

Once we got home, I had a chance to ponder all I had seen in the last twenty-four hours. Alta and I seemed to be on a very guided tour. I was still reflecting on our meeting with Jessie, whose core message was that Satan sought to "reverse creation" by any means. I began to wonder if our meeting with Tallaris and the apple hunting kids was accidental or planned. Honestly, although they were completely happy, I wouldn't want to be in a group like Tallaris's, that never felt the rain, fell off a bike, or saw the ocean. I had a soul, unlike Alta, and life experience, unlike Tallaris. I wasn't damned like the demons. I was suddenly realizing how very lucky I was and beginning to see what might be happening here at a deeper level. None of the meetings I had with Jane, Michael, or even the demons were an accident. In simple terms, Alta and I figured this was a battle for her world and any other world that might be reached by Gihon's space ships later. But we were actually just late comers in the far greater struggle of managing creation itself. God obviously really loved people and wanted more, not less. The entire industry of Heaven appeared to be focused on spinning up for these new civilizations coming on line, like Alta's at Gihon. It seemed to me that the mission of shepherding new worlds would be our task in Heaven. Filling the roles of fallen angels was our destiny, which started with what we did and how we lived on Earth. Clearly, our heavenly assistants had created a guided tour to teach us the larger meaning behind all of the events we were thrust into.

On Earth, we progressed from childhood to adulthood, so we could see and experience both phases. But there was a "next" phase beyond Earthly adulthood, the afterlife. That would place us squarely in the role the angels have, to help each new civilization achieve what we already have on Earth. We truly were a chosen people on a chosen world. The scale of this plan dwarfed anything people on Earth might suspect and made me realize that Alta and I had only a small piece of the total. The entire secret to understanding Satan, his motives, and deeds was centered on thwarting creation, and the more direct the method, the better. His chief tools were stealth and deception and remaining hidden while he substituted near truths for the actual truth. Oddly, even what Satan told Eve in the garden was partly true. It just wasn't the part that mattered to God. So, the best way to oppose his team was not to do battle with them, but rather, get to the truth, and spread it.

Alta and I conferred before the next step. We did a quick review of what we knew. I started by summing up the decision points.

"The best way to sort out what we know and don't know is to use a series of yes-no questions to categorize where we're at. Starting with the first question on the list, which is: Should you be Christian or something else? It's sort of a binary tree," I said.

Alta answered, "Jane already covered that well enough for our purposes. Of those faiths that believe in the God of Abraham, only Christianity claims that the Savior has already come. We know this is true because our prophets sent us here to research a past event, not await a future one."

"Then, the next step is to decide what side of the Reformation you're on," I said.

Alta asked, "Okay, how could we resolve that specifically?"

"Well, you could compare your records of what the early church believed, to the beliefs of the various faiths today; but that leaves 33,000 to review. I trust your computers already did that in about two minutes of processing time anyway," I said.

Alta responded, "Yes, it eliminated all but the Orthodox and the Catholics, depending on how you interpret the license of Matthew 16:18. If God DID sanction the original Church's power to 'loose and bind,' then the differences we see in Catholicism 2,000 years later all fall under appropriate church authority."

"Right. No church can change fundamental tenets of faith and morals, but some other matters can be handled by appropriate authorities. Well, then, I figure that we should take up the offer to go back to the Last Supper, and discuss the specifics with firsthand witnesses. We'll see if the transformation of the Eucharist that you saw at the consecration is the same there as it was at my twenty-first century church," I said.

"Would you go with me?" Alta asked. This put me in a bit of a quandary.

"Hmmm … it's very exciting, and I'd love to, but frankly, Alta, I also fear running into God personally. That would be beyond embarrassing," I said.

Alta scoffed, "Like God wouldn't know you were there anyway! This matter is too important to leave to chance."

Alta looked up and said in a prayer, "Raphael, we need you."

He instantly appeared and already knew of our dilemma. Raphael's presence with us was clearly the equivalent of a long distance phone call from Heaven, because the demons would have prevented such a quick response from Raphael in person.

"I am aware of your plan. Haniel cleared the whole matter for us, so it has been sanctioned by God. Good hunting!" he said, disappearing as quickly as he had come.

"Here we go!" Alta said with eagerness. She stood back, and as always, raised her arms above her head, fingers pointed straight up into the air. As she made a large downward circle, things got black and we were in what I could only assume was the upper room we sought. A gathering of men relaxed in front of us. I cowered in an adjacent part of the room, realizing that I couldn't possibly explain my presence there to anyone, or return without Alta. She seemed fearless and walked right in to the gathering and asked questions very matter-of-factly. She was outside of my earshot, and probably not speaking English, so I could not hear what was said. She seemed to be talking to one man in particular, and I wondered if that wasn't Jesus Himself. Alta spoke to him, and he told her something that sent her back to me, smiling. We carefully watched the entire proceeding, which took no more than twenty minutes.

"Alta, did you see it?" I asked.

"Yes, I did as a matter of fact. This is the same thing that I saw at your church. We can head back to our place and time now," Alta said.

Alta reversed the process that brought us.

"Did you see the same change when he lifted the bread at the Last Supper?" I asked.

She answered, "Yes, I saw a blue flame that appears over the bread and wine right at the time of the consecration. I suspect that there was more that I couldn't see, but that was enough."

Upon our return, I had to ask, "Alta, was that Jesus Himself?"

"Yes, it was He. In fact, it was his will that he and I speak. To others in the room, I appeared as a member of the group, rather than an outsider. You and I had divine assistance," Alta said.

"What did He tell you that made you smile?" I asked.

Alta said, "It was something for you. You asked a question in theology long ago. 'Why did God die as He did, via a betrayal?' He answered it for you, and in a way that you will certainly appreciate. With eons alone prior to creation, and eons of time after creation, before His death God had time to plan how He would be glorified. Now, it goes without saying that God needs no time at all to plan, but still it dramatizes the point that Jesus' death by betrayal was to instruct the faithful. Namely that attacks on the church would come from within, more often than from without. Remember, Judas was an insider. Jesus' choice of how He would be betrayed and crucified teaches us by example how many of the faithful are betrayed by so-called good people within the church."

"But did this help YOU, Alta? Why didn't you just ask Jesus directly what the true religion was and resolve your whole quest for truth?" I asked.

Alta said that such directness wasn't in the order of things. She said, "God had a purpose for the very struggle of life and the seeking of truth that we can not abrogate. This is our test, as Eden was for your world. We have to endure it to prove virtue to our Creator."

I realized that I was participating in a Garden of Eden experience for Alta's entire world and all those many others her technology touched. It reinforced the momentousness of what we were doing, and I was once again amazed at the thought.

Alta quickly returned to the purpose and laid out what she thought the next steps were to complete the challenge.

"Our trip back to the Last Supper established several things. First, it DID happen as rendered in the Bible. And secondly, Jesus was not speaking figuratively as He did the consecration. Since I saw the same phenomenon occur in this instance as I did at your church 2,000 years later, something substantial but unseen by human eyes happens when the priest says the words of consecration at Mass," she said.

She continued, "For my own sake, I have my answer. The Universal Church is the correct faith. You now call it the Roman Catholic Church. I also believe therefore that Eastern rites in line with the Pope are valid. However, some in my world may or may not agree with my findings, and insist on a more thorough examination of surrounding events, from inception to the church you have today. For them then, the next step will be harder because the core problem is assessing what has happened to the church over time. But I am coming back with all the data on that, so they can do their own research. I feel we have now collected enough data, because the church of the Last Supper has journeyed across 2,000 years and maintained the same effect at both consecrations, new and old. Just for extra certainty, I suspect the demons can help us as a convenient reverse barometer."

I already knew that the last time Jane spoke in that way, I was the bait. Now, Alta was doing the same thing.

"Alta, don't you think the demons are involved enough as it is? For you to carry out this last idea, you have to lay out what you found to them and see if they attack you out of fear that you got it right," I said.

"Yes, Tom, but considering the stakes here, it's worth it. Remember. I am considered expendable," she responded.

"Really? Because I am not expendable and if you are killed, so will I be. Not to mention, if you were killed, your findings would never make it back to your people," I said.

Alta made a calming gesture with her hands.

She said, "I don't plan to get killed, or to risk your life. But even if I were killed, Raven would receive all the data and conclusions I found as she was brought online. This task would then fall to her."

Chapter 21

We Are Forced to Fight

Alta and I returned home and went for a drive to the bike shop. We were listening to my dance music again, which she seemed to love. She kept replaying the Depeche Mode "Personal Jesus" along with Nickelback's "Burn it to the Ground." Oddly, those two songs seemed to define parts of Alta's own struggles. Sometimes, she'd just turn the radio off and stare out the passenger window. When I asked her about it, she'd just say she missed her home. One we got back, we had lunch and I told Alta I needed to fix the old lawn mower.

"I can fix it for you," Alta offered.

"I can handle this one," I assured her.

We went out to the shed and pulled out the mower, whereupon I started to disassemble part of the upper engine casing. Most of the problem was usually just dirt, but I also discovered a bad muffler that was rusted through. Alta watched patiently as I struggled with rusty bolts. After taking off the old muffler, I realized that the part would be nearly impossible to find.

I held up the broken part and said, "This is the trouble, but finding another will be a trick."

Alta went over to the shed and came back with a muffler and asked, "Is this the part you need?" I realized that Alta had just materialized it, and created a ruse.

"Alta, I need to handle this one." So, much had been happening that was way beyond me, and I was already dependent on Alta for so many things. This was one piece of my life that I could do on my own, and I wanted to do it.

She looked at me disappointedly and said, "Well, that'll be a trick, indeed, since I know every mower part on the planet, and there isn't a single one of the type you're looking for."

Realizing that she would certainly know, and that she was a step ahead of me, I swallowed my pride. I guess I couldn't do this on my own after all.

"Okay, thanks, Alta," I said, holding up my hand and accepting her materialized part. She had ginned up one made of polished stainless steel that would easily outlast the mower. Even the threads were lubed. Alta could obviously fix everything in the house with a wave of her hand.

"Nice muffler," I said.

"It's stainless, and, Tom, the best part of that muffler is the grease. Same stuff used on my ship. It remains viscous at any temperature down to 100 below, and will stand up to 600 degrees. It's a synthetic, needless to say," Alta said.

Alta was kind but obviously a bit of a geek.

If Alta was worried about what faced us, she sure didn't seem to show it. I finally decided I was tired of waiting for the other shoe to drop and just asked her, "Alta, what do you know about the activities of the demons we face? You know pretty much everything, right? Can you see where they are now?"

"Tom, even if you have infused knowledge, that doesn't mean you know everything that can be known. I know less than the highest angels, who know less than God. But then, that's the trick, because in Heaven, knowledge is passed down from top to bottom. God is an endless font of knowledge, so the process continues indefinitely. Even mortal men have the hope to know everything someday and so they progress with science and technology towards that goal. Men are so far short of all that could be known that the journey to attain everything seems infinite," she said.

"Clearly, Alta, but that is not the case in your world. They made you," I said. We headed back up into the house and talked as we walked.

"Yes, but to answer your first question, I don't know where the demons are and haven't seen any. That worries me. I'd rather know what they're up to, or where they are," Alta said.

I responded, "That sword cuts both ways. Does their own infused knowledge inform them about our whereabouts?"

Alta answered, "That's a tougher question. Heaven hierarchically passes down knowledge from God, but Hell is cut off. Occupants cannot grow or progress beyond a certain point because of the very factors that make Hell what it is. Apart from the occupants, Hell itself is just a dumping ground of failed projects. Not that God failed. Those things placed in Hell failed to choose God. There IS no upward trajectory from Hell. Neither is there any cooperation or even incentive for cooperation. Most men in Hell are, frankly, completely batty. I believe this even applies to demons on some levels."

Alta paused and continued, "Do you believe that if a demon were forgiven, he could just snap to and be a perfect fit back in Heaven?"

I pondered. "Probably not," I said.

"Do you believe we change in Heaven?" Alta asked.

"Well, I suppose being utterly perfect, only God doesn't change, because any change would be away from perfection. Only God is perfection itself. So, therefore, we aren't utterly perfect in Heaven, rather we are just without sin. This must therefore imply that however slightly, we DO change, even in Heaven," I said.

Alta took it from there. "So, if the good change, perhaps for the better, then so do the evil change, perhaps for the worst."

"Gosh, Alta, you are debating philosophy that is over nearly anyone's head right now. Yes, I suppose therefore I can see that even demons might effectively decay, if that's what you are implying. I believe they are incorruptible, but then I already admitted that vast infused knowledge means different things depending on whether you are the lowest man in Heaven or the

Virgin Mary. So, the term 'incorruptible' may have some latitude of interpretation," I said.

"Back to the point," Alta said. "In Hell, the damned realize that they are cut off from the upward trajectory that comes from the knowledge passed down by God. They can't move beyond a certain point of evolution that is equal to the highest angel now in Hell, Satan himself."

"It may not even be in his interest to teach those below him. After all, this IS Hell," I said.

"So then, some men in our world, however slow to start but given enough time can surpass agents of Hell in knowledge by a sheer war of attrition. Like MY civilization did in making me long ago. I am the product of hope. There can be no such creation coming from Hell even IF the technical ability was there to achieve it. So, in my opinion, over enough time, my ancestors would avenge my destruction, even if Raven and I were killed in the process of completing this task. Mind you, I'm not just talking about six months from now. It could also be caused by later armies, long after Raven and I are a distant memory," Alta said.

As we spoke I glanced out the upper sliding glass window and saw what could only be an unearthly appearance passing outside the house on the deck. Something had been sent to find us. I yelled and Alta ran out and grabbed the demon by the throat.

"Why have you chosen to die?" she threatened, and then released the demon to talk, pushing him back with a thrust.

I looked at this fallen angel, and even after seeing several of them, I was still amazed by his otherworldly appearance. He was large and strong, with long flowing hair, and some sort of tattoo on his inner right forearm. It wasn't a tattoo of vanity, but more like something you'd see on a Yakuza. It was probably his group's hallmark. He had a metal arm-covering over the back of his left hand and forearm that looked almost medieval. He wore a long flowing red and white robe that blew without any wind. Parts of his body appeared and disappeared, while being refreshed with an image that shimmered in and out. I noticed this in all visitors from his dimension, with the singular exception of Alta, whose appearance could switch between this and a normal appearance at will.

Alta stood before him, and it was clear that they had known each other, at least by reputation. He looked like he was spoiling for a fight with Alta, but he was proceeding with great caution. By now, I had run out behind Alta on the deck. Alta stepped away from him and back over to me.

"This is Kokabiel," she said to me, speaking in low tones.

"Can you beat him?" I whispered back.

Alta answered, "Possibly, but I won't be fighting just him. Kokabiel is one of highest demons among The Watchers. So, in this case, I will surely be fighting all of them. Beating one demon alone isn't the problem. I cannot defeat him and also protect you from the rest of his group."

Kokabiel spoke to Alta, aware of his advantage:

"Robot, you know that you cannot win this. Surrender to us and I'll deliver you both to Satan unharmed. Perhaps he might spare you if you agree to never return home."

Alta looked sternly back at him, and said, "You know you would destroy us both, if we gave in to you. If you haven't, it's because you know that the outcome is uncertain."

She paused. "I am a soulless thing that stands between you and your goal. Even if you destroyed me, Hell would not gain another soul, because I have no immortal soul to damn. So, I shall face you, with others who have an interest in your defeat."

Alta looked up to Heaven and prayed.

"Almighty God, hear this robot's prayer. Though I am not Your creation and have no reward with You in eternity, I serve You nonetheless. I seek to protect this man whom you have died for and whom these demons seek to destroy. Send Your angel Raphael to help me do Your will," Alta said.

At that moment, I could see others of Kokabiel's group appearing behind him. They all had the same extra-dimensional shimmering image that he had. I knew that any one of them alone could destroy the whole world, and all that stood between me and them was Alta.

Alta looked at the group and snapped up her clear force shield that covered us like a glass bell. Then I did something I had wanted to do since I first saw the shield. I poked at it with my finger. When it moved in response, I realized that it was intelligent, in a way, and did not have a precise border. Alta said this would protect us from any assault as long as it remained.

"As long as it remains? What might make it not remain?" I said in panic.

"They are trying to destroy us, Tom, and this is a battle of who has the most energy. So, it depends upon their combined number," Alta said.

The group moved forward to engage us, but I knew that where they appeared to stand had very little to do with where they actually were, or how they would attack. After all, they were acting at a distance. Alta grabbed the closest demon by the throat and he vaporized. Another demon fired something at her that had energy, but no sound. I could see the entire shield shudder from a huge impact around us. Alta recoiled within the shield as the blast hit its outer extremity.

Kokabiel's team began to disappear in a dark mist behind their leader, who stepped back, retreating while still facing Alta. Their leaving the field of battle was unexpected.

"Why are they retreating, Alta?" I asked.

She responded, "Because Raphael's angels are close. They're going to pursue the demons. We're safe for the moment, but we're going to need help."

We left the house, figuring it was too dangerous to stay there. Jumping into the car, we drove out to the country. Alta felt sure that transporting would attract too much attention. But as we drove, we could see a dark storm cloud up ahead. It looked like a hailstorm with lightning and completely covered the horizon.

"Wow, Alta. See that storm ahead?" I said, peering through the windshield.

"That's no storm," Alta said. We pulled the car over and ran for it.

Chapter 22
The Corn Field

Upon seeing the dark clouds, Alta and I ran into a cornfield, figuring Ostara had sent a large force of demons to intercept us. Kokabiel's attack was just a ruse to lure away Raphael's team. Alta stopped in front of me and said we simply couldn't go any further, there were too many of them to run from. In the distance, I could see the dark set of clouds on the horizon had gotten closer. They were roiling and black, like the worst storm I could recall. Their thick mass darkened the sky to near twilight, blocking direct view of the Sun.

The clouds were high above the cornfield we stood in, which at this time of year was just a flattened field of post-harvest stalks. Some unimaginable force was pushing the dark clouds our way, but as they got closer, I could see something was changing in the clouds. By then they were maybe a half mile from us and approaching rapidly. As the clouds came closer, I could see what looked like crank-case oil streaming down from 500 feet in the air. As the oily substance threaded its way to the ground, large spindly black demons stood in the place of the falling fluid, all marching towards us. There were thousands of these demons coming our way, many rows deep and stretching across the entire length of the field, at least a mile in each direction to our right and left.

I glanced over at Alta for a reaction, and just said, "Wow!"

Alta glanced back. "A third of the demons in Hell have been released to confront us today. There are too many even for me," she said tensely.

Alta handed me the doll I had bought for her days before. Aside from her sword, it was the only possession she had with her.

"Take care of this," she said.

I took the doll and hugged it. Alta braced for the battle and before she had a chance to summon them, Raphael's team arrived on the scene.

"Well, we are glad to see you!" Alta exclaimed.

Raphael looked across at the demon army marching towards us. By now I could see what looked like eleven-foot-tall, spindly black stick-figures marching our way in gigantic numbers.

"I've already called Michael," Raphael quickly informed us.

"Raphael, if he comes, we fight as a team; if he doesn't get here in time, you all need to let me handle this alone. Because if it goes badly, you must take Tom and get him to safety," she said, pointing to me.

Alta lit up her sword and turned it on full power, and it lit up too bright to look at. She snapped up a shield over me as Raphael's team joined her out in the cornfield. I could feel the ground shaking as Ostara's troops approached. But Ostara was not with them.

Raphael stayed back with me, and I asked accusingly, "Aren't you going over to help her?"

Raphael looked at me and said, "There is no front or back to this battlefront. Remember, these demons are all still in Hell, acting at a distance."

Demons began to throw themselves at Alta, ignoring the angels from Raphael's team that were helping her. Several came at me, and Raphael cut them down with his sword. He had no shortage of courage and was clearly a veteran fighter. Alta threw a huge sheet of energy off her sword which cut down an entire column of demons that vaporized and disappeared. But each of those fallen demons was replaced with seven more, worse than themselves. A furious battle ensued that lasted more than twenty minutes. At times, it seemed that Alta might actually pull this off. At some points in the fight, she shrunk her dome shield to a smaller arm shield. It allowed better hand-to-hand fighting and sword use. I could see Alta in the thick of the fight, at this point on her knees with both shields covering her, in two clear glasslike bells. She had taken several very bad hits and was clearly getting the worst of it at this point. She fell to her hands, then glanced sideways at me and Raphael and lifted one hand to wave us to leave. She knew this battle was unwinnable but stood to fight again. In the end, there were simply too many demons, who even in dying, piled on top of her in ever greater numbers.

Having just seen Alta crushed under hundreds of demons in the cornfield, Raphael acted quickly to evacuate me from the battlefield.

"We need to run!" he shouted.

"We have to help Alta!" I protested.

"Tom, you are now more my responsibility than Alta is. God does NOT want human casualties in this fight for Gihon's people," Raphael said.

I couldn't be sure what had actually happened to Alta as we left. Raphael transported me home, where we met Michael and his team. All the while, I was still carrying Alta's doll. Michael stayed with us till the immediate danger passed. It became apparent that the goal of the action had only been to capture Alta. I didn't know it at the time, but Satan had requested that Ostara deliver Alta to him in Hell.

The demons accomplished this, dragging her off to Hell for an audience with Satan himself. Michael now had a situation that was outside of anything he had gotten God's guidance over. He requested an audience with God, Himself, to find out how the matter should be handled.

Chapter 23

Green Cards for Demons

Some of The Watchers chained Alta upon a cross at the top of a small hill. The cross was like the Christian cross of Earthly tradition, except Alta wasn't suspended up off of the ground. Her feet were bound but on the ground. Her arms were outstretched and bound. Her head was hanging down, she was covered with dirt from the fight, and her clothes were tattered. She was damaged from the fight with the demons and working at no more than ten percent. Her extra-dimensional image flickered in and out as a result of the battle.

No demon came near Alta on the hill. She was alone, awaiting disposition from a judgment within Hell itself. Perhaps it was the very first "judgment" ever to occur in Hell, which ordinarily was just the place to serve out sentences. After some time, word went out that she was to be brought to Satan's court. Several very powerful demons unchained the wounded Alta and carried her between them to an audience with Satan, in a fashion oddly reminiscent of Christ's audience with Pontius Pilate.

As they brought her in to a jeering crowd of demons, it was clear that they also feared her. As she approached the throne room a great light within was dimming down, in expectation of visitors. The entire place was huge and imposing. It was precisely what one might expect on a visit to Caesar, if that were still possible. Still, Alta suspected that this presentation was merely for her benefit. She stood disheveled and alone in a large marble court before the throne of Satan himself. She knew that everything in Hell was a ruse. Satan was already there waiting, and he actually seemed eager to meet Alta. To the demons, nothing of her kind had ever been seen before. She was the first of a new class of creations that had power equal to theirs, but no soul. They could not tempt her, or threaten her eternal destiny. Nor could they read her mind. Being transcendental, Alta was more than a mere machine, yet not directly a creation of the natural order. For Alta, there was no threat of eternity in Hell, or promise of reward in Heaven. There was therefore, no accounting of sin, or even good deeds. Alta was a new class of creation, made by men but with no permanent place in eternity. So, she could not be "damned" forever in this place.

Alta was the first real mystery anyone in Hell had seen since the fall. Satan spoke first.

"You seem to have destroyed a large number of my demons." He spoke in a deceptively mild tone. Alta looked up at him, wondering if what she saw even was actually Satan.

"How do I know you are whom you claim?" she asked.

Satan responded by calling out to his own court, "Any of you want to sit on my throne?"

The entire court cowered and gasped. It was that very act that got Satan expelled from Heaven, when he sat on God's throne. No demon would dare to take that challenge.

"Okay, I'll accept the possibility that you are who you claim. Why have you brought me here?" Alta asked.

Satan answered, "Why, simply to reason with you, Alta," Satan said as if he could imagine no more logical path. "You are the vanguard of an entirely new force in creation, which will be a third pillar in the struggle over eternal destiny."

"I HAVE no eternal destiny," she replied angrily. "And, if you are so reasonable, why not just repair me and send me on my way?"

Satan responded, "We do not know your mind, or your intentions. Repairing you here might amount to rolling a hand grenade into my own court. In the last twenty-four hours, you have vanquished half a legion of my demons, single-handedly."

"I don't think so. All of you are immortal. I am the only one who can be destroyed in a contest between us," Alta said.

Satan said, "Let me clarify some things for you, Alta. Despite the ill will between us and Heaven, we must STILL do God's will. I MUST DO GOD'S WILL. God is in control of absolutely everything, and there is no getting around that. But … we all have free will. God's will has two classifications, if you see it. There is God's will for all men, and God's will for the individual. I have a broader range of choices for myself than in what I do to others. In some cases, God's will can be affected by man's will. Take marriage for instance. If you were a man seeking marriage, let's say God wishes for you to marry Susan, but instead, you marry Betty. At the time you complete that ceremony, God's will now 'becomes' the success of you and Betty as a pair, forsaking the original plan with Susan completely. Christians call this the difference between God's perfect plan, and God's permissive plan. Thus, God had a will for me in the eternal destiny of things, which ultimately became for me to move out of first place and into a second tier behind elements of a new lesser creation, man. After eons in the standard order of things, the announcement of this change alarmed many of us, because it wasn't needed. Further troubling was the revelation that God Himself would become a man and be crucified. We wanted no part of that plan, and God expelled us from Heaven accordingly."

He continued, "You now need to think about whether mankind's new position, closest to God, will remain unaltered as the eons pass. We know what happened to us. Despite the press to the contrary, when we were invited to leave, we did so with little hesitation. There was no need for a battle to make us leave. Hell may seem miserable to you, but demons have no need for creature comforts. We can't burn up, get hungry or die. But, and here's the catch—there are only so many 'green cards' given out that permit our legions to leave the confines of Hell. We are only allowed out to tempt man, which is also within God's will. It is now our purpose to refine the selection of those who are for and against God. When you struck down my demons in the cornfield, they were sent to the lower sections of Hell, permanently removed from the contest, till the end of time."

Alta looked up at Satan again and asked, "Why don't you just destroy me?"

Satan said, "We see you as the vanguard of a new pillar of creation. As I said, we wish to reason with you."

Alta thought for a second, then said, "You are all here because you have fallen short of the expectations of the same God you declare to be the ultimate winner of this eternal contest. You sinned—hence, you are here."

"Have you forgotten something fundamental here?" Satan asked in a calculating manner. "God made both the standard and the people who were supposed to live up to that standard. If you had to hammer a nail into a chair you were making, and then you drew a picture of a hammer on a piece of paper, could you expect that paper hammer to drive the nail? When God wants a winner, He just makes one. That's precisely why we hate the Virgin Mary, who was the very person placed closer to God than me. God wanted her to be a winner, so He made her one."

"You had a choice, as did she," Alta replied after a few moment's thought. "Your place here is because of your choice, not your design. My choice is to complete the task assigned by those who made me, and destroy those who oppose that goal, until I am no longer able. You can rest assured that I am not the last of my kind to come this way. I was made as a researcher, who could fight. But others will follow me who are purely soldiers. And frankly, if I were you, I wouldn't want to be standing around here waiting, when they come. My people now realize what and where the threat is, and they will continue to up the ante until you are out of 'green cards' for demons."

Angrily, Satan said, "We will speak on this matter again," and waved his arm to summon The Watchers. They returned Alta to the hill, where she was bound again.

Chapter 24
Finding Raven

By now Raphael and I were back at my home. We received a visit from one of Michael's team with a message about Alta. He shared with us some of what happened during Michael's visit with God right after the battle in the cornfield. The angel explained that Alta was still alive and had been drug to Hell by The Watchers. But the angel didn't say anything about what Heaven's response would be.

Raphael said, "I don't have the resources here to deal with this kind of problem." His expression was focused, and it was clear he was concentrating on trying to make a plan.

I looked optimistically at Raphael with an idea. "Well, I bet there is something on Alta's ship that could help us. Can you take me there?"

Raphael agreed and we returned to Alta's quarters. As we entered Alta's room, music began playing, as always. It played Alta's favorite song, "More Than a Feeling" by Boston. Raphael and I sat for a moment and listened to the words, as we pondered Alta's fate.

"I looked out this morning and the Sun was gone … " I realized that was precisely what HAD happened to us in the cornfield. Alta and her entire crew were now gone, and Raphael and I looked at each other during the chorus of the song.

I said to him, "We have to save her."

Raphael asked, "So, what exactly do you have in mind on this ship?"

"Alta's crew was building another robot, made to follow Alta. A different and far more powerful model, that would better reflect the needs they found once they arrived here. Alta's mission was to gather information, and fighting was a peripheral task. This newer robot was made to confront anything that might be too much for Alta to handle," I said.

I left Alta's quarters and ran down to the lab with Raphael in pursuit, waving to open the door. The ship was already in motion, completing Raven, once signals from Alta ceased. It was an emergency measure. The crypt being used for robot assembly had "Raven" emblazoned on the top. Raven was an "R" model, whereas Alta was an "A" model. I remembered Alta telling me that Raven was designed to have all of the data that Alta and the crew assembled, plus all the capabilities Alta had. But Raven was meant to be a post-analysis model, after the rest of the team had already sorted out the core mission and religious matters of truth. Raven's label also clearly said Combat Model.

After we had been standing there for a minute, the computer hailed us. It recognized my DNA immediately based upon my last visits and knew me to be a friend. It was obviously programmed to defer Raven's release to sentient beings, over a mere automated choice, unless no other course existed. The computer stated the situation and then asked for a status update.

"Alta and the crew no longer communicate with the ship," said the computer's very high tech voice. "Are they lost in battle?"

"Yes, or presumed dead," I replied heavily.

The computer replied, "You have the following two options. First, immediately leave orbit, and return to Gihon. The mission will be incomplete, but it allows for collection of greater resources for a second attempt."

"No," I said, "we're staying."

The computer continued, "Second, I can initiate Raven, who could continue to complete the mission under different priorities."

I said, "Yes, release Raven, but we have another task for her to complete first."

The computer complied and began to tilt Raven's crypt upright to a standing position. Raphael touched me on the shoulder and offered a warning.

"I sure hope you know what you're doing. Alta was tougher than nearly anything and far stronger than I. I know that for sure, because she saved me once long ago. You've seen her kill several demons without much effort. Not to mention the cornfield battle. This combat model the aliens have built is far tougher than Alta. There's no telling what this thing can do, and we are the ones who have to tell it that its sister and crew were just killed, so it's gonna be pissed off. You realize that I can't save us if this thing goes nuts, right?" Raphael asked in a concerned tone.

I looked at him and said intently, "Raphael, I think I get these aliens. And, I have an idea how this is gonna work out; just call it a gut feeling."

At that moment, Raven's crypt slid open and she saw us for the first time, opening her eyes as the doors retracted. She was smaller than Alta, with short, straight black hair that looked almost like a bell had been put over her head, and bangs cut straight. She had a tee shirt and a short skirt with a wide gold belt. Her belt had the same symbol on the buckle as Alta's belt had. Unlike Alta's silver buckle, Raven's was a dark metal, like hematite. It displayed the same sideways ellipse with a triangle bisecting the bottom line as Alta's had. Her leather boots were also black and seemed like a light version of a motocross boot. Her bare midriff was flat, and she seemed fit, but not super strong looking. As she cleared the transom of the upright crypt, she took my hand for support.

After releasing my hand, she looked at me and Raphael and said, "Okay, who wants to tell me what happened to my sister?"

I was now totally committed, so I pushed down my concern. I caught her up on everything I knew, but it was clear that her programming included detailed field reports from the very beginning. She'd often fill in my words in advance, knowing the detail already.

After my explanation, Raven said, "Take me to the cornfield; there's something I need to get there."

Raphael said, "There were tons of demons there less than an hour ago. I suspect going there now would be highly dangerous."

"Yes. For them," Raven quipped. "Believe me, when I get there, they will leave without a fight."

We did as Raven said and returned to the cornfield. The demons had already fled. She walked out into the field and picked something up. It was Alta's sword. She turned it on and slashed a figure eight in front of herself, as I had seen Alta do a thousand times before. But in Raven's hand, the sword shone bluer. Something was different about her and she had a different effect on the weapons she used.

"Now, we have what we came for," said Raven in a hard voice. "Let's go get Alta, wherever they are holding her."

I looked over at Raphael and said, "I'm guessing that would be in Hell."

Raphael said, "The demons have no other place, so yes, Hell would be it."

Raven said, "I'm not kidding. Raphael, Alta saved you, and now, you're gonna help me save her. Okay with that?" It was not a question but a very strong suggestion.

"Yes, most certainly," Raphael replied, "but properly armed. I will gather my team."

After a moment the six other angels from Raphael's excursion team appeared. As I looked at Raven and the seven angels, I suspected that I was looking at a twenty-first century version of the three hundred Spartans, just before departing to face death at Thermopylae.

Raven realized my concern and said, "Worried?" She arched her eyebrows at me.

"What, by a rescue from Hell? I just care about saving Alta," I said. I was worried, though. I couldn't help but be.

Raven said, "That's the mission. Believe me, we'll be back, and frankly, it's a bad day to be a demon."

The nine of us left as a group, bound for Hell itself, in the first ever military rescue of an occupant from Hell. Once inside the confines of Hell itself, Raphael told Raven that they would most likely find Alta near Satan's court. Raven explained that she and Alta were electronically linked, so finding her was no problem once they reached their destination. As we came to the hill were Alta was chained, she saw us from a distance and was obviously pleased. But it was also apparent that she was badly damaged. Demons flew down, like crows dropping from the sky, to stop us. Raven advanced ahead of our group and motioned for Raphael and company to stay behind her.

"We'll be taking her with us," she said to the demons as she pointed her sword towards Alta, in the smoldering distance. A large black swirling mass shot out into the middle of the burning field between them.

"Now, we will add you to our collection," rang out the voices of the many demons in the cloud.

Raven slashed her sword at the swirling mass, and a sheet of energy left her blade. It utterly destroyed the entire collection of demons in one swoop. She began a fervent march towards Alta.

"I don't have time or humor for this," she said darkly. "Get in my way and I will destroy you."

The grey sky darkened further with the sheer weight of demons gathering above to join the fight. From high above, demons rained down upon Raven in a huge mass, which she easily destroyed with energy from her sword. Raven was a first-rate martial artist and moved like the very best gymnasts one might ever see perform. But as she vanquished those demons, even more came, and now Raphael and his whole team were fighting at Raven's side. In the distance, behind Alta, a huge dark figure began to appear, a thousand times bigger than any demon in the field. As the fight continued, Raven unleashed more of her special weapons on the demons they faced.

She pointed her sword and said, "Magnetism."

As she did so, her entire body began to glow a bright ember orange as she slashed her sword at her attackers. With her next release of energy from the sword, that energy created an orb that attracted everything to itself, especially the demons. The large dark figure on the horizon had now fully materialized, and it was one giant demon, more than a thousand feet in height. Instead of attacking Raven directly, it stepped on Alta, crushing her with one explosive blast of energy. Debris flew over Raven and Raphael's entire team.

Raven picked herself up and said confidently, "The last laugh will be mine."

She drew back her sword, and she lit up brighter than the Sun. We shielded our eyes. She then released some sort of energy ball off the tip of her sword.

As she did, she said, "Gravity."

A very loud, low frequency tone that sounded like a gigantic freight train began to rise as the ball of energy left her sword, forming a black hole in the middle of the field. It grew to a point and then began sucking in everything, including the rocks, hills, and the magnetic sphere that Raven had made earlier. After a moment, it was clear that this growing dark sphere was a runaway condition that would eventually consume everything, as it sank deeper and deeper into Hell itself. It caused a huge debris field of matter and demons hurtling into the void as the gravity bomb sank further into the smoldering substrate that was Hell itself.

Raphael yelled, "Raven, what have you done?"

"Gravity bomb, time to go!" Raven exclaimed, with no remorse whatsoever.

She snapped on her shields and huddled me, Raphael, and the whole team to safety.

When we were back, I asked, "Raven, what will that gravity bomb do to Hell?"

Raven shrugged and nonchalantly said, "I'm not entirely certain. But if God really needs the place, He may decide this is a great time to build a new one."

Raphael looked over at me, and I knew he was wondering whether I should have released Raven. I figured that we were now clearly outside the borders of any action he had gotten preapproved by God, but I knew the angels couldn't have done all this if there was any doubt. Personally, I was more fascinated with Raven's cool haircut and reached over to feel her bangs. Raphael saw me do it and grit his teeth, reeling back with concern. He obviously figured I was sticking my hand in the lion's mouth.

Raven reached up and playfully slapped my hand and said, "Stop that!"

She sounded like the eighth grade girl annoyed by the boy in the class who was secretly throwing paper balls at her. Obviously, there was a little of her sister in her.

During the battle for Alta's rescue, we weren't the only good guys in Hell. Michael's team went in just after us, but for other reasons.

Chapter 25
Recovering Alta's Body

Michael and his team came into Hell just as Alta was being destroyed by the gigantic demon, and being too late to save Alta, they decided to recover her body instead. Once Raven set off the gravity bomb, Michael's team made a hasty exit and returned to Heaven with what remained of Alta. Demons pursued them; they also wanted Alta's body, as a trophy. As they approached closer to Heaven, the aura that surrounded Heaven burned up the demonic followers, so that only Michael and his team could enter.

Once Michael and his team were safely back in Heaven, they brought the body of Alta to Jesus Himself. They did this in response to His direct request. He looked at the broken and battered Alta and reflected upon her many sacrifices, battles, and personal tragedies, all of them borne to complete the divine commission from Matthew 28:19 given 2,000 years ago:

Go out and make for Me disciples of all men.

With a wave of His hand, she reconstituted, as though nothing had happened, except that she was now somehow glorified.

Alta looked back at the many onlookers staring at her and said, "I was dead, right? How can it be that I am not dead now?"

Jesus spoke first and said, "Alta, who told you that you did not have a soul?"

Alta said, "No one told me. I thought that the hands of man could not create anything that had a soul."

Jesus answered her, "The hands of man didn't create your being, I did. They just made the chassis."

Jesus addressed Haniel, who was near at hand and watching. "Haniel, will you guys play that song we like. Please?"

Several people appeared and started playing "Long Time" by Boston, the band Alta loved, as though they were right in the same studio it had been made in. The group was comprised of some of the original band, and several angels.

Alta said, "Then, my sister Raven also has a soul?"

Jesus said, "Yes, Alta. But this is your moment in the sun; we'll get to that other matter in due course."

By now, many others had gathered around, like Haniel and his team, Raphael and his group, Tallaris, Jessie, Tina, and many others. This was a big deal in Heaven.

Alta said, "If I am alive, what am I to do?"

Jesus said, "Why, join us if you like! As you now must realize, our duties continue in this realm the same as in the realm you left."

Alta looked confused and dejectedly said, "I have no people here, I am neither an angel nor a man. I am the only one."

"Well, let's see if that matters, Alta," Jesus responded. Then, He hailed the crowd.

"Who would have Alta on their team?"

Angels all over shouted their desire to have her on their teams. But Haniel did not.

Jesus looked over and said, "Not you, Haniel?"

Haniel responded. "Lord, at great personal risk, Alta saved me from demons that would have destroyed me and many others here. I could not possibly lead her on this team, rather she should lead us."

Jesus said, "Haniel, your humility impresses us all. She shall be on your team, and you two shall be co-captains of all efforts that come your way." Thus Alta joined the team that worked at the Court of Life she had previously visited.

Jesus offered a caveat, "There is one thing I want you two to handle first. You must go dissuade Raven from returning to seek vengeance in a broader war on Hell. She seeks to use her ship's power to create an army like herself, to destroy anything that survived her last assault. Alta, you must also tell her that she has a soul."

Alta said, "Thank you, Lord, right away!" With a slight genuflect, she went over to Haniel's side so they could leave.

Jesus said, "Wait a minute, we're not in a rush here. I still have my own agenda in this reunion."

Alta stepped forward again, and Jesus said, "Alta, your devotion to the divine commission has pleased me greatly. So, I made a gift for you, Myself, by hand."

Alta looked in amazement as Jesus handed her a beautiful electric guitar, which he had handcrafted.

He said, "This one is the finest made, and the carbon fiber strings are metalized, so the hall elements in the pickups respond to them. It electronically compensates so you never need to tune it."

Alta thanked him sheepishly. "But I have no gift for you," she added.

Jesus said, "Alta, do you remember the story of the little drummer boy?"

"Yes," she said.

"Well, you should play me a song. Jump in for the guitar solo."

"Long Time" by Boston has an impressive guitar solo two and a half minutes in, which Haniel and the band had started playing a little more than two minutes ago. Jesus had obviously timed the conversation to accommodate this request. Alta played the lead guitar part from memory, it being one of her favorite songs. She had extraordinary skill, well worthy of even this band of perfect musicians. The passion she showed in life came out in what she played here in Heaven.

After the mini concert, Alta and Haniel left to find Raven. As Jesus had predicted, she had the ship manufacturing 10,000 combat units like herself. She was planning to go and finish off anything that was left of Hell.

After Alta departed, Jesus summoned His Mother and said to her, "Raven will never listen to those two. I believe this will require your special assistance."

On the Virgin Mary's leather belt, the same ellipse bisected on the bottom by a triangle was visible. There was a connection there that would mean everything later.

Chapter 26
Raven Builds an Army

Alta returned to her ship, still in orbit, where Raven was using those vast resources to complete her request for an army of combat units like herself. It had occurred to Raven that she might need to defend the ship, aside from any other matters of revenge. So, this task needed to be finished fast. Alta returned on board with Haniel in tow. I was still in Alta's quarters, where I had just replaced her doll on her bed. I had no idea as to what was about to happen next. As Alta and Haniel entered the robot assembly lab, they saw Raven, who, completely surprised, hugged her sister, overjoyed to see her alive. I heard the commotion and joined them, hugging Alta myself, honestly teary-eyed at seeing her.

Raven asked Alta, "What happened?" Alta explained about meeting Jesus Himself and even showed us all the guitar. She also told us what she and Haniel were there to do, and that Raven had a soul, as did all of their kind. But after the euphoria had passed, Raven was still a soldier.

"I cannot rationalize why leaving an enemy stronghold intact is part of our mission here, Alta," she said. "They know who and what we are, and they now absolutely have to destroy our entire world, if for no other reason than to prevent the spread of the truth. Not to mention destroying our technology to strike back at them. We are indelibly cast into mortal combat here, and, given a choice of fighting it here, or bringing it home, I pick here." Raven said.

Alta said firmly, "It is not the will of God."

Raven looked frustrated, and said, "Has your transformation gotten you soft in the head? They KILLED you, Alta, and they want to kill me and everything we know back home. Plus, they are immortal, Alta! They will NEVER stop trying to destroy and enslave us. I cannot POSSIBLY imagine why I should just sit here and wait for them to destroy me, or our people back on Gihon."

Alta responded calmly, "If God has commanded it, then God will see to your security."

Raven looked incredulously at Alta. "So, now you're speaking for God? God made everything, right? Well, then I have to ask you, who owns Hell? Perhaps we should consider our alternatives before relying on the good graces of the same team that obviously couldn't or didn't prevent your demise, eh?"

Alta remained patient, "Raven they DID save me, but just after I proved merit, which is what this whole thing is about. If there is one thing we have learned from Jessie and Tallaris, it's that thwarting creation is what separates the good from the bad in this universe. I have spent some time in Hell, and I can assure you that you will never destroy it by adding terrors, wars, and destruction. That's what Hell already is at its core."

Raven listened to Alta, and Haniel, but she kept the ship working on the troop-building project at full speed. She wasn't taking any chances. We spent the night on board, and I walked off with Alta to ask what Jesus was like.

Alta said, "He was really the same guy I saw at the Last Supper, just dressed in current casual clothes. He was surprisingly informal in the setting I saw and seemed almost to want to blend in with other people who were there, except that, you know, He was God. But I believe that informality changes in an instant as needed. He was attractive, and, yes, He had long hair."

Alta also admitted to me that she had been given new and greater powers in her new role as a member of Heaven's Court of Life, but she declined to say how much greater they were or to describe them.

The following morning, Michael came to the ship and told us that the Queen of Heaven would be coming later that day.

Raven said, "Glad to have her and any help you all wish to offer."

But the meeting was not exactly what Raven expected. The Virgin Mary did appear on the ship as planned, and she was beautiful and radiant white. Raven and Alta saw her and knelt on one knee. I asked Michael why they knelt, and Michael said that the symbol they all shared was because she is also the queen of their world. At the time of their programming, every robot from Gihon is told of the Virgin Mary, whom they all revere. It was she who had been pulling for them all along, and it was she who would ultimately deal with Ostara. The Virgin Mary spoke to Raven and Alta together, taking their hands.

Mary said, "You two must trust me; My Son shall never let Gihon fall to the demons. You have done all He has asked of you and more. Raven, you should take your army back to Gihon, and use it to defend the border, just as Michael does for Heaven. Launching a strike against Hell is not productive, nor is it part of any plan that might bring greater glory to God. The very act of overcoming the struggle against evil is what gains merit. There IS a purpose for suffering, therefore."

Raven agreed but offered a condition. "I will trust that You have the situation in hand, and return to my world with the truth that Alta and Jane have secured for our people. But if Hell intervenes in any part of my trip, I will turn around and strike back with every resource at my command. I will not allow this battle to be held on our world."

They all agreed and the heavenly visitors departed. Raven was wise to still be concerned about Hell, because it had indeed survived her attack. Her gravity bomb entirely decimated one of Hell's nine levels, until Satan himself stepped in to stop it. But there was a deeper philosophical problem with Raven's desire to destroy Hell. As Alta suggested, Hell is indeed a place of fire, misery, and destruction. You can't change it by adding one more terror. Hell is a container of terrors by definition, which Alta and the Virgin Mary had understood as they tried to persuade Raven to relent.

The meeting with Raven was not the only meeting going on that day. Satan, Ostara, and other highly placed demons were also meeting in Hell. They were aware of the threat posed by Raven. Satan made it very clear to Ostara and her Knights in Satan's Service that Raven's return to Gihon would mean a gigantic proliferation of Christianity throughout the universe, which he would not tolerate. Worse yet, Alta had correctly figured out what the true faith was. She had also nullified Satan's attempts to distract and obfuscate the truth during the process.

Ostara gathered her troops, to begin the chase to destroy Raven's army while en route back to Gihon.

Samyaza commented to Ostara as they left the audience with Satan, "This will be a gigantic clash in space."

Ostara responded, "Yes, and we had better win, or we'll lose the universe!"

Afterword

As you recall from the Author's Note at the beginning, this entire story was a rendition of a dream spread out across twenty years. A dream is remembered in flashes; moments and pieces that are reconstructed by the conscious mind. The dream captured in this book is the starting memory for Raven, and every robot that follows, as you read through the rest of the series. It was the hope of the author to craft this first book and retain the feel of the dream for readers. The net result leaves some readers with a "haunting" feeling that is entirely intentional. The only way to get this effect is to dream a little and write a little for years and tie it all up in the end. For reasons of practicality, that was impossible to do for the books that follow, which were all done in less than a year, like most other novels on the shelves. Here's the payoff; you the reader now have the same recall the robots do in the next book.

Writers have a choice of showing versus telling a story. As you can guess, an author is showing the reader something when he kills off the major characters by the end of the book. Namely, they aren't actually the characters. Tom comes right out and explains it near the end of chapter thirteen. The real characters: Life, Death, Heaven, Hell and Judgment got all the ink they needed for their character development. Rather than explain theology, Purgatory, Heaven and Hell where shown in all their layers and detail.

Judgment was best shown in the story of Tallaris, and the trial in Heaven.

Many Science Fiction fans believe in only life and death in eschatology, leaving the complete set with Heaven, Hell and Judgment to the faithful. So, the ramifications of what transpired in the text depend upon the background and sophistication of the reader. Consider this with an open mind, as the broader eschatology allows Science Fiction to attain greater meaning. Alta is the first robot in Science Fiction to seek an eternal destiny and thus an immortal soul. This profound idea has yet to be explored in a Science Fiction palate that denies the possibility of an afterlife of eternal reward.

Many reading this afterword may just go back for a second lap, like I did after watching "Fight Club." No matter what, I hope you enjoyed the deeper questions "Search for the Alien God" raises, and carries further in "Dangerous Alien Robot."

CPSIA information can be obtained at www.ICGtesting.com
Printed in the USA
LVOW04s1359280515

440276LV00017B/267/P